# Days of Blessing
## *A New Ulster Novel*

By

## *Karen MacDowall Haggerty*

**_Days of Blessing, A New Ulster Novel_**
© 2015 by Karen M. Haggerty

# ACKNOWLEDGEMENTS

Heartfelt thanks to those who supported and encouraged me
in the writing of this book:

Richard Haggerty
Cheryl McNeace
Lisa Wright
Michelle Clark Higgins
Debbi Romano
Peter Romano
Layton Romano
Laurel Romano
Vanessa Lowry
Joy Edwards
Virginia Chryssikos
Vicki Johnson
Kristin "Trixie" Johnson

"Are You Afraid?" in Chapter 20, page 171 by Leo Robin. Used with permission.

*An áit a bhuil do chroí is ann a thabharfas do chosa thú.*

Your feet will bring you to where your heart is.
−Old Irish Proverb

# Table of Contents

To Rich

*a chuisle mo chrói*

# Chapter 1     Broken

It was a sunny autumn afternoon when I drove through the mountains toward Mama's house. I didn't understand how the colorful leaves and the vivid blue sky could look so outstanding. Inside, I was demolished. I thought the least the weather could do was give me a little fog so I could feel hidden for a while.

I was leaving Kentucky and going back to New Ulster, South Carolina, where I'd grown up. My husband had recently told me he was divorcing me, and I needed to get out of his house. We had had an argument, and I asked him what I needed to do to make him happy. His reply still scorched my memory: "Pack your things in that car and get lost. I don't care where you go. I can't stand the sight of you anymore."

Hearing those words sear through my memory again made my heart physically ache, and I had to pull the car over. How appropriate that my stopping place was right beside a waterfall on the side of the mountain. In the shadow of an overhanging rock, and the noise of the water tumbling down over it, I clutched the steering wheel and sobbed. The mountain and I cried together.

When I'd been given my "notice of eviction," I called Mama. She was trying to talk to me through my tears, but I couldn't understand her because of my crying. But finally I heard her say, "You come on home, Mo. Come on home to where you're loved."

So here I was, pulled over on the side of a mountain road, my eyes swollen from more sobbing. "Lord," I prayed out loud, "When will the pain end? How will I make it through?" And then I remembered a scripture verse: "My grace is sufficient for you."

I dried my eyes on the sleeve of my sweater and started the car. "Okay, Lord. My time is in Your hand."

It was late in the night when I got to Mama's. I pulled up the long dirt driveway and felt as though I had never been away. As I looked at the little frame house, I couldn't believe that I was back here to live. I had been gone so many years. But a feeling of comfort washed over me when I saw the familiar landscape of trees and flowers—some I had even planted myself as a child—within the warm glow of the porch light that

Mama had left on for me. I was so tired. I decided to leave my stuff and unpack the car in the morning. All I grabbed was my overnight bag.

Just as I reached the porch, the door opened and Mama held out her arms for me. I fell into them sobbing again. We stood out on the porch like that, with her stroking my hair and saying, "It's okay, Mozie. You home now."

We finally went inside. Mama was still holding my hand. "You hungry? You want somethin' to eat or drink?"

"No, thanks, I'm okay. I just want to get into my pajamas and die."

"Girl, you may as well forget that idea. I ain't through payin' for your burial plot yet, and you ain't about to use *mine*." She winked at me. "I got your room ready." The house was small, only five rooms, but it was home, and its loveliness and comfort wrapped around me like a winter blanket. "I put a extra quilt at the foot of the bed in case you need it tonight. It's done turned off chilly."

I tossed my overnight bag down and sat on the edge of the bed. Mama sat with me. "Mo, everythang's gon' be alright. You just give it some time. When you ready, we'll talk about it, okay?"

"Okay, Mama. I'm sorry. I'm sorry I let you down."

"Let me down? What do you mean by that?"

"It's just—you and Papa were married for so long--I'm the only one in our family, ever, to get divorced. I can't tell you how ashamed that makes me feel, and add to that the shame I've brought to the family. I just never saw it coming, Mama. I never saw it coming."

Mama put her arm around my shoulder. "Girl, I could never, *ever* be disappointed in you. You didn't ask for this. But now here it is, and I know you'll pull through. Don't ever doubt that God has His hand on you. He never promises things'll be perfect, but He does promise He'll be with us all the way t' th' end."

"Yeah, I felt that today, coming through the mountains." I sighed raggedly. "But I just never thought anything could be so hard."

She hugged me, and I kissed her. She smelled of Dove soap. Her hair, red but turning white, was tied back in a knot, and there were soft wisps around her face. I thought how pretty her skin still was.

Mama got up and kissed the top of my head. "We'll call Maggie in the mornin'. It's too late to be callin' her tonight. I don't know what time

Rose'll get t' th' airport, but she said she'd rent a car so we don't have to worry 'bout pickin' her up."

After she left, I looked around the room. It had been my bedroom, mine and my sisters'. But now Mama had it all done up in white. *She could never have had anything white when we were little*, I thought, and felt myself smiling.

**********

Maggie showed up early the next morning. I was still in bed, having only gone to sleep shortly before dawn. I heard voices coming from the kitchen, and Mama was doing a lot of shushing, and Maggie said something about "breaking his dad-blamed neck." Then Mama said, "Don't wake her, Maggie," but Maggie was not one to be turned around, and she was coming through the bedroom door.

"Mo?" she asked in a whisper, which I thought was a bit incongruous after all the drama in the kitchen.

I rolled over and looked in her direction. "Hey, Maggie," I mumbled.

"Law', I hope I didn't wake you up, but I wanted to see how you were doin'."

I peered at her over the blankets. Raising up on an elbow and rubbing my eyes, I said, "I'm alright, just exhausted."

After seeing that I was not near death, Maggie jumped right in. "Well, lemme tell you right now that that ol' b-hole had better not be callin' 'round here once he starts regrettin' what he's done! I will land him with a left hook!"

*Some things*, I thought, *never change*. Of the three of us girls, Maggie was the most out-spoken. She had a big heart and would help anyone in need; but when it came to someone hurting her family, she was ready to draw blood. As much as I appreciated her support of me, I couldn't deal with it right now.

"Maggs," I said, "you don't need to worry about that. He's not about to change his mind. He won't be coming around here, I can guarantee that."

"Well he better hope not!" Once Maggie was riled up and on a jag, she was like a freight train. She was already pacing the room with something akin to fury. I was relieved when Mama walked in and in a

9

bubbly voice said, "Who wants French toast?" I seized the opportunity to escape and said, "I do!" and throwing the blankets back, I was up and heading for the bathroom. Maggie was right behind.

"I'm tellin' you, Maureen, that boy is a' *idiot*! I hope he *does* come down here. I'll tear his head off and hand it to him in a *paper bag!*"

As I was closing the bathroom door in Maggie's face, I heard Mama say, "Margaret, get away from that door an' leave her alone. Give her a chance to pull herself together. And pull your *own* self together 'fore you throw a rod!" At that point I turned the water on and could only hear muffled voices.

Leaving the water running, I sat on the bathtub edge and began considering my plight. I was losing my marriage, I was bruised and shaken, unsure of my future, unemployed, 36 years old and back living with my mother. Grim. But at least I was in a safe place, and I had time to rebuild my life. I may color my hair, and I smiled at the thought. I got up and turned off the water. It was time for some French toast.

**********

Rose blew in from the airport about half-past four. She had rented a car and was there on the spot. She lived in New Mexico and had made arrangements to come home as soon as she heard. Rose was the eldest and referred to herself as "the old maid." When she saw me, she shouted, "Mozie!" and had her arms around me in seconds. She squeezed me so hard that I almost lost my breath.

"My baby Moze," she said and looked in my eyes. "What can I do for you? Are you okay?"

"I'm still shaky, Rose, but I know I'll be alright. I may feel I'm out floating in the wind, but I know God has His hand on me."

With her arm around my shoulder, we walked into the house. Rose was still beautiful. Maggie and I had red hair and blue eyes like Mama, but Rose got Papa's blond hair and green eyes, and she was the real beauty of the family. Although she was six years older than I, she looked younger than her years. She had not cut her hair since college. Today it was tied in a bunch at the back of her head. Maggie and I had our nicknames, but not Rose. Rose was "Rose," and she would answer to nothing else.

Maggie had gone home to tend to her family, so the house was quiet, as Mama was not one to cause a stir. There was something about Maggie's presence that got everyone in an agitated state, or as Mama put it, "their bowels in a' uproar." So the three of us had coffee and considered the moment.

"What do you think happened?" Rose was looking at me with such kindness in her face.

"You reckon it's 'cause y'all didn't have children?" Mama asked.

That was a sore spot for me. I had desperately wanted a child, but it never happened. Maggie was married for years before George was born, and that was totally unexpected. I had always hoped the same would happen for me, but it didn't.

"I don't think so, Mama," I replied, trying to pretend my eyes weren't stinging.

We talked about how this divorce must have been in the works a long time before it ever surfaced. Marriages just don't fall apart after one argument. The more we discussed it, the stronger I felt. I had no idea of the rollercoaster my emotions would be on for weeks and months following. There were times when I enjoyed moments, like now, of real calm, and then the gravity of the situation would fall in a heap upon me again, and the sadness felt crushing.

While I was washing the supper dishes that evening, I had a memory of happier times, and I began crying, my tears dropping into the soapy water. Maggie had by now returned, and that got her going on another jag. Mama told her to hush up, and I again began trying to pull myself together.

When I finished the dishes, I sat at the little card table in the front room, pretending to work a crossword puzzle. Mama was in her chair in the corner as she crocheted a new blanket. Rose and Maggie were on the sofa, not saying anything, just looking at me. Maybe they were waiting for me to throw a fit or something.

"You doin' alright, Mo?" Maggie asked.

"No, Margaret, I'm not," I replied, not even looking up from my puzzle. "My marriage is over. I'm a complete failure. I have no job, no home, no husband. I'd say that pretty much sums it up."

"Well, don't you worry," she said. "You'll find somebody else."

"Honey, the *last* thing I want right now is another man. Just another opportunity to get kicked in the teeth and thrown out like the trash." I didn't want it to happen, but tears started falling out of my eyes, and I wanted to cry.

"Aw, Mozie, don't cry. Someday a *real* man is going to see you for who you are and treat you good," Maggie said. She had gotten up and was standing at the table. "Don't base all of them on *that* thang. They not all like that. You'll get married again. Every woman ought to marry a man at least *once* in her life."

Rose stifled a giggle. Then she suddenly took on a serious tone and said, "Maureen, no *man* would have done this to you."

"I won't ever get married again. How could I trust anyone enough?" At that, I could no longer hold back crying. "And besides," I said between sobs, "I'm too old. Who would want me, anyway? My own husband didn't!"

Maggie got an edge to her voice. She was absolutely no-nonsense. "Now, look, Mo. You ain't old. You just feel old because that ol' b-hole *made* you feel old. And he did that because *he's* old."

They were both now standing beside me at the table. "He was *born* old," Rose added.

Mama, who had been quiet up till now, never looked up from her crocheting. She said, "Honey, that boy was born *dead*."

I looked up, shocked, and then burst into laughter. That was music to Mama's ears.

"That's what I like to hear! Mozie, you're too purty to be messin' up your face with tears. Now!" She got up and said, "I declare! It's time for a drink." She held with Thomas Jefferson who had said that coffee was the favorite drink of the civilized world. We followed her into the kitchen and watched as she mixed up her favorite coffee beans and ground them. The aroma of coffee filled the little house.

I stood by Mama, watching the coffee drip, and she said in a very serious tone, "Mo, sometimes the first step in forgiveness is realizin' that the other person was born a' idiot." I laughed and hugged her.

"Mama," Rose, seeing the opportunity to change the subject, said, "I can't believe how that property next door has grown up. That's absolutely scandalous!"

"I know," Mama replied as she took down coffee mugs from the shelf. "Ain't nobody lived there in decades, and you can hardly see th' house anymore for all th' overgrowth."

"Y'all remember that one man that lived there when we was growin' up? I don't think we ever knew his name. I think we just called him ol' Creeper Man." Maggie sat down with me at the kitchen table and Rose joined us. Mama hummed as she put the coffee tray together.

"Yep," she said, "Ol' Creeper Man. He was such a' ol' sot. I didn't want y'all gals anywhere 'round him. He just give me the idea that he could go off his nut any time!" She looked at me as she put the tray down on the table and sat. "You remember that dog, Mozie?"

I didn't right away, but a faded memory began to unfold, and I remembered a fall day when I was six years old. I began telling my sisters the story.

**\*\*\*\*\*\*\*\*\*\***

Mama and I were out at the clothesline. "*Humph.*" Mama put her hands on her hips and regarded Creeper Man's house. From the distance, we could hear a dog whining. She stooped down to get another towel out of the basket and began hanging it on the line, a look of disgust on her face. Her jaw was set. I knew she was mad.

"That just burns – me—*up*," she said through tight lips. "He's got about as much business havin' a dog as I have a herd o' pigs. That po' dog. That's just plain cruel, *that* is."

Mama put out her hand for another clothes pin. I gave her one.

"Yep," she continued, "One o' these days that boy gonna get what's comin' to him." Suddenly she put her hands on her hips again and snapped her head in the direction of the whining. "An' *this* is the day."

She dropped the clothespin in the basket and let the towel dangle. With purpose in her steps, she marched off toward Creeper Man's house.

I was frightened. "Mama! Where you goin'? You told us never to go around Creeper Man's place! You said he was a lunatic!"

She ignored me and kept walking, and I followed close behind her, my heart pounding. I was terrified.

"Mama! You could get *killed*!"

She stopped, whirled around and looked me in the face. Her cheeks were bright red and she was breathing hard. "Lookahere, little girl," she said to me, "sometimes you have to do thangs in this life that ain't pleasant, and may be downright dangerous. All I know is there's a little dog up here sufferin', and I can't abide by that. You get on back to the house and lock th' door. Make sure y' sisters stay inside."

"They in school, Mama."

Ignoring me, she pivoted on her heel and continued through the briars that grew all over the property. I ignored her order and kept following. The thorns ripped through our clothes, and we were getting scratched up. Mama's stockings were torn and her legs were bleeding. As terrified as I was, I wasn't about to leave Mama. I was afraid for her. And she was going to tear a strip off Creeper Man. When Mama told someone off, it was brutal and lasting. I kept up right behind her.

We got close to the house and Mama started shouting for him. "Mr. Man! Come on out here! I got somethin' to say to you!"

The only greeting we heard was the dog whining and trying to bark at the same time. Mama stepped up on the back porch and rapped hard on the door. "Mr. *Man!*"

Nothing. Mama came off the porch and took a deep breath. She was beginning to calm down. "Well, I don't know where that ol' rascal done got to, but this ain't over." I thought she would start toward home, but instead she went around the corner of the house where the dog was tied. He was a little coon dog, smaller than he should have been, and he was starved. He tried to look fierce and scare us away, but Mama would have none of that. She knelt down just out of his reach and started speaking to him.

"Hey, baby," she cooed. "I ain't gon' hurt you. Come on over here." She extended her arm and made her hand into a fist. Never taking her eyes off the dog, she said to me, "Don't ever stick your hand out to a strange dog, Mo. He can take your fingers easy. Put your fist out and let him smell you. And don't ever look a strange dog in the eyes. They see that as a challenge."

I was taken aback. I never knew Mama knew so much about dogs. I didn't know she knew anything about dogs. I could feel pride welling up inside me, my fear forgotten. I wondered what other good stuff my Mama was keeping secret.

After the dog had sniffed her, she inched closer and closer to him and was actually petting him. He was licking her.

"This baby's tongue is dry as a bone," she said, thoroughly disgusted.

"You want me to run home and fetch a bowl of water?" I asked, knowing this house possessed neither water nor electricity.

"No, no time. We got to get out of here. Gimme your pocketknife."

My heart stopped. How did she know I had a pocketknife? I wasn't supposed to have it-- she had let me know that in no uncertain terms-- but there I was with it. I could almost feel it burning in the pocket in my corduroys. Before I could open my mouth with a lame denial, Mama said, "Look, I know you have the pocketknife. We'll talk about that later. Just give it and let's get outta here."

Shame-faced, I drew it from my pocket and handed it to Mama, avoiding her eyes. With deft hands, she opened the blade and neatly cut the rope that had the dog tethered to the house. She stood, wrapped the cut rope around her hand, and headed toward the house. The little dog followed her.

I stayed behind, wondering what Mama's pocketknife talk would be this time. Then the thought of Creeper Man coming back and finding me lit a fire in my legs, and I raced off through the briars and down the hill toward home.

**\*\*\*\*\*\*\*\*\*\***

I could hear voices. "Take a look at that dog, Sheriff Delaney. You just tell me he ain't been starved an' abused."

"Well, Miz MacKenzie, it does appear so."

I looked through the crack in the kitchen door and could just barely see them. They were on the back porch, where the dog was still drinking water. He'd eaten his fill.

"And what you reckon you gon' do about it? This po' dog is tied out there to that house in all weather, rain or shine, heat or cold, and by the looks of him he don't get enough t' eat. And them marks? Them's *burns*!"

"Well, I'll go talk to him."

Mama's voice rose. "You need to do more than *talk*! That man is mean as a strip-ed snake! I won't let my children anywhere *near* his place. He's abused this defenseless dog. And you tell me you gon' *talk* to him? I don't know why I wasted my time callin' you out here!"

"Now look, Miz MacKenzie, there ain't no law about keepin' a dog tied up. The law says that what a man does with his own property is his own business."

That really set Mama off. "Then the law needs to be changed! This is a *dog*, not some ol' abandoned *car*!"

Sheriff Delaney sighed and put his hat back on. "Okay, I'll go up there and see if he's in yet, and then I'll see what I can do."

Mama's voice calmed just a little. "Well," she said, "I'll tell you right here and now that this dog ain't goin' back there with you. No sir. Arrest me for stealin' if you want, but this dog is *not-- goin'-- back*."

He stood there a minute, regarding the dog, a look of pity on his face. "Well, Ma'am, I don't rightly see this as stealin'. I reckon it's more of a case o' savin'."

A smile broke out on Mama's face and then suddenly tears came to her eyes. "Thank you, Sheriff. You are so kind. I'm sorry if I got too huffy with you. This has just been really upsettin'." Her anger was completely gone. She moved to come back into the kitchen, which sent me skittering back around the corner into the hall.

"Here, have some peach cobbler," she said. "Made it fresh today. These are Gaffney peaches! I put 'em up over the summer. Take the dish with you—I can get it some other time."

The lawman had no time to protest; she was already slipping the dish into a brown grocery bag and pushing it into his hands. I guess he knew there was no need to say no. If he knew nothing else, he knew, as all men knew then, that a Southern woman was going to grace him with as much food as possible.

Mama said brightly, "I think I know somebody who'll take this dog. They got a lot of property and some nice children who'll just love him."

"Don't tell me anything, Miz MacKenzie," the sheriff said, holding his hand up as he made his way to the front of the house. "The less I know, the better."

Mama disappeared out the front door behind him, and I knew she was watching as Sheriff Delaney safely delivered the cobbler to his police car and then headed up the hill.

I was standing at the sink, making a pretense of washing my hands when Mama came back in the house. "What'd the sheriff have to say?"

Mama gave me the look. "You know very well you heard ever' word," she said.

My face turned red. I was beginning to suspect that Mama knew a whole lot more than she ever let on.

"Okay, I'm gon' take this dog to th' country. He'll have a fine home waitin' for him."

"Can I come?" I never missed an opportunity to ride in the car. With Rose and Maggie in school, I would have the front seat—and Mama—all to myself.

"No. As a matter of fact, I should have the sheriff come back here and haul you off to the reform school for playin' hooky today."

She stood over me, looking down. I felt my face growing hot again. Tears burned my eyes. This day was not going so well. "I'm sorry, Mama. I'm sorry. It's just them boys at school are so mean." My voice was starting to quiver.

"What boys?"

"Them Grigsby boys. They always sayin' mean things an' bein' mean to me on th' bus. Ask Rose and Maggie. They get it, too."

Mama was silent. I wondered what was going through her head. "The Grigsby boys, is it? Well, we'll see about *that*. Now don't cry, Mo. You shoulda told me. I'll fix them Grigsby boys. Have mercy, they just like their triflin' daddy. He was a terror when we was in school, too. Low-life trash."

Mama took my hand and with the other took the dog by his rope, and we headed out to the car. She kept looking around, but there was no one around to see anything.

I ended up sitting in the back with the dog. I started calling him Blue. Over and over I would say, "Blue, you good dog, you. Blue, you *good dog*, you!" Blue loved the attention. He showered me with affection in the form of a wet tongue. He finally had enough water in him to slobber a little. I didn't mind at all.

**********

It turned out that when Sheriff Delaney went up to Creeper Man's house, he didn't find him at home, but what he did find was very interesting. The little house only had two rooms, and one of them was filled with stolen goods. The sheriff recognized them from some reports that had come across his desk. He waited awhile for the thief-and-dog-abuser to come back. He had to go back to the office, though, so he left about an hour later. However, later that evening the sheriff's phone rang in with a complaint of a disturbance down the road and something about a drunk neighbor yelling about a stolen dog. Delaney seized on the opportunity, and before Creeper Man had time to sober up, he was handcuffed and taken to the county jail.

It was an awful ruckus. We could hear Creeper Man screaming. We all gathered on the front porch to get a better listen. We had no shame about standing in the open, eaves-dropping. Besides, it was dark.

He was hollering fit to be tied, yelling about how he'd come home and somebody had taken his dog and left all this stolen property in his place. "I done been *framed*!" he wailed. He wasn't about to go peacefully. We couldn't see anything, but we could hear a scuffle ensuing, and then more shouting, and then something like a muffled thump, and all went quiet. A few minutes later we saw the Sheriff's car pull out of the long dirt driveway.

We were all quiet. Papa finally broke the silence with, "Great time o' day," muttered under his breath. "I wonder what *that* was all about?"

"Ain't that somethin'?" Mama said in return. She squeezed my shoulder once we got back in the house, an unspoken word of encouragement for having kept silent.

Earlier that day, when we had pulled into the Caldwell's driveway with Blue, Mama turned around and put her arm over the back of the seat. "Listen, Maureen," she said, "I don't want you tellin' nobody about what happened today. Loose lips sink ships, as the sayin' goes. If anybody else finds out about all this business 'bout this dog, Creeper Man may find out and come down here and get him. That's why we can't keep him. He'd never be safe at our place. You understand?"

From the back seat, I nodded grimly. We were on a secret mission of mercy.

"Good girl. Now let's go see about findin' this baby a new home. Oh, and by the way," she said, handing me my pocketknife, "I guess you should hang on to this. It come in mighty handy today. Just don't take it to school. Or church." She paused, the look on her face. "And try to remember you a *girl*."

Mama and I never discussed Blue again. It was hard not telling the story, because it had been so exciting and frightening, but I had made my promise.

**********

"I don't believe you've never told us that story!" Rose was incredulous. "Mozie! How could sit on that for so long?"

"Don't think it was easy! But I swore I wouldn't tell. And you know how it goes when you're little. Things get tucked away and forgotten." I finished off the last of my coffee.

"Oh, it didn't end there," Mama said, and she began telling us about Creeper Man showing up a few years later.

For a short time, I felt better. Reliving those days of my childhood made me feel safe. I was where I belonged.

# Chapter 2     *Stitching Things Up*

New Ulster, South Carolina, was founded in 1798 by a large group of Irish immigrants who had come to practice their faith in the way they deemed right and necessary. Led by Reverend Eamonn Delaney, they settled in the Piedmont of South Carolina after a long journey from the north. There were still many Delaneys living in New Ulster who shared ancestry with the original immigrants. Initially a little settlement of Irish Presbyterians, it grew into a thriving town, attracting other Irish and Scots-Irish to the area, Presbyterian as well as other faiths. According to family history, the Doyles came in during the influx of immigrants escaping the famine. The MacKenzies arrived just in time for the Civil War. Now in New Ulster there were Presbyterians and Baptists, Catholics and Methodists, and even a few Pentecostals.

There had been two main occupations in New Ulster: milling cotton and farming. There were several cotton mills in town, and every year the town grew. After the textile industry fell, New Ulster's city planner got on the ball and came up with a workable plan for rebuilding the town as a vacation getaway. Now, years later, there were cozy bed-and-breakfasts that were doing quite well; a golf course that held a huge charitable tournament every summer; cottage industries that sported everything from hand-made quilts, breads, and local honey; and fruit and vegetable stands with produce from the still-working county farms.

Maggie, her husband Wash, and their son George lived near downtown New Ulster. They had a nice little place on a corner lot. Maggie loved it, but Wash was a big outdoorsman, and he said the city cramped him. I had to laugh at that because the "city" we lived in had a population of only eight thousand. Neither one of them had ever lived anywhere else but New Ulster, so they, like Mama, retained their Southern accents mixed with some old Irish expressions still found there.

When they married, Wash moved out of the woods away from his family and bought a house in town for his bride; he wanted nothing more than for her to be happy. As he got older, he vowed that he would be back in the countryside one way or the other. Maggie would roll her eyes and say, "I guess the honeymoon is over, Wash." I had the feeling that after 25 years together, *that* honeymoon had been over a long time. They had married when Maggie was 16 and Wash was 18. A lot of water had gone over the dam in those years.

My nephew George was turning 15 the next summer and would be heading off to boarding academy that fall. He was looking forward to going, more so than his mother thought was respectable. She had tied the apron strings in a bowline knot. He went to church every Sunday, minded his parents, but speaking with him gave me the impression that he was about to explode.

I took him out for ice cream the Sunday after my arrival. He was in a good mood. We talked about football, fishing, cars, and the upcoming year when he would be leaving New Ulster.

"I can see why you wanted to leave," he said. "There is *nothin'* goin on here."

"New Ulster is a great little town. I left to go to college and ended up working for a company near the school." I didn't tell him, but I wanted to "escape" my hometown when I was his age, too.

"Why did you come back?" He played around with a plastic spoon.

"Well, my marriage ended, and I needed to be with family." It hurt me to talk about it, but I had always been honest with George.

He frowned, his green eyes looking like sparks. "That husband o' yourn, he's a b-hole." He sounded just like his Da. "He ain't good enough to scrape your shoes on, Aunt Mo. You're better off."

I just looked at him. He was trying so hard to be grown, and it touched me.

"I appreciate that, Georgie, and I know everything will work out, but this is tough."

"Huh." He sounded disgusted. "He ought to be horsewhipped. Daddy said he ought to go up there and punch him in the nose."

"You never cared much for him, did you?"

"Well, he wadn't exactly warm an' fuzzy. And lazy? Sheesh! I ain't *never* seen anybody as lazy. Wouldn't hit a lick at a snake."

When George was six, we had come to visit and celebrate his birthday. Wash had gotten him a new rod and reel, and the birthday boy could hardly wait to get down to the river and do some fishing. Unfortunately, Wash had broken his ankle at work and was laid up, so trekking down to the riverbank was out of the question. George excitedly ran to his uncle and asked him to take him fishing, and the reply he got puzzled and stunned him. "I don't do fishing," he'd said behind his book, not even looking at his nephew. This was the last straw for Georgie, who had often tried to engage his uncle in some fun, and he had held it against him ever since.

Wash didn't care too much for him, either, as he had tried to solicit his help in the garden, and had invited him on several fishing trips, and the answer was always no. It wasn't until after the divorce that I knew how my family really felt about my husband. Maggie left out no details.

"Like I said," George reiterated, "He's a' ol' b-hole."

"As eye-opening as it is, I find the topic of this conversation is making my stomach churn. Let's change the subject. How is school this year?"

George rolled his eyes. "Why do grown-ups always want to talk about school?"

"Well, what do you want to talk about?" I finished my ice cream and wiped my chin with my napkin. I could never eat ice cream without making a mess.

George again screwed his face into a frown and I held my breath; I knew it was going to be a doozy. "Do you really belong to a secret society?"

I dropped my napkin. "No, I do not," I said. "Where in the world did you get that idea?"

"From Daddy. He said you go to church on Saturday and belong to a..." He was searching for the word. "A... *cult*. I never thought about it before, but I do remember every time you visited, you'd be gone on Saturday most of the day. So you was at church? How'd you get to be in a cult? Do y'all have secret handshakes and sacrifices?"

"Oh, for Pete's sake. George Washington Connolly, I do *not* belong to a cult, much less a secret society. And I don't know any secret handshakes. I tell you what. Why don't you come to church with me some Saturday and find out all about it?"

**********

It was time for Rose to go home. She'd taken an emergency leave from the university where she taught, and her time was gone. She'd said her goodbyes to Mama and Maggie. I walked her out to the rental car where we lingered. I hardly got to see her anymore since she'd moved to New Mexico. In those years, she had changed. She'd lost a lot of her New Ulster ways. But I noticed from time to time they came back full-force. She also carried herself with more confidence than I'd ever seen. The same teenager who'd worked in the cotton mill was now a grown, educated woman. As Maggie put it, Rose "had it goin' on."

"You're going to be fine, Maureen," she said. "You're strong. I know it'll be tough going for a while, but you're going to come out on top. I know it."

"Thank you, Rose." I felt tears starting to sting my eyes. She put her arms around me and gave me a big hug. "You sure you don't want to come with me to La Paz?"

"And what would I do there?" I asked, smiling and wiping my eyes.

"Anything you want. New Mexico is wonderful. The university is fantastic. You have a degree; you could find something. You could even go back to school and get your Master's."

"I may do that someday, Rose, but right now I just need to think and look at all my options. I appreciate your suggestion, though. I do think it would be fun living out there with you in New Mexico. Imagine the trouble we'd get into!" We both laughed. "But right now, this is where I'm supposed to be."

"Okay, Mo, but you know the offer always stands. We would be two single chicks out on the make!"

I threw back my head and laughed. "Rose, some man is going to snatch you up one fine day and you're going to wonder what took him so long!"

"Not in *this* lifetime, Sweet Cheeks." With that she got in her car, blew me a big kiss, and headed up the long driveway. My heart pounded. I missed her already. Too many goodbyes, I thought, and walked toward the house.

**********

Mama wasn't exactly the most graceful thing on two legs. One Friday morning we were visiting Maggie. Mama got up after having offered to make coffee, tripped over her own feet, and crashed to the floor, banging her head on an end table as she went.

"Oh, Lawsey!" Maggie screamed, and threw herself on the floor next to Mama. "Mama! *Mama*! Are you alright?"

"I ain't deaf, Margaret, at least not yet," she replied. When she rolled over, blood was gushing down her face. Maggie started screaming.

"Mo! She's *bleedin'* to death! Call an ambulance! *Call 911!*"

Mama was looking at her in disbelief. I had gotten a kitchen towel and began pressing it against the gash in her head. "We don't need to call anyone, Maggs," I said, trying to sound reassuring. "You're okay. Right, Mama?"

"Well, I don't reckon I'm gonna die *that* easy."

"But Mama," Maggie wailed, "all the *blood*!"

"Margaret," I said, "why don't you go get another towel and put some cold water on it and bring it to me? Mama's okay. Head wounds bleed a lot, but she's fine. Okay? Go get me that towel."

After she'd gone, I said quietly, "I think you need a stitch or two, Mama."

"Well, dang, girl. You said I was alright!"

"You are! But you laid your forehead open pretty good."

Mama looked disgusted. She could never be bothered by doctors. Maggie came back with the towel, and together we helped Mama into a chair.

"I'm going to take her in for a few stitches," I told Maggie.

"I'll get my coat. I'll drive and you can hold the compress."

She went for her coat. Mama looked at me. "Thank you gigantically," she said with more than a hint of sarcasm.

I told her I thought it was a good idea to have an extra pair of hands.

She put her hand to her head and murmured, "Lawd, have mercy."

**********

There was a doctor on East Main Street. Mama didn't know his name, but she wanted to go there. Since her doctor retired, she had not seen a regular doctor. "I will not go to that boy who took over his practice," she said.

"Boy?" Maggie said. "Mama, he's got to be at least 40."

"Yeah, but I saw him at the county fair, an' he was pickin' his nose. No, thank you."

So we stopped at the office, which was run more like a clinic. Appointments were taken, but they weren't necessary. The waiting room was almost full. Life behind the receptionist's window was a madhouse. The phone was ringing off the hook, and there was only one girl working there. She was trying unsuccessfully to answer the phone and check patients in and out at the same time. She looked at me with an apologetic, wilted expression in her eyes and handed me paperwork on a clipboard. I took it and started filling it out for Mama.

"I didn't know it would be like *this*," Mama said.

"Should we go to the emergency room?" Maggie asked.

"Mercy no! That's the chamber o' death! I'll stay here and take m' chances."

As we waited and filled out the papers, two people got up and left. We all looked at each other. "Think they know somethin' we don't?" Maggie asked in a hushed tone. I shrugged. Mama was cool. "Less time to have to wait," she said.

Given Mama's open gash, we were bumped ahead of a few others. The receptionist took us to a tiny room that faced the back alley. "Are you sure it's my turn?" Mama asked the girl. "There were some ahead of us that didn't seem too happy."

"Triage," the girl replied. "Dr. Liske'll be with you shortly." And she was gone.

Mama said, "Triage? What does that mean?"

"It means you rate gettin' seen first," Maggie offered. "Mercy, it's cramped in here," she groaned. She was somewhat claustrophobic.

"Well, look," I said, "Mama's okay, and I can manage things. Why don't you go out front and finish your magazine? Lots more room out there."

"Is that okay with you, Mama?"

"Actually, if you wouldn't mind to go down the street to the Little Cricket and get me a Coke, I'd be much obliged. I'm a mite parched."

Maggie wasn't gone long when the doctor walked in. In spite of the chaos in his office, he looked completely unruffled. He was nice-looking, looked to be in his mid-to-late 50's and had a pleasant smile. With a slight German accent, he introduced himself as Dr. Liske.

"So, what's going on with you, Mrs. MacKenzie? Did you take a fall?"

"Yessir, I did. Hit my head on the corner of a' end table. How's it look?"

He removed the towel and inspected the gash. "That looks pretty nasty," he said. "You need a couple of stitches. I can take care of that right away. But I'm really concerned as to *why* you fell."

Mama held her leg straight up in front of her. "See this big foot?"

"Yes."

"It looks just like *this* big foot," and she held up the other one. "I got 'em crossed and went down like a stone."

"So you experienced no dizziness? Nothing unusual?" Dr. Liske asked.

"No, just klutziness."

The doctor smiled. He began his examination, listening to her chest and asking her to follow his finger with her eyes. He questioned her as to her medical history. Then he patted Mama's hand. "Well, let's get you fixed up. I'll use a nice herringbone stitch, eh?" Mama and the doctor looked at each other and smiled. "Go on with ya," she said.

While he was cleaning the wound, he explained that he would have to inject the area with a local anesthetic. "That's the worst part," he said. "The rest will be a day at the park."

Mama was still while he made the injection, though I saw a tear roll down from the corner of her eye.

"Now," Dr. Liske said, smiling, we'll give that a few moments to do its work, and then we can finish."

"Thank you," Mama told him. "I don't mean no disrespect, Doctor, but your office seems to be a looney bin. Where's your staff?"

My jaw dropped. I was mortified. Dr. Liske seemed to be a little taken aback himself.

"I lost an employee this morning," he said. "I can't seem to find anyone who wants to work!"

Mama never skipped a beat. "My daughter needs a job," she said matter-of-factly. "Maureen here, she needs work. She works like a mule. You'd be lucky t' have her."

Dr. Liske looked at me. I stammered, "I was an office manager for the same company for 15 years." He simply smiled. "See my receptionist out front," he said. "Fill out an application."

He turned his attention to Mama, who was looking mighty smug at the moment. "Now, Missus, let's get that head stitched up." As he guided the needle into the skin, Maggie opened the door. She saw the shiny curved needle in Mama's head, and she and the large fountain soda hit the floor.

**********

That afternoon, Mama was resting in her recliner and watching judge shows on television. Maggie and George came over to check on her, and he and Mama watched television together.

"I love me some Judge Judy," Mama said, turning up the volume.

Maggie and I went into the kitchen.

"I take it you're feeling better," I said.

"Don't remind me. How embarrassin'." We couldn't help giggling, however. "Do you think you'll get a job there? Mama said she really talked you up!"

I rolled my eyes. "Girl, with the state that office was in, my application is probably lost already." I started pulling food out of the refrigerator to make supper. "Tomorrow I'm going to start looking. I need a job in the worst way."

"Not much around here, Mozie. You might have to go over to Greenville or Spartanburg."

The phone rang. Mama was calling my name. "It's for you," she said, waving the receiver in the air.

It was Dr. Liske. "Can you start Monday?" he asked.

## Chapter 3        *Kilts and Cousins*

Papa was 21 years older than Mama. They met when she was 19. New Ulster held a St. Patrick's Day dance every year at the Veteran Lodge, and that year Mama went with a group of her girlfriends. Papa saw her walk in and, as he said in telling us, his jaw dropped. "I never saw anythang so purty in all my life. Your Mama was wearin' a green dress, an' her red hair was fallin' over her shoulders. I thought I was lookin' at a' angel."

He walked right up to her and asked her to dance. To his surprise, she accepted his invitation. She didn't see the age difference. Mama said that when she saw Papa heading her way, her heart stopped. He was wearing the kilt of the MacKenzie clan, and he looked, she said, absolutely dashing. He had thick blond hair. She noticed his deep dimples before he got close, but Papa's green eyes took her breath away.

They danced with no one else that night. It was the best dance, Mama said, that she had ever been to in her life. At the end, Papa asked to see her again.

Her friends gave her a hard time about the age difference, asking her what she saw in "that old man," but Mama would have none of it. She enjoyed Brance MacKenzie's company, and she wasn't going to let age get in the way.

Her parents liked Papa right away. Her father especially liked him, considering he was only 10 years older. They had a lot to talk about. My grandfather was only 2 years older than my grandmother, but he had been forced into adulthood at an early age to help support his family. He felt that a woman needed a strong man, a mature man, not some playboy with nothing but sport and deviance on his mind. Brance MacKenzie was solid, a man who would take care of his daughter.

Papa had been married once before, when he was 20, but his wife died of pneumonia only two years into their marriage. He was not interested in marriage again until he met Mama. Then, he said, his whole world changed. He was ready to live again.

I loved hearing Papa talk about his courtship with Mama. Even after all those years, he still had that light in his eyes. To him, Elizabeth Doyle MacKenzie hung the moon. I can still see Mama standing behind

Papa as he sat at the table, telling us about her. She'd smile and kiss him on top of his head and say, "I couldn't resist a man in a kilt."

We never noticed the difference in our parents' ages until we went to school. Then it became an issue. The other children would make jokes about us having an old man as an "old man." We took it in stride until we got to be teenagers, but I think Rose took it the hardest.

Papa loved telling jokes, the cornier the better. Unfortunately, he told them over and over. I would still laugh because I was the youngest, but Maggie and Rose would groan. We were at the supper table one night and Papa said, "Hey, Rose, why did the rubber chicken cross the road?"

"So she could stretch her legs," she answered, not even looking up from her mashed potatoes.

"Now, little girl, that just goes to show you got too much book learnin' if you don't find a joke like *that* funny!"

Rose got up from the table and said, "Really, Papa, can't you find some new ones?" She went to our room.

Papa looked a little hurt, but he said, "What you reckon's eatin' at Rose, Bessie?"

Mama just shook her head in an *I don't know* and went on with her supper. Later Maggie and I heard her go in to Rose and talk to her. Of course we had no shame and listened through the door.

That day at school, Rose had gotten into an argument about Papa with someone who didn't care too much for her. She could have handled it alright, she said, except that Matt Brody was in earshot, and she was a little sweet on Matt Brody. She just felt humiliated and was embarrassed to have the oldest father of anyone at school.

"Listen here, Rose," I heard Mama say, "Your Da is a hard-workin' man. He works in that cotton mill an' still manages to keep this place up. An' he's worked all these years so you can have the things you have now. He has been a blessin' from God, and don't you ever forget it. If them silly brats at school have nothin' better to do, then just stay away from 'em. Low-life trash!"

By the time Mama came out the bedroom door, we were intently studying math and English at the kitchen table. As she breezed through to the front room, she said, "Catch all that, girls?"

**********

When we were growing up, all the MacKenzies and Doyles got together at our house for the yearly Christmas dinner. How that little house held all those people is still a mystery to me. The yard would be full of cars from our town and all over the state. Mama started cooking early, and we all chipped in to help with the festivities. We had to really steel ourselves to get ready for all the aunts, uncles and cousins, especially Cud'din Willy, whom we didn't like one whit because he was such a pain. No matter what anyone got for Christmas, he got something better. He was an only child, born late in his parents' lives, and all the coddling had made him insufferable. Uncle William thought his child was the best thing since pasteurized milk.

Cud'din Willie was not what you would call an attractive boy. He had unruly curly hair and was missing his front tooth. I certainly could have looked beyond all that, but he had the personality of a scrub brush. Mama said it was because he was born on Halloween.

Uncle William was Mama's older brother, and he had never really forgiven Mama for leaving the Catholic church and becoming Presbyterian when she married Papa. His wife was Aunt Doris, a woman trembling on the edge of death whenever she had an audience.

The middle sibling was Aunt Melba. Her husband, my Uncle Clive, was a genuine sweetheart. They had five children: Clive Junior, but we called him JuJu; another Margaret, but she was always called Margaret, never Maggie; Bryce, Henry, and Little Melba. (When she was 30 years old, she was still called "Little Melba," much to her dismay.)

Papa's side of the family was slightly older, so there was another generation to come in with them. Papa's brother, Uncle Richard, who had been a widower since he was 32, had never seen fit to remarry. His two sons were grown and living in Ireland, so he always came alone. He was a striking figure of a man, still very handsome, and a snappy dresser. Every bit of an old-fashioned gentleman, he still stood whenever a woman came into the room. Sometimes Mama would joke in front of him, "If I'd-a met Richard before you, Brance, well, I believe you'd probably be out in the cold!" Everyone would laugh, but I noticed that Uncle Richard always looked a little embarrassed. He was very a straight-laced, card-carrying Presbyterian. We were Presbyterian, too, but nothing like Uncle Richard. He should have been a reverend, Papa always said.

There was Uncle Michael and Aunt Sally. Their daughter Lois, her husband Martin and their children always came over. There were so many of them and we only saw them once a year that we girls called them the Columbia Cousins and let it go at that. There was also Ida Rose, whom our Rose was named after. She and Aunt Lois were twins. Her husband Jerry was an atheist, so Aunt Ida Rose would never allow him to come for Christmas. "Huh! He can spit in God's face all he wants if that's the way he wants to be, but I'll hanged if he's gon' get a feast on the Lord's birthday!" So she came with her daughter and son, Anna-lee and Robert.

Always the last to show up was Aunt Minnie, Papa's baby sister, and Uncle Russ. They had never had children, something that caused them great sorrow, so they lavished us and the other cousins with love and attention. They always brought a black walnut cake, chocolate cream pie, kitchen sink cookies, and a coconut cake, all made from scratch. Uncle Russ would also bring fireworks, and that assured us all of a grand time.

On this particular Christmas, when I was seven, I was in the front room as it was filling up with relatives. Aunt Doris had a history of being deathly ill from something whenever we had family gatherings. On this occasion, she left her death-bed to grace us with an appearance, her hand never leaving her head. Watching her feign a headache and fanning herself with her handkerchief, I thought that if I had a child like Cud'din Willie, my head would have rotted plumb *off*. Weary of her moaning, I went in the kitchen with Papa while he made his eggnog. Papa made the best eggnog in the world. It was so rich and thick and delicious that it only took a small cup to fill me up, but the taste left me wanting more. I never learned his recipe, and that always made me sorry when I grew up.

Cud'din Willie came in and watched Papa as he stirred the ingredients. "What ya doin', Unka Branch?" he asked. For some reason most of the cousins thought our father's name was Branch. Papa went with it.

"Makin' eggnog, boy," Papa answered. "You like eggnog?"

Cud'din Willie nodded his head.

"I think I make pretty good eggnog. Want a taste?"

Cud'din Willie nodded and held his hand out for the cup. He drank deeply from it.

"Whatcha think, boy?" Papa asked.

"It's alright, but my Mama makes it better than that." He wiped his mouth on his sleeve.

"You don't say," Papa said, and went on mixing. He kept his eyes on Cud'din Willie. "Say, boy," he finally said, "Do you know how to make holy water?"

Cud'din Willie nodded his head. "Of course I do. Everybody knows *that*."

I couldn't stand Cud'din Willie. He thought he was so smart. I knew he didn't know how to make holy water, even if he *was* Catholic. I didn't know how to make it, either, but I wanted to learn.

"Papa, how *do* you make holy water?" I asked. Papa gave me the greatest smile and said, "Well, you take regular sink water, put it in a pot, and then..." he leaned down and said, "you boil the hell out of it."

Cud'din Willie let out a shriek and gasped, "Unka Branch said a *bad* word!! MAMA!" He went running to the front room, and we could hear him scream, "Mama! Unka Branch said a *real bad word*!"

Papa threw back his head and laughed. He went on to finish his eggnog. I looked at him for a minute then said, "What do you mean, Papa?"

He gave me a startled look, and then he laughed out loud and kept laughing. "Mo, my girl," he gasped between laughing, "don't ever lose that!" Of course, I didn't understand what "that" was, either. I reckoned I was not going to learn how to make holy water that day, so I decided to put on my coat and go outside to play.

I wasn't out of the house one minute when some of the other cousins came out. Two of the Columbia Cousins came, but they didn't stop to play with me; they made for the tire swing. Anna-lee, Margaret, and of course, Cud'din Willie, followed. I groaned. Just when I thought all was lost, Robert came out. I was relieved because I figured the two boys would play together and leave us girls alone.

But Cud'din Willie thought he was the recreational planner, and he took charge. "Let's go play in the woods at the old outhouse!" It wasn't a suggestion; it was an order. For someone who was only 10, Cud'din Willie Doyle thought he was a big shot.

"Shut up, Cud'din Willie," I said. "We'll play where we want to."

"I'm gon' tell Mama you won't play with me, and you'll be in trouble." Cud'din Willie looked at me without blinking.

I hated it, but I knew he was right. My mama was ferocious when it came to manners and being a good hostess. If word reached her ears that I was being anything less than gracious to our visiting cousins, she'd make me do dishes when it wasn't even my turn. The other cousins were looking at me and waiting for my answer.

Finally I said, "Alright. We'll play in the woods." I sighed deeply in resignation.

We went behind the house and down the path to the place where we played. The old outhouse was something of a mystery. It was there when our house was built, and no one knew who built it. We suspected it had been built for the Creeper Man house, but it was situated on our property, deepening the mystery. We loved it though, because it often came in handy when we were playing in the woods.

Cud'din Willie passed the outhouse, however, and made his way down the hill. "Lookit that deadfall!" he said, as though it were a miracle of nature.

"So it's a deadfall, Cud'din Willie. What of it?"

Cud'din Willie looked at me like I smelled of limburger. "We can play on that," he said, and ran up to it. "We can climb over it, and then when we're done, we can set it on fire!"

"You're crazy!" I retorted. "You want to burn the whole place down?"

"Not the whole place, you dope. Just the deadfall. I have *matches*!"

Cud'din Willie *would* have matches. He was fascinated with fire.

"No, Cud'din Willie," I said flatly, "we ain't gon' be burnin' *nothin'*!"

Anna-lee and Margaret looked alarmed, but Robert said he liked the idea. "A bond fire!" his little voice shouted.

That seemed to give Cud'din Willie the courage to go on with his plan. "See? *Robert* wants a fire. Let's have a fire!"

The girls started shouting, "No!" together, but Cud'din Willie only chided them by telling them they were wimps. Margaret grabbed Robert's hand and she and Anne-lee tore off running. I was left alone with Cud'din Willie. He began gathering dried leaves for a starter.

"Cud'din Willie, gimme them matches," I demanded, trying to sound mean, but my voice quivered a little. I was angry but also terrified.

My beloved woods—not to mention our house—could soon be swallowed up in flames!

"Wimpy!" he shouted and laughed. I tried to wrestle the matches out of his hand. He was bigger and stronger and his hands broke away from mine with ease. He began climbing the deadfall, laughing, and I followed.

"Cud'din Willie! Gimme them matches!" I was fully angry by now. He continued taunting me. He was loving this game. As I got closer to him, the deadfall began to collapse, and I felt it give out from under me. I screamed as I fell. As Cud'din Willie was laughing, the deadfall collapsed even further and gave out from under him as well. With a loud crash, Cud'din Willie landed in a heap on the ground. He began screaming.

When he looked up, I screamed again, too. A stick had pierced his eyebrow clear through and just missed going into his eyeball. Blood was spurting everywhere. I was horrified.

"It's your fault!" he screamed. "It's your fault!" And he got up and looked around to see which way was home. He was stumbling around.

"Give me your hand, Cud'din, an' I'll he'p ye!"

He just shouted, "It's your fault!" again and refused my offer of help. I jumped in front of him so he would at least follow me. We went a few steps, and I could hear someone crashing through the woods.

Papa and Uncle William were coming through the trees. I was so relieved. "What in the world happened here?" Papa asked as Uncle William swooped Cud'din Willie up in his arms.

He began crying, "Mo pushed me down in the deadfall! *She* did it!"

Uncle William gave me a look that would have killed a wild boar, turned on his heels and began stomping back to the house.

"Papa, that ain't what happened! I *swear* it ain't!" He picked me up, not looking angry at all but very concerned, and wordlessly made his way back toward home. I felt something warm on my face. *I must be cryin'*, I thought.

We got to the back yard and were greeted with shrieks coming from Aunt Doris. She was running across the yard. Papa put me down and took a step toward her with his hand out, but before anyone could take another breath, Aunt Doris had pushed past Papa, and her hand struck me across the face. I gasped. Blood splattered everywhere.

I put my hand on my face, and it was sticky with blood. There was a big gash on my forehead that I had gotten from the deadfall. Mama was suddenly there, picking me up and carrying me inside. She had me on the sink, cleaning my face, and telling me not to worry. There were loud voices coming from the hall and bathroom. Cud'din Willie was in there with Aunt Doris, who was carrying on like her baby had been wounded by mortar shell.

She came out of the bathroom with Cud'din Willie, who still had the stick piercing through his eyebrow, and without another word, they left. The house was deadly quiet for a minute, and then everyone started talking. Anna-lee and Margaret told everyone what really happened. Aunt Doris never did apologize for hitting me like she did.

It took a while, but we finally settled down to eat. I had a bandage on my head, and on my cheek was a big welt in the shape of Aunt Doris' hand. I was sitting beside Papa, and he picked up my hand and gently kissed it. He leaned down to me and said, "What did Santy Claus say to Mrs. Claus when he looked up in the sky?"

"What, Papa?"

"It looks like rain, dear!"

I giggled, "Awww, Papa!" No one else heard the joke because they were all talking at once. No one could out-talk the Doyles and MacKenzies.

After dark Uncle Russ brought out the fireworks. I thought it had been a fine Christmas.

# Chapter 4     The Office

Doctor Wolfgang Liske's office was worse than unorganized; it was chaos. He'd had only two receptionists working for him, although it was an office for at least three. The day we took Mama in there was the day one of the ladies quit, and the other was threatening to quit, too, if he didn't hurry and hire someone else. The place was in such a state that I think he would have hired me if I had been a gorilla with a pencil.

I arrived early Monday morning to get briefed on what was going on. I couldn't believe the mess. Patient files were everywhere. There were different stacks of papers that had to be filed away in them. It wasn't even time to open, and the phone was already ringing off the hook. My coworker, Jean, tried to present herself as calm that morning when she was showing me around. She was so happy to see me, she said, and hoped that I would stick around.

Jean was probably in her 20's, but she wore so much make-up it was hard to tell exactly. Her hair was done up in a wild angular-cut style that started off as brown at her neck and ended up bleached blonde on top.

"Don't mind the phone," she said. "The answerin' machine will get it. We don't *open* till nine, so I don't *answer* till nine. And at lunch break? Take your break. Let the machine get it. And we close at five, so be *out* by five, or you'll end up spendin' the night."

She was whizzing through instructions on the computer so quickly that I hardly had time to come up for breath. I was totally lost. I was beginning to wish I were still at home having a cup of coffee.

"Here's the list of patients we're seein' today, and these are all their files right here." She patted a huge stack of stuffed manila folders. "If someone comes in needin' attention right away, put 'em in front of everybody else."

By the time Jean unlocked the door, patients were already waiting to get in. "Here goes nothin'," she hissed and called out the first patient's name.

**\*\*\*\*\*\*\*\*\*\***

At four fifty-five that afternoon, Jean already had the answering machine set and the computers shut down. "At five o'clock, we're gone," she said. "He doesn't pay us after five, so we are gone."

Just then Dr. Liske walked up front from his office, smiling and rubbing his hands together. "So, Maureen, how was your first day?"

I resisted the temptation to tell him that passing a kidney stone would have been more pleasurable. "It was...busy," I said. "I'm sure I'll get the hang of things around here."

"Oh, I am certain that you will," he replied, smiling and looking so happy. "I think you did a marvelous---"

"Bye!" Jean nearly shouted, and was, as she said she'd be, *gone*.

**\*\*\*\*\*\*\*\*\*\***

By the time I got home, I was exhausted. I noticed Mama had a troubled look on her face when she met me at the door. I braced myself for bad news.

"What is it?"

She handed me a slip of paper. "Some man called for you today. Said he was your attorney. Wants you to call him back."

"Don't be alarmed, Mama. It's the guy who is handling the divorce. I'll call him tomorrow on my lunch break."

Mama looked relieved. "Whew! I thought you were in some kind of trouble, girl. I've been worried all afternoon."

"Well, why didn't you just call me at work?'

"I *tried*! But I got put on hold every time. I finally hung up and tried again, but got the same thing."

"Oh, Mama," I groaned. "What a nightmare! I hate this job. I can tell already that it's going to put me in an early grave." I took my shoes off and sat at the table. I was spent.

"Well, look," Mama said, "let me get you some supper. How about a nice sweet tater? Ain't nothin' better on a chilly day than a good hot sweet tater. You want me to dress it for you?"

I thought I was a little old to be waited on by my mother, but I was so tired, and the idea of a hot sweet potato sounded so good, especially if I didn't have to get up to dress it.

"Please. Thank you, Mama."

She put butter on it, a sprinkle of cinnamon, a splash of maple syrup, and topped it off with pecans. It was delicious. We ate together in silence. Once I had something to eat, I began feeling better, so we chatted a bit about the job. I told Mama how miserable it was.

"Do you know he's a tight-wad? He can't keep anyone because he tries to get by on as little as possible. He got rid of the cleaning company because it cost too much. Mama, he expects Jean and me to clean that place! And he tries to have just two of us working out there when we need a third. I could see that today. And get this, Mama—he doesn't even have a *nurse!*"

"Good land!" she remarked. "No wonder he was doing everything hisself when I was there! Is he lookin' for one?"

"I don't know, but he'd better be. More days like today would kill me. As a matter of fact, I'm thinking I may just give my notice tomorrow."

"Mo! You're not a quitter!"

"Listen, Mama, this man would have made Winston Churchill give up. I just don't think it's a good fit."

I left it at that. Mama didn't argue, but I knew she'd worry if I didn't have a job.

Tuesday I went to work early to make sure I was a step ahead of the game. Jean came in at her usual time and said, "Girl, if he sees you came in early and he has to pay you overtime, he'll have a fit. When Nancy quit, I stayed over to get things in order, and when he saw I had overtime, his face turned the color o' blood. I'm surprised he didn't go out and break his hand just so he wouldn't have to write a check."

I laughed out loud. Then I realized she was serious. I started to tell her I was quitting, but thought better of it. First thing in the morning was not the right time. Besides, I owed it to Dr. Liske to tell him first.

"Why is he so tight?" I asked, not really expecting an answer, but I got one.

"Girl! That man can't handle *money*! He had some hare-brained real estate deal on the side, and loaned somebody some money to flip several houses he was gonna use as rentals, and he got taken to the cleaners. We're talkin' big, fat money. That's when he let the cleanin' service go. It's been downhill since--and don't get me started on his wife. She spends like nobody's business--- and we used to have three girls out here, *and* a nurse, but all that went bye-bye soon after. The third lady we had here asked for a raise, he wouldn't give it, so she up and quit. The nurse quit soon after. Then it was just the two of us, and everything has fallen apart. I told him I was gonna quit if he didn't hire somebody else. So he got you. I'm glad you're here, but I don't see how the two of us can keep this place goin' much longer. He's got to hire somebody else *and* a nurse."

I felt a surge of guilt. I knew my time was limited there. I didn't respond, but I went to the file cabinets to get the patient charts for the day. Dr. Liske breezed in, smiling as always, and wished us a good morning. He went on back to the kitchen to make coffee. Jean followed him. I heard the door close, and voices. After a while, the voices got louder. All this time the phone was ringing, ringing, ringing. It was time to unlock the front door.

At my lunch break, I went into one of the patient rooms to use the phone. I was really too frazzled to have a logical conversation, but I had to make that call.

"Maureen, so glad to hear from you!" John Hobrick was always the gentleman.

"What's up John?" I needed to get straight to business.

"Well, I've spoken with your husband's attorney, and these are some things he wants in the divorce settlement."

I was mildly interested, because I figured it would be the house and property and everything else he already possessed; I left with a few things that were mine before we married, and some clothing.

"He wants the house and property. He said he owned that before the marriage and thought he had the right to keep it."

"Fine," I said.

John continued, "He also wants the car that's in your possession."

"What? He's lost his mind. I have to have my car. He has his own!"

"Apparently, the engine blew in his, so he wants yours. I've already told them to forget that, and his attorney agreed. And you want to let the house and property go?"

"Yes. That place means nothing to me."

"Maureen, if it were sold, it would mean several *thousand* to you!"

"John, he probably owes more on the house than it's worth. He's refinanced a couple of times. I'm surprised he didn't try to stick me with *that.*" My heart began to ache, not from sorrow but from anger. I left without any ugliness, and now this was how he was repaying me.

"Let him keep the house. What else?"

John Hobrick cleared his throat. "Well, Maureen, you know none of this is set in stone yet. Nothing will be decided without serious consideration by the judge."

I felt my scalp tingle. "What is it, John?"

He paused then said, "He's asking for maintenance."

"For what?" I asked.

"Alimony."

**********

Mama nearly had a fit when I told her the news.

"Whatever you do," I said, "don't tell Maggie. Until I know how this is going to turn out, I don't want her to know. She'll throw a rod."

"Honey," Mama said in a serious tone, "she'll send him a letter bomb."

We talked all evening about it, wondering how in the world he'd ever win alimony. We agreed that he was lazy, but laziness never won anyone alimony. His attorney must have been as crazy as he was to go along with such a thing, unless he knew something we didn't. At any rate, it would be decided by the court. I got a sick-to-my-stomach feeling knowing I'd have to make a trip to Kentucky to see this thing through. I would fight it, though.

The next morning I went to work early again, trying to get ahead on some filing, never having spoken to Dr. Liske the day before about leaving. There was just never a moment, and at five he promptly left. As much as I had wanted to go home, I stayed and worked a few more hours.

Jean came in that morning and began helping me file. I could tell she was still upset about the day before. She'd gone in to see Dr. Liske in his office, again, about hiring a third staff member, and from what I gathered from her, it didn't go too well.

"He's tighter than Dick's hat band," she told me later through clinched teeth. "'I have to hire a nurse,' he said, and I said, 'I know, but you also need someone else at the desk. It's a fulltime job just keepin' these charts current!' And he had the nerve to say, 'You need to file away patient information as it comes in,' and I said, 'Are you *kiddin'* me?

When am I supposed to answer the phone, and check patients in and out, *and* verify insurance?' He said, 'Let Maureen handle that,' and I nearly went off. The man is thick as a *rock*!"

Jean's eyes got big as saucers when she was upset. At one point I thought they were just going to fall out of her head. "So I finally told him, I said, 'Dr. Liske, you either get some more help in here, or I *quit*!' Well, he didn't like that one little bit. Said three workers aren't in the budget. I started to say, 'Well, budget *this*!' But I didn't." When she finally came up for air she said, "Have mercy, I'm going to have to go to confession this week for *sure*!"

I said, "I hope you're okay with me being hired as office manager. After all, you've been here longer."

Jean kept filing, never looking up. "I don't have a problem with it. I wasn't hired on as the manager. But I know how *I'd* manage this office."

"Hm."

"I'd burn it to the ground." She nodded her head in the direction of Dr. Liske's office. "With *that* thang *in* it."

Later that morning, we had a visit from a woman who barreled in, acknowledging neither of us, and headed back to Dr. Liske's office. She had on a tight, short skirt and leopard print blouse, her hair done up in a tease. Her high heels clicked as she disappeared down the hall. She left a cloud of very loud perfume.

"Great," Jean said. "Just what we need to make the day brighter."

"What *was* that?" I asked.

"*That*," she said, "is Mrs. Wolfgang Liske." I could tell by her voice and the expression she wore that Jean didn't care two whits about Dr. Liske's wife.

I lowered my voice. "Wolfie—you *dog*."

Jean snickered. "I never woulda put that pair together," she said. "Get ready for fireworks. I could tell by the look on her face that she's not here for a social call."

Jean was right. In a short time, we heard loud voices come from Dr. Liske's office. The patients could hear, too, so Jean went in the waiting room and turned the radio up louder. Within minutes the walls trembled from the slamming office door, and Mrs. Liske, wearing a horrible scowl, banged her way back out and into the parking lot. Her tires squealed as she pulled into the street.

Dr. Liske appeared, frowning, and said he was ready for the next patient. Jean and I acted as if nothing had happened.

By the end of the week, we had settled into a rhythm around each other. We worked well together. Dr. Liske noticed the semblance of order, and he was happy. "Let's not make him *too* happy," Jean said, "or we never *will* get any more help."

I finished up my time card on Friday. I had worked over a couple of evenings, plus with coming in early, so I had a total of 52 hours.

Jean looked at it. "You're kiddin' me, right? You're gonna turn that in for him to sign? Hm. When Dr. Liske sees *that*," she said calmly, "he's gonna go out and saw his fingers off so he won't have to sign your check."

"Well," I responded, "if that's the case, I'll just have to take it in cash." Then we laughed.

I held my breath as we approached Dr. Liske's desk with our time cards. He glanced over Jean's and promptly signed it and wrote her out a check. He took mine, looked at it, then stared at it, then put it down flat in front of him on the desk. "Maureen," he asked coolly, "why do you have twelve hours overtime?"

At this point, Jean spun around on her heel and headed out the door. I was left to face the firing squad alone.

"I came in early every morning. I worked over evenings, too. I *had* to, Dr. Liske, or we would never have gotten ahead."

The smile that he always wore was gone. He picked up his pen, rolled it between his hands and slowly said, "Alright, but don't let this happen again."

I started to remain quiet, but I spoke up instead. "Dr. Liske, I put in all those hours to get this office in order. This place is chaos! There is still a ton of work to do to get it in decent shape. You hired me to do a job, and there is no way under heaven to get it done in a few days with just the two of us out there working no overtime. I don't know what you expect me to do! I'm not a miracle worker!"

"Your mother spoke of you as if you were."

We regarded one another. I figured now was the time to hand in my notice.

"Dr. Liske," I began.

Before I could say more he began speaking. "Maureen, I apologize. You *have* done a good job, Jean likes working with you, and in spite of the fact that you can't remember the patients' names, I think they like you, too. I think this will work out alright. Have a good weekend."

He was writing out my check while he was speaking, and he then handed it to me. I forgot all about my notice. I left his office, got my keys, locked the front door, and headed home. On the way in the car, I was humming happily. Then it occurred to me that Dr. Liske had done a sharp about face there in the office because he probably thought I'd quit. At any rate, I had the next two days off.

**********

The days rolled by and were heading into November. It was still busy at the office. I never did get a chance to tell Dr. Liske I was leaving. Despite what a pain the job was, I was falling into a comfortable spot, and it looked like I was going to stay there for a while. Jean and I got to know one another better, and I found myself going along with some of her hare-brained ideas.

On Halloween, she had talked me into coming to the office in costume. Although it wasn't planned, we both showed up Goth. We screamed with laughter at each other.

"You look *great*!" she said.

"So do you! Mama said I looked like a zombie street-walker!" We fell into a fit of giggles.

When Dr. Liske walked in, he saw us and stopped dead in his tracks. The look of confusion on his face was worth any reprimand we might be getting, but after looking back and forth between Jean and me, he shook his head in surrender and made his way to the kitchen for coffee.

# Chapter 5    Bad News and Pity Parties

Aunt Melba's husband Clive was retiring, so for the first time in 40 years, they would be living in New Ulster. Mama was excited, because she and Aunt Melba were not just sisters; they were best friends. They were only a year apart in age, Mama being the younger of the two. Ever since Aunt Melba left town because of Uncle Clive's job, she swore when he retired they'd be back. And now the time had arrived. With his retirement and the money they'd saved all those years, they secured a house in town, only a block from the Catholic church in one direction and a block from the hospital in the other. Aunt Melba said she wanted to be close to God and the doctor for whichever event might come first. If all went according to plan, they would close on the house by Thanksgiving. Mama's joy could hardly be contained.

"Just think, Mozie," she said, "by the time they close on the house, your court date will be over an' we'll have all that business behind us! I know you still hurt inside. But I make the promise to you right now, that this will be the best Christmas we've had in *years*! You can forget Ol' Thang for a while an' be happy."

Mama's joy was contagious. I was already feeling happier than I had in a long time. Most of that was seeing Mama so happy. When Papa died four years before, she went into a terrible depression for over a year. She had bounced back somewhat, but she was never quite the same after that.

Papa was 81 when he left us. He'd caught a cold and was nursing it himself.

"Brance, you need to get to the doctor and have him look at you," she said.

"No, Bess, I'll feel better tomorrow. You know how colds are, stubborn things." He had always enjoyed good health, and for 81 years of age, he was still very active.

That Sunday Mama prepared lunch before she left for church. "Maybe I should stay home with you today, Brance. You don't look too good around the gills."

He made a face like a fish and Mama couldn't help laughing. "You get on to church, girl. I won't be havin' a heathern for a wife. I'm just gon' flop around in my easy chair till you get back." She kissed him on the cheek and went on to church.

Mama left right after service so she could check on Papa. Usually she lingered and gabbed, but she didn't like the idea of being gone too long when he was sick. In all their years together, she could count on one hand how many times he'd ever had an ailment, the worst being appendicitis when he was 60.

When she walked in the front door, Papa was in his easy chair like he said he'd be, looking at her. Taking of her jacket, she said, "Law', Brance, you won't believe the story ol' Miz Kearse told o' what she done this week. She done drove down t' Birmin'ham, an'," in her bustling around, she looked at Papa, but his eyes were still staring at the door. Whispering, hoping he was trying her on, she said, "Brance?" The silence of the room filled her ears. Mama knew that he was dead. In what seemed to her slow motion, she called for an ambulance, but there was nothing the medics could do for him. Papa was gone.

It turned out that his cold had developed into pneumonia. Mama was beside herself with grief. She blamed herself for not being there. The doctor assured her, though, that even if she had been, she could not have saved him. It happened that quickly.

Now Mama had a light in her eyes I had not seen since those dark days. Her Sissy was coming home.

\*\*\*\*\*\*\*\*\*\*\*

I wondered if New Ulster was ready for Mama and Aunt Melba. Aunt Melba had come to visit one spring, when I was about 13, and she and Mama kept the road hot. Every day they would go out somewhere shopping. Once they went all the way into Greenville. I was so disappointed that I couldn't go, but I was still in school. Aunt Melba brought me back a new dress and Mama bought pair of stockings for me, and I had never worn such things before in my life. That was the most grown-up thing I owned, and I cherished them.

Aunt Melba was always dressed to the nines and fully made up; she would have died before she let anyone see her without make-up, even Uncle Clive. And we always knew when she'd been around because she left a trail of Estee Lauder everywhere she went.

I got off the school bus one afternoon, and they had just pulled up in Aunt Melba's Coupe de Ville. They were howling with laughter. Aunt Melba could barely catch her breath. "Mo," she gasped, "wait to you hear what your Mama done!" She had laughed so hard that her mascara was running.

Apparently, she and Mama had been breezing through the country that afternoon enjoying the spring foliage. As they were heading back into town, Aunt Melba spied a doughnut shop on the side of the road. "Oooooo, Bessie! Let's stop and get us some doughnuts! I've been hankerin' for a cream-filled chocolate!"

Quick as lightening, she wheeled into the parking lot of the Do-nut Hole. Aunt Melba was graceful, but behind the wheel of a car, she was a savage lead-foot. The car came to an abrupt stop which knocked the hat right off her head.

"This place don't look too clean," Mama remarked.

"Oh, Bessie, don't worry. I bet it's clean as a pin inside. You know how these little country stores are!"

So they got out of the car and went inside. They were greeted with clouds of cigarette smoke and loud country-and-western music. Ferlin Huskey was singing about falling for some gal. A tattooed man behind a grim-looking counter sat looking at a magazine.

"Whut kin I hep you ladies with?" he asked.

Mama spoke up. "We'd like a dozen a-doughnuts."

The tattooed man took the cigarette out of his mouth and asked, "Do whut?"

Thinking the man was a little deaf from the loud juke box, Mama spoke louder this time. "*I said we'd like a dozen a-doughnuts!*"

Aunt Melba had been looking around, and it was beginning to dawn on her the exact nature of the business they were in. She grabbed Mama's arm and hissed, "Bessie, let's get out of here! This here's a *pool hall!*"

Mama said, "You said you wanted a chocolate doughnut!"

At that, the tattooed man threw back his head and laughed, and shouted, "Hey, fellas, these two gals want some *doughnuts!*"

As Aunt Melba hustled Mama out the door, they could hear laughter coming from the back of the Do-nut Hole. "Well, I declare!" Mama protested, not understanding what was going on. She hadn't understood what her sister was trying to tell her.

They got into the car, Aunt Melba gunned the motor of that blue Coupe de Ville, and the tires squealed as she sped back into the road. Once she calmed down, she was finally able to tell Mama what had just happened. By the time they got home, they had seen the hilarity of it, and they were nearly hysterical. They laughed about that for years, and it became a joke between them whenever they were together. "Come on, Melba," Mama would say. "Let's go get them doughnuts!"

**********

I was dreading the trip to Kentucky. Jean was dreading it as well because that meant she'd be alone in the office for a few days. In a last-minute plea, I finally convinced Dr. Liske to hire someone temporarily to take my place while I was gone.

With a straight face I told him, "If you don't hire someone to cover for me, Jean will quit. She told me so this morning. She said she'd be out the door without so much as a notice. I think she means it, Dr. Liske." Of course, that conversation never happened. I would apologize to Jean later.

"Alright, *alright*, I will hire a girl, but only temporarily, do you understand? If I hear any more about this, my brain will collapse!" Then he said something in German, which I'm sure was ugly. "Now go make me some coffee. I deserve a little pampering."

I made his coffee.

When I hit Jean with the news, she was overjoyed.

"Don't get excited," I warned, "it's only temporary. As soon as I get back, he's kicking her out."

"Huh! That's what *he* thinks," Jean replied, and I knew she meant it.

**********

The temp worker was a disaster. She hardly spoke English. And she was Dr. Liske's niece. Jean took one look at her and scowled. She thought the girl looked like a poster child for hot chocolate, with her blond hair in braided pigtails. Jean was not just in a bad mood--she was *furious*. She and I had to work our hardest to train this girl in the short time we had.

"After the things I've thought about that man, I'd better go to confession on my lunch break," she snarled. "*And* again after work."

I didn't know if it was the added stress of training this girl, Katja, or the stress of the upcoming trip for my court appearance, or the combination of the two, but in the days leading up to my leaving, I felt really unwell. I was tired, intermittently hot, and my throat began to hurt.

Dr. Liske looked at me on my lunch break and decided to take a throat culture. "This is a rapid test," he said. "We'll know by the time your break is over." He looked concerned.

"Know what, exactly?" I asked.

"Whether or not it is strep throat."

"Strep throat? I can't have *strep throat*! I have to go to *Kentucky*!"

"If you have it, you have it. Now please stop speaking and go lie down in the lounge while we wait."

I felt too ill to argue. I lay down on the sofa and closed my eyes. I must have fallen asleep, because it only seemed like minutes later that Dr. Liske had his hand on my shoulder, gently trying to wake me up.

"Well, Maureen, I'm afraid to say you indeed have strep throat."

**\*\*\*\*\*\*\*\*\*\***

I called John Hobrick to let him know I was sick and asked if we could change the court date. He said he would do all he could, and if the case was presented, he would fight it for me. He even had prayer with me before he hung up. Right after that, I went to bed. I slept till the next evening.

Mama came in to check on me. "Girl, I was beginning to get worried. How you feel?"

It was too painful to talk. Although Dr. Liske had treated me there in the office and sent me home with antibiotics, he said I was going to be really sick, maybe even for several days. "Strep throat won't kill you," he'd said. "But you'll think it will." He was right; swallowing was torture.

To answer Mama's question, I waved my hand in the air, signifying, "I'm alive, but that's all I can claim." I noticed that when she came up to my bed, she had a dish towel tied over her face. All I could

48

see were her eyes. I almost laughed, but the pain was unbearable and stopped me cold.

"That nice Mr. Hobrick called," she said. "I told him you was near death, so he said he'd call back later."

After that I went back to sleep. I felt so sick, I didn't even care about the divorce hearing.

**********

Later I could hear voices in the kitchen. Maggie and Aunt Melba were visiting. I strained to hear what they were saying, but it was useless. Looking at my watch, I saw that it was the next day. I found out later that Mama had been coming in and giving me my antibiotics, but I didn't remember. Good ol' Mama!

I finally was able to get up. I went out into the hall and peeked into the kitchen.

"*There's* m' girl!" Mama said heartily. She, Aunt Melba, and Maggie were sitting at the table. They were all wearing dish towels.

**********

Later that afternoon when everyone was gone, I tottered into the front room to use the phone. It was late and I was afraid John had already left the office. He picked up the phone himself.

"Ah! Maureen! I'm glad to see you're back from the dead." I smiled, not that he could see it.

"I'm not over it yet, but I am much better than I was." I paused. "So what happened at the hearing? Is it all over?"

There was a momentary pause at the other end of the line. My scalp got that tingly feeling again.

"Well, the divorce was granted. Your maiden name will be legally restored. The judge agreed on the house and property agreement."

"John," I interrupted, "get to the main event."

John Hobrick cleared his throat. "The judge awarded your ex-husband maintenance for a total of five years."

I could feel my ears fill up with white noise. John was still talking, but I couldn't understand him. "What?"

"They looked at his circumstances, the fact that he has no education and currently no job. When you were married, Maureen, you made more money due to your education and training."

"I made more money because I stayed with one company and didn't change jobs every time I got mad at somebody!" In the 14 years we were married, my ex had almost as many jobs. He could never be happy in one place. If someone made him mad, no matter how insignificant, he'd up and quit. I took it in stride because I had a good job and we lived within our means. The first time he refinanced the house, he wanted the money to open a restaurant. The place was a money pit and was a financial disaster before it could even open, which it never did. His work life was a string of failures, but I stood behind him because he was my husband. Now I wished I had just driven by the church that day and had never gotten married in the first place.

"The bottom line, Maureen, is that the court looked at his circumstances as opposed to yours. He lives in a house that's underwater, and he's unemployed. You work fulltime and live with your mother. As the court sees it, you have no outstanding bills or obligations to speak of, so they awarded him maintenance so he can go to school and get training. I didn't agree; I fought it, but that was the judge's decision. I'm so sorry, Maureen. And, um..." He hesitated.

My throat was killing me again by now. And I knew there was more bad news to compound how lousy I already felt. "Just spit it out, John."

John Hobrick spoke slowly and quietly, as if to soften the final blow. "You were also ordered to pay all court costs on his behalf."

**********

I finally returned to work after having survived "the strep," as Mama called it. It was difficult going back because I was so depressed. Nothing could have prepared me for the way things turned out.

Jean convinced Dr. Liske to keep Katja on for a little while longer to get the filing caught up. I think he agreed because when I came back to work, I was pale and drawn, and I think he actually felt sorry for me. He asked me how the hearing turned out but I couldn't answer him because I was afraid I would start crying. He seemed to understand and never pressed me about it. I got my work done, but the days went by in a mist.

Aunt Melba and Uncle Clive closed on their house and began moving in. Everyone was so happy, and I really tried to get into the spirit of things, but I felt lost. I began giving in to self-pity. I could never have a place of my own, at least not for five years, because I couldn't afford it. I was feeling really down, and I made the mistake of lying down in it and wallowing.

On Sabbaths I went to church but found no comfort. I wasn't looking for it, actually. I figured if I remained miserable, I'd get all this grieving over in one chunk, and then I'd be able to get on with my life. I left church right after the sermons were over. I didn't want to chat with anyone. I hadn't been there long enough to really make friends, and I deliberately didn't get involved. I avoided everyone as much as possible.

Mama went to church the Sunday before Christmas, and when she came home, I was still in bed.

"My land, girl, what has happened to you?" She sat down on the bed next to me.

"I don't know, Mama. I just don't care about anything anymore."

"That's not *my* Mo talkin'," she said. "You're a fighter, always have been. What has happened to you? I know you've been through some bad business, but you have to keep goin'. Listen, when your Papa died, I wished I'd-a died, too. I thought it was too much to bear. But I had to remember God's promise, 'See, I have engraved you in the palm of My hand.' Sometimes God allows us to go through trials 'cause He knows they'll make us stronger, better. But all the time, He's got us cradled in His hand. You see that, don't you, Mo?"

"I thought this divorce was horrible, but I figured once it was over, I could move on. And now I have all *this* to contend with, for five years. I'll never be free, Mama. It seems like never, anyway. How can God bring anything good from *this*?" I pushed my face into the pillow.

"Well, Mo, I can't honestly say, 'cause I don't know. Only God knows that. I lost your Da, but he didn't leave 'cause he *wanted* to. He didn't have a choice. What you're goin' through is somethin' I can't imagine. And I'm sorry for that, 'cause I ain't got no way to comfort you."

I left my face in the pillow but held out my hand. Mama took it in hers and kissed it. "Prob'ly what you need right now is just a great, big ol' pity party.  But one thing about pity parties, girl," she said as she stood up.  "Nobody brings refreshments."

# Chapter 6    *The Christmas Cousins*

Aunt Melba was hosting Christmas dinner. She wanted an excuse to show off her new house, so Mama agreed to have it there. It had been held at our house all my life. This would be a new experience.

"She's really puttin' on the dog," Maggie said. "There ain't a' *inch* o' her front porch not decorated!"

"Well, when Melba puts on the dog, she puts on the *whole* dog," Mama said. "I ain't never seen nobody to take to decoratin' like my Sissy. You got a lot o' that from her, Maggie. Even when you was little, you made your own decorations and was hangin' 'em on everything! I remember one time," and she laughed, "you'd made these little bells out of tin foil. You came out of th' bedroom wearin' two of 'em on the front of your church dress! It killed me and your Da, 'cause you had 'em hangin' right where your breasties woulda been, if you'd had any!"

Maggie and I hooted.

"I don't remember that," I said.

"Mo, you was just a baby then. We was all ready for church and here Maggie come with them bells. I like to never got Brance t' stop laughin' and put his tie on."

We were all in Mama's kitchen making Texas Lizzies for Christmas gifts. They were little fruitcake cookies that Mama had made for years, and they were delicious. Maggie and I were cutting up the fruit and nuts.

"You know what I just thought of, Mama?" Maggie asked. "Do you remember that underwear we got you for Christmas?"

"Lawsey, I sure do! As a matter of fact, I still have it! It's in my cedar chest."

I was six, Rose was 12 and Maggie was 11, and we pooled our money together to get Mama a nice Christmas present. In those days, department stores had "shoppers," ladies who would help choose just the right gift for someone special. Mama took us to Belk and handed us over to a shopper named Miss Lundley. She was gorgeous. She wore a green sheath dress with matching heels, a pearl necklace, and a charm bracelet that made the most wonderful tinkling sound when she moved her hand.

Miss Lundley was blonde and had beautiful blue eyes surrounded by fake eyelashes. She had full crimson lips and smelled even better than Aunt Melba. She was Christmas personified.

"All right, ladies, let's see what we can find special for your mother this Christmas!" We loved her right away because she spoke to us like we were grown ladies, not three girls in plaid skirts and saddle oxfords.

We were going past lingerie when my eyes spotted something on a table. It was pink and green and yellow, and it was the prettiest thing I'd ever seen in my life.

I stopped short in my saddle oxfords. "I want *that* for Mama!" I yelled, and Miss Lundley and my sisters turned around to look in my direction.

"Oh, dear, I don't think your mother would like that," Miss Lundley said, trying to be diplomatic and adding, "Don't you think it's a little cold for something like that?"

My sisters were standing at the table, eyeing the form that was modeling the lace teddy I had seen. "Oh, *no*, ma'am," Rose said, "I think that's the purtiest thing I've ever seen in my life! We want *that* for our *mama!*"

"Really, ladies, wouldn't you rather look around awhile and see if there is something else she might like?"

I was getting upset. As much as I adored Miss Lundley, she didn't seem to be paying attention to our request. We wanted the teddy for Mama, and that was *that*.

"I want *that*," I said, pointing to it, and began to sob.

"Oh dear," Miss Lundley said as people began turning around looking at us. "All right then. This is what we'll get. We want our ladies to be happy. Don't cry, dear." She looked at the little paper Mama had given her that had her measurements written on it. She then took a teddy out of the display case.

"No!" I shouted. "We want *that* one!" and I pointed to the display again.

Miss Lundley looked at the size of the model and said, "But, dear, this one won't *fit* your mother. You wouldn't want to get her something pretty that she couldn't even *wear*, would you? Imagine how disappointed she'd be on Christmas morning!" She showed it to us so we'd know it was exactly like the one on display.

We were so happy after that. Miss Lundley helped us check out and even saw that the teddy was gift-wrapped. We had a little money left over and were able to buy Papa a nice tie. Miss Lundley looked relieved when we asked her to pick it out. We had that gift-wrapped, too, and then Miss Lundley returned us to Mama.

"You have some very sweet ladies here," she told our mother. "It was a pleasure serving you. Merry Christmas!"

"Thank you kindly," Mama said proudly. "Well, you girls didn't waste no time! And I'm so proud of you for bein' ladies. That makes me happy."

When we arrived home, Rose placed the gifts under the tree, just so, and then we stood and admired them. Saving our money all summer would be worth seeing the look on Mama's face.

Christmas morning arrived and we were up before daylight. Rose, Maggie and I piled into the front room and stood amazed in front of the tree. There were more packages there than when we went to bed! From the looks of it, we had been good girls that year.

Mama and Papa stumbled in, bleary-eyed, and sat down on the sofa to watch us open our gifts. I have no memory of what I got for Christmas that year, but I remember what Mama got! Rose handed Mama the beautifully-wrapped package from Belk, and we girls stood breathless as she opened it.

All Mama saw was the lace, and she said, "Why, girls, this is beau—." By this time she had it out of the box and was holding it up. Silence. "Beautiful," she continued, and her face was three shades of red. Papa looked like he'd been hit in the face with a hammer, his jaw hung down so low.

"You really like it, Mama?" Maggie asked.

"I've never had anything like this in my life," Mama said, certainly meaning it.

"Let's see it on you!" we shouted, but Mama declined, saying it was a little too cold that morning.

"Besides, that would be like me walkin' out here in my underwear!" She laughed. "I tell you what. I'll wear it under my dress when we go to church Sunday, and I'll let you peek at it under my blouse. Okay?"

We were satisfied with that.

Unlike Mama, Papa was willing to model our gift to him. He put his tie on with his pajamas. We all laughed, but he still had that hung-jaw look to his face.

After breakfast, Mama and Papa went their room to get dressed.

"Sure is takin' a long time for them to put their clothes on," Rose remarked.

**********

Mama and I drove into town to the family Christmas dinner. Maggie was right; Aunt Melba had really put on the dog. Even the cedar trees in her yard were decorated.

"Law' murdah, it'll be Easter 'fore she gets all this taken down," Mama said as we went up the sidewalk.

"Better her than me," I muttered, but inside I was thinking how beautiful it all was.

Mama and I had baked all morning. She fixed some of her specialties. I made a pecan pie; it was all I could manage to get in with Mama busy in her kitchen. I also tried my hand at eggnog, but I knew it would be nothing compared to Papa's.

I was pleased to see Uncle Richard. He was getting on in years, but he got along wonderfully. He always said the secret to staying young was keeping busy. He was 87 now, and he vowed to live to be at least 100. I was certain he would do it.

Aunt Melba's children were married and had children of their own. "They're scattered to the four winds," she'd say, and getting them altogether was no easy task. This year, though, Bryce and Henry, who had both settled in Charleston after college, were coming with their wives, and Little Melba, who was single, managed to make it to New Ulster all the way from New York. She was an attorney and found it very difficult getting away for any length of time. Uncle Clive said she was a workaholic. JuJu lived in Florida with his wife. They had eight children and stayed home every Christmas.

Uncle William and Aunt Doris, who lived in Greenville County, weren't coming. Mama and Aunt Melba were secretly glad.

"Doris must be dyin' again," Aunt Melba said and rolled her eyes.

Mama nodded her head in agreement. "Honey, to hear her talk, she'd have to *die* to get better."

Nor were they too crazy about Uncle William, who always complained about money, politics, and how his son had practically killed him when he left the church. If Uncle William held it against Mama, he certainly found no more forgiveness in his heart for Cud'din Willie.

Cud'din Willie surprised us all by not ending up in prison on charges of arson. He actually grew into a fine man. In high school he felt the call to the priesthood. In his sophomore year in college, he met a young lady named Hannah and fell in love. Hannah, he said, changed his world. He wanted to marry her, but knew he could not do that and still enter the priesthood. He ended up leaving school over his dilemma, much to Uncle William's ire, and got a job and an apartment for a while so he could think. He and Hannah stopped seeing each other so Cud'din Willie could be clear-headed. In the end, he converted to the protestant faith and became an Episcopal priest. He and Hannah married and had two children. Their son, William III, insisted on being called Bill now that he was 13. Their daughter, Grace, was 11. They lived up in Asheville and would have by no means missed the family gathering.

Ida Rose was coming. Her husband the atheist had died several years ago, and her children were grown, so she was coming alone. Maybe, she said, Anna-lee and Robert would show up. She didn't make too much fuss whether they came or not because they both were "away from the church an' livin' in sin." Ida Rose loved her children, but their chosen life-styles embarrassed her to no end. "Anna-lee changes boyfriends more often than she changes socks. At least Robert has been with the same gal for several years now!"

I knew the last to show would be Aunt Minnie and Uncle Russ. Aunt Minnie was 72 now and Uncle Russ was 80. They never missed a family gathering. Uncle Russ still brought fireworks and put on a pretty good show. I noticed he was a little slower-going these days, but he and Aunt Minnie held on to each other, looking like young lovers rather than a couple who had been married for 54 years.

Aunt Minnie still kept her kitchen hot for the holidays, bringing the same cakes, pie, and cookies she'd always brought. Maggie and I greeted them at the door. Then she and I went to their car to bring everything inside.

"You reckon we'll have fireworks this year? I'm not sure about city ordinances about fireworks," she wondered.

I had never considered it before. Our house was in the country where such things didn't apply. "I suppose it'll be alright," I said, balancing coconut cake and a huge tin of cookies while trying to close the car door. "If it isn't, I guess the sheriff will send someone over."

Christmas dinner was a success. Aunt Melba had to squeeze everyone into every nook and cranny available in the house because the dining room was too small to accommodate the lot of Doyles and MacKenzies and all the in-laws and offspring. She loved it. Aunt Melba never backed down in the face of a challenge.

The only failure of the day was my eggnog. "Who in the world made the eggnog?" Bryce shouted, which I thought was unnecessary. When I told him I did, he dumped the rest of his glass in the sink and said, "Girl, Unka Branch was the eggnog king. Don't spoil his memory!"

It took Uncle Russ most of the afternoon to get things ready for the fireworks. To speed up the process, Bill offered to help him. They seemed to be enjoying themselves. Bill had taken a liking to Uncle Russ.

Once it was good and dark, we were all ready for the show. Some of us stood on the porch and some out in the yard because there was such a crowd. While we were waiting, Mama said to Maggie and me, "Y'all gals remember when y'all had some firecrackers left over one Christmas?"

Maggie and I laughed and said that we did. The cousins around us wanted to know what happened.

"Well," Mama began, addressing the cousins, "the mornin' after Christmas, your Uncle Brance took all the used wrappin' paper and such out to the trash to be burned. Well, there musta been some of them firecrackers mixed in, cause as he was walkin' back to the house, he heard POW, POW, POW-POW! He dropped to the ground and crawled the rest of the way to the house. He got in all out of breath, eyes big as tractor tires, an' said, 'Bessie! They's somebody in them woods, and they's a-shootin'!' When we figured out is was them firecrackers, we had a good laugh over it. But, boy, I'll never forget the look on his face when he come bustin' through th' front door!"

Over the laughter, someone shouted, "Hey! The show's startin'!" Uncle Russ let Bill light the first fuse, and it lit up "Merry Christmas" spelled out with sparklers on a wire frame. We saw it year after year, but we always gasped in the wonder of it. The way Uncle Russ had everything set up, it was non-stop fireworks. Most of the neighbors came out and were watching from their porches. We were watching the bottle rockets explode, and the younger children were screaming with delight, some covering their ears, when Bill appeared on the front porch next to the decorated shrubbery.

"*Firecrackers!*" he screamed, and threw the entire lit package into a bush. The firecrackers were going off, and suddenly the entire bush, with all its decorations, went up in flames. I couldn't believe my eyes. I saw Bill run down and set one of the trees on fire the same way. He was laughing and having a big time. People were running and screaming.

Someone had called 911 because in no time, the fire trucks arrived and had everything under control. When it was all over, Aunt Melba had lost 2 big cedar trees, all the shrubbery in front of her porch, and the porch roof was scorched. Aunt Melba and Uncle Clive were both in tears, not just from the damage, but from the sheer terror of the events. Mama kept trying to calm them down by reminding them that everything was all right and that no one was hurt. I heard Cud'din Willie tell Bill as he hauled him up the front steps, "Well, that's not entirely so, 'cause this one's going to think he's facing the wrath of God once we get *inside!*"

Mama shook her head and muttered, "Um, um, um. I don't feel the least sorry for Bill. But I can't help thinkin' that th' apple don't fall far from th' tree."

# Chapter 7    Supper Guest

It was a long winter, and especially cold. We had a big snow in January and another in February, just before March. I made it through one day then the next, and one day I looked up and the trees were starting to get green, and I felt my mood lifting. The depression that I had been living with seemed to be giving way to something else. Hope, perhaps.

The situation at work had even improved. Dr. Liske had let Katja go, just as he said he would, so I thought it was time to have a throw-down with him. I trapped him in his office and told him exactly how things were.

"Do you care about your practice, Dr. Liske?" He seemed insulted by the question, but before he could answer, I plowed straight into it. "Well, you're about to lose it. You can't keep anyone here because the work is overwhelming. The patient load is too high. I have some suggestions. Take them or leave them. But I can tell you right now, if things don't change around here, this place is going to fall apart right around your ears.

"First of all, take down that 'Walk-ins Welcome' sign, because that is costing a huge amount of time and causing grief. If they're that bad off, they need to go to the emergency room. You're cheating your patients who have been waiting with appointments. And another thing, you *have to hire a nurse*. I don't think I need to say any more about *that*. And unclench your fists from the bank account and hire back the cleaning company. Jean and I can't keep this place as clean as it needs to be. It should be *spotless*! They're the professionals; we're not. I managed an office for 15 years, and I can tell you right now that this is the biggest mess I've ever seen in my *life*. You're going to start losing patients if the service doesn't get better. If you take the advice I've given you, you'll see a huge improvement. You may not be seeing as many patients, but I guarantee your practice will eventually grow."

With that, I got up and walked out. I had no more to say, and I didn't want to hear him complain.

When Jean and I came in two mornings later, we noticed the "Walk-ins Welcome" sign was gone. In its place was "Appointments Only." We were stunned. Inside was full of surprises, too, as Dr. Liske had had a cleaning crew in the night before. Everything sparkled. We looked at each other in total disbelief.

"Wow, I guess he took to heart what you said," Jean remarked as she put her purse in her desk. "I haven't seen it this clean in ages!"

"Hey. Do you suppose this means we're getting a nurse today?" I asked.

"Or even another girl for the front?" she asked.

We stared at each other. At the same time we said, "Let's make him coffee!!"

When Dr. Liske came in, he seemed rather pleased with himself. "All right, ladies, we're going to give this a try. A nurse is coming in today. I expect you to show her where everything is."

"Yes, sir!" we said enthusiastically.

"And I will have Katja come in a few hours after school to file. Her English has improved, so she will eventually be able to help with the phones. After today, I don't expect to hear anymore grumbling out of either one of you, or I will do some *firing*. And I like this—I like having my coffee waiting for me, so please repeat this tomorrow and every day following."

"*Now* we've done it," I said to Jean, and we smiled.

"Not so fast with the humor," Dr. Liske said to me, looking a little stern. "I also expect *you* to improve with the patient names."

I frowned, not understanding. "I'm good with that," I replied.

"Oh? Have you forgotten the Goldie Smith debacle?"

No, I had not forgotten the Goldie Smith debacle, but I had sure hoped *he* had. One particularly busy afternoon, several patients came in at once, and I was trying to get them checked in. A man was at my desk, telling me his appointment was at one, and he hoped to be seen right away since we'd just opened from lunch. Dr. Liske came to the desk, saw him, and motioned him back to an examination room. Jean hopped up with his chart and delivered it. I looked at the afternoon list, and Goldie Smith indeed had an appointment at one o'clock. Jean and I were scrambling trying to check patients in and out as well as answer the phones.

Dr. Liske walked out with Mr. Smith, handing him three prescriptions off his pad, and he walked off saying, "Next!"

He always left the names blank and we had to fill them in. I thought it was because he was afraid of misspelling their names and so he left us to do it. What in the world was so hard about "Smith"? So I filled them out and handed them back to the patient. Suddenly the man snapped at me, "Who the heck is *Goldie Smith*?"

A lady in the waiting room jumped up and said, "*I'm* Goldie Smith!"

Jean dropped the phone receiver on the desk and said to her, "This way, Miz Smith!" and took her to a patient room.

I was completely confused. Then I had to apologize to the man, who sternly told me his name was Aldous Brandywine. In all that chaos, I remember thinking it was surely a made-up name. I just stood there for a second, looking at him and blinking. With my tail tucked between my legs, I had to go back and explain to Dr. Liske what I had done. It was not pretty.

So no, I had not forgotten the Smith debacle, thank you very much. "Yes, sir," I said, suddenly feeling very humble, "I will be more diligent."

With that, his old smile returned, and he left with his coffee.

Jean and I looked at each other. It was going to be a great day!

**********

It was nearly April. I was sitting in the sunshine in the back yard, my sweater pulled around me because it was unusually cool. Church had been a blessing that morning, and I was feeling better than I had felt since last fall. I was still humming the closing hymn, "Lift High the Cross," one of my favorites, when I heard a car screech into the driveway. It could be none other than Aunt Melba. I walked around the house and greeted her as she was getting out of the car.

"Hey, gal!" she shouted. Give me a hand with this, will ya?" In her back seat was a cardboard box that held a pie and a platter of fried chicken. Aunt Melba refused to remember that I was a vegetarian.

"What's this about, Aunt Melba?" I asked.

"Just some leftovers I thought I'd share. Have you eaten yet?"

"Yes ma'am, a while ago." I said.

"Well, we'll just have an early supper!"

I followed her into the house, carrying the box of food. Mama was making fresh iced tea. "Nothing better than sweet tea," she said as I put the box on the counter. "Mo, why don't you go change back into your church dress and show your Aunt Melba? I'm sure she'd love to see it!"

"Yes, I *would!*" Aunt Melba chirped. She was getting vegetables out of the refrigerator. "I always like seeing you in a purty frock."

I stood there in the kitchen regarding them. They were up to something. They both were trying too hard to be nonchalant.

"Maureen," Mama said, "hurry and get changed."

"Okay, so what are y'all up to?"

They ignored me and went right on talking. "Bess, I think I'll warm this chicken up a smidge," Aunt Melba said.

"That'd be good, and I'll put the finishin' touches on this coleslaw."

"I *said*, what are you *up to*?" I demanded to know.

"Watch your tone, Mo," Mama said, not looking at me.

"Uh-oh," Aunt Melba gasped. "Somebody's comin' up the drive!"

"Who could *that* be?" Mama said, taking off her apron. "Maureen. Put. On. Your. *Dress.*"

Well, that was it. I knew that whoever had just pulled up to the house wasn't a surprise to them, nor was this any regular ol' chicken dinner. I felt like I was about to be involved in something that smacked of match-making, and I was having none of it.

Mama was already at the door, so I snagged Aunt Melba by the arm. "Hold it," I hissed. "Who is that out there, and why have you invited him? What are you and Mama up to?"

"Oh, Mo, your mama and I thought you'd like a little company. Somebody to talk to, you know? Somebody to hang out with, or whatever you call it these days. We invited Joseph Thickett to supper."

"*Joe Thickett?*" I could have died on the spot. I had gone to school with Joe, and he made fun of my freckles all the time. He didn't seem to mature as we got to high school, either.

"Now *hush*," Aunt Melba said. "He's here, and he's gon' eat with us, so just be nice and' don't embarrass your mama!"

I groaned at the prospect of being trapped behind a table with Joseph Thickett. I swore to myself that Mama would get an earful later.

"Maureen, you remember Joe," Mama said.

"Yes, I do," I said, politely putting out my hand. He shook it and there was more power in an earthworm. "How are you, Joe?"

"Jus' fine, Mo," he said, sporting big white teeth. "Good to see ya! Gotta say I was really surprised when your mama invited me to supper like she done. Just happened to see her in the grocery store. I had to pick up some pig feet, and I heard somebody say, 'Well, Joseph Thickett!' An' I looked up, and thar she was, carrying a big ol' mess o' greens."

I smiled, but inside I felt my world crash. This was going to be the longest supper in history. I considered bolting for the door, but Mama was already pushing me behind the table, guiding Joe in behind me so we would be sitting together. She and Aunt Melba brought the food to the table and sat down.

Mama said prayer as we all held hands. This was common practice in our house, but Joe seemed a little surprised and didn't let go of my hand right away after the prayer. It was an awkward moment for me, but I could see Aunt Melba with a smile on her face. I made a mental note to give *her* an earful later, as well.

"Aunt Melba, where's Uncle Clive this evening?" I asked.

"Oh, you know *him*. He stayed home to watch golf on the TV. I can't stand golf. I gave up on watchin' that stuff years ago. But Clive? He loves it. Anyway, I couldn't have pried him away from the TV for *nothin*'. I said, 'Clive, honey, I made chicken!' And he just said, 'Leave me a coupla pieces!' And that was th' end o' *that* conversation."

Aunt Melba continued speaking but turned her attention to Joe. "So what you been up to, Joseph?"

"Not much, Ma'am. Not lately. Me an' my wife busted up about a year ago, an' I been makin' a go o' thangs on m' own. It ain't been easy."

"I reckon not!" Mama interjected. "Why, Mo here done got herself divorced, too, and oh, I've seen this child suffer. Ain't it awful, Joe, what it does to you?"

"Yeah, it's awful, ma'am. I never thought in a million years it'd happen to *me*."

Much to my distress, we spent most of the evening listening to a blow-by-blow account of Joe Thickett's divorce. Before it was over, I wanted to slash my wrists. I could feel a headache coming on, so when we decided to have pie with coffee, I begged off and went to my room. Mama followed me.

"Don't start, Mama," I whispered. "I can't take another minute of it. I can't believe you would try to set me up like this!"

"I was *tryin'* to do somethin' *nice*. Now get back out there and you and Joe have a good *time!*"

I stood my ground. "No, Mama. I'm developing a blistering headache, and I just want to go to bed." I turned my back on her, so she gave up and left. I heard voices in the other room but didn't strain to hear them. It made my head hurt worse.

That night I dreamed about my ex-husband. I was still married to him in the dream, but I was also married to Joe Thickett, who brought his ex-wife to live with us. I kept saying how this was all wrong, but all my ex would say was that it didn't matter to him one way or the other. I woke up in a sweat. Daylight couldn't come soon enough.

# Chapter 8        *More than a House*

With the alimony payments I was making, I could not afford my own place. It was time for me to go, too. The night before, I heard Mama holler out from the bathroom. "You okay, Mama?" I shouted from my room.

The bathroom door flew open. Mama was stomping to her room. "I—just—brushed my teeth—with—your *hair stuff*!"

*Oh no*, I thought. Even though I couldn't see her face, I could tell her teeth were clenched. I had left a tube of depilatory cream on the sink. I jumped out of bed and hurried to her room.

"I'm sorry, Mama!"

"Why in tarnation did you leave it on the *sink*? I just picked it up and squirted a big pile onto my toothbrush and started brushin'. I thought, 'What happened t' the *mint*?' Gol—ly *bum*!"

"I was going to do my legs in the morning, and I didn't want to forget to use it," I said weakly.

She was furious. "If my teeth fall out o' my head, I'll haul off and throw a rod! I *swannee*!"

I couldn't help chuckling about it on my way to work the next morning. But I knew I was stuck, at least for the next five years. Just thinking of that wiped the smile off my face.

It was still a little early for me to be at the office, so I decided to ride around the neighborhoods and look, enviously, at the yards and summer flowers. On one of the corners I spotted an old American Foursquare with an overgrown yard. Empty. Immediately I was drawn to it and wanted to stop and get out.

All around the front yard was a wrought iron bow-and-picket fence. I stepped up on the long porch and peered through the windows. The floors were hardwood, and as far as I could see the staircase, it was stunning. I gasped at how pretty it was, even with all the neglect. The walls were in desperate need of paint, but I could see that this house had once been a beauty, and could be again. I went to another window and saw what I was sure had been the dining room. The fireplace was lovely. I was falling in love with this house and wanted to see all of it. Although I knew it was hopeless, I wrote down the phone number of the realtor and planned to call on my lunch break.

"You mean the house on the corner of Cork and *Monroe*?" the lady at the real estate office asked that afternoon.

"Yes. It looks like it's been empty for a while. I'd really like to see it."

The voice on the other end of the line hesitated. "Well. Ok. I can meet you over there at five."

I could hardly wait for the work day to be over.

********

The realtor, Mrs. Kennedy, who sported a white, blue-tinged up-do, met me at the house on Cork Street. I could hardly wait to get inside. "If you don't mind," she said, "I'll give you the keys and you can let yourself in and look around. I have some calls I really need to make. Is that okay with you?"

"Sure," I replied, but thinking how rude and unprofessional that was. Still, my heart was pounding as I slipped the key inside the lock and opened the door.

The inside was more beautiful than what I had seen through the window. It needed paint and work, but it could be a showplace if someone wanted to put the work into it. The kitchen was large and still had all its original cabinetry. There was a butler's pantry off to one side that separated the kitchen from the dining room. Upstairs were three bedrooms and a bath with the original claw foot tub. I could hardly stand it. It was more than a house; it could be my home. I wanted to rescue it and live the rest of my days in it. But I doubted it would still be on the market in five years. My heart fell.

I looked out the front bedroom window and saw Mrs. Kennedy leaning on her car, evidently waiting for me. I was puzzled as to why she didn't come in. She had a worried look on her face.

Mrs. Kennedy smiled when she saw me come back outside. "Any questions?" she asked.

"What can you tell me about the house?"

"Well, it was built in 1900. Electricity was added later and the box and wiring were updated about 10 years ago, but you may still see some of the old knob and tube that was left behind. New plumbing was run in about the same time. All the woodwork and built-ins are original. It's never been renovated as far as I know. There is a bathroom off the back that was built on in the '50's, I believe. Maybe '60's."

"How long has it been since it was lived in?"

Mrs. Kennedy frowned in thought. "Several years, but it was just put on the market again last year."

"Again?"

"It's changed hands several times."

"I see. Well, I can't imagine why it hasn't sold. It's lovely!"

A look passed over her face, and it made me curious. I felt there was something she wasn't telling me. I decided to press her. "What's wrong with the house, Mrs. Kennedy?"

Her cheeks blushed. I knew there was something.

"Well," she began hesitantly, "there were some things that happened in the house that just puts some people off."

"Such as?"

Mrs. Kennedy took a deep breath. "Back some time ago, about 30 or so years, I think, a woman was murdered here. Poisoned. Her husband was arrested for the murder but hanged himself in jail before it ever went to trial." She stood looking at me as if I'd be appalled.

"Mrs. Kennedy, I don't mean to sound ugly, but people die in houses all the time. I don't understand what you're trying to tell me."

She gave a little nervous laugh. "Well, you know how superstitious people are. There are stories that it's, well, haunted."

"*Haunted*?" I couldn't help laughing. "Oh, Mrs. Kennedy, I don't believe in that nonsense."

"Well," she said, "people have heard things in there."

I shook my head. "So you're telling me that's why it's been empty so long?"

"Yes." Mrs. Kennedy looked a little relieved that I didn't take the matter seriously.

On the way home, I started formulating a plan. I wanted that house. Of course, I didn't have the money for it, but I could certainly put back and save every bit I could. If the house would just stay empty, I could get it in another five years' time. Five years would pass by whether I saved for the house of not, so what did I have to lose by planning? It would make a nice down-payment. I couldn't wait to tell Mama.

"That house on Cork and Monroe Street? Mo, you hafta be kiddin'. Don't you know about that house?"

"I know someone died in it, if that's what you mean."

"Not just *died* in it, Mo—was *murdered*! I guess you don't remember because you was just a little girl, but it was in the papers all over the state. This lady's husband decides he wants a new woman, so he up and poisons the one he's got. Kills her dead. Buries her in the back yard."

Mrs. Kennedy failed to include *that* little tidbit.

"She didn't show up for church for a coupla Sundays, so people start askin' questions. He tried to say she run off, but that just didn't make sense. Anyway, he finally confessed, showed 'em where the body was, and then the ol' dawg went and hung hisself in jail. Didn't have the nerve to face the law. I reckon he busted hell wide open. Anyway, other people have lived there, but nobody stays long 'cause of the weird noises in the house. They say it's haunted by the wife *and* the husband. She's probably chasin' him around with a skillet for him killin' her."

I looked at Mama for a few seconds without saying anything. "Anyway, Mama, I thought if I could save all I could in the next five years, I could put a down-payment on it as soon as I'm free from my ex. It's such a beautiful house."

"You'd want to live there, knowin' what I done told you?"

"Mama, it's not the *house's* fault what happened there, and it was a long time ago. What do you think of my plan? Is it crazy?"

Mama looked at me with a little pity in her eyes. "Are you unhappy here, Mo? I know I raised a fuss last night."

"Not at all, Mama! This has nothing to do with *you*. It's just for the first time in a long while, I feel like I have a future again, and I just want to plan for it. It's such a beautiful house, Mama, and I know it's been waiting for someone like me to come along and love it. That house and I, well, we *need* each other."

"If I had th' money, I'd hep ye get it right now."

"I don't doubt that one bit, Mama. But if it's meant to be, it'll still be waiting on me. I'm going to call Mrs. Kennedy tomorrow and ask her if I can clean that yard up. It's a sight!"

**********

69

"You mean you want to cut the grass for *free*?" Mrs. Kennedy couldn't believe her ears.

"Yes. It's a shame the place looks so run-down. I know you need to ask the owners, but I doubt very seriously they'd say no. I just want to clean up the yard a bit and give the place back some dignity."

Mrs. Kennedy was quiet on the other end of the line.

"Mrs. Kennedy?" I said.

"I'm here," she said. "I just don't think I've ever heard-a such a thing in my life. Ok. I'll tell the owner what you want to do. I don't think there'll be a problem. They live out of town now and have a hard time gettin' anybody to cut the grass."

After work, I picked up Mama's lawn mower and headed back to town. Cutting that grass was no easy task; it had been left to its own devices and had grown tall and tough. Although the front yard was of no great size, it took me an hour to finish the job. It was getting late, so I decided I'd cut the back the next day.

That one-hour amount of work made a huge difference. I raked up the cuttings and piled them to the side. Then I swept the sidewalk and the porch and stepped back to admire the sight. I was pleased. I was planning to bring Mama to see it that weekend.

I stopped by Maggie's house on the way home. She and George were cleaning fish out back.

"Ooo, girl," I said as I approached the picnic table, "better you than *me*!"

"Weenie," she chuckled and went on scaling. "Wash and George caught a big ol' mess of fish today, so we got to get 'em in the freezer. I'll give you some to take to Mama."

"Thanks. Spring break, huh, George?" I asked.

"Yep." He was sucking on a jawbreaker. I couldn't understand how he could eat *anything* and have his hands in fish guts at the same time.

"Yeah, so Wash took the day off so they could get in some fishin' together." Maggie looked at me for the first time. "Good land, girl, you look like you just come off the farm. Don't tell me ol' Dr. Liske got you doin' his *yard* work now."

I laughed. "Nooo, not at all. I, uh, have my eye on a house here in town, and I cut the grass over there today."

"A house? Girl, how can you afford a *house*? Ol' Thang got you choked for four and a half more years. What are you goin' on about?"

I told her about the Cork Street house. She stared in disbelief. George stopped sucking on his jawbreaker and was staring, too.

"Ain't you heard about that place?" she asked.

I assured her I knew all about it.

"Mama, you mean the one that's haunted? Cool!" His eyes were huge with fascination about the history of the Cork Street house.

"George," Maggie warned.

"Well, I won't be moving in anytime soon, so no worries there. All I'm doing is getting the yard clean. But I'm going to start saving back, so when all this alimony trash is over, I'll have a nice down-payment. I'll have my own place. Won't that be fun?"

"I don't expect *I'll* be comin' over there too much," Maggie said flatly. "That place ain't fit. Poor woman murdered over there, in cold blood, mind you..."

"*Murdered*??" George interrupted, nearly screaming with delight.

"Hush up, George. Polite people don't talk about such things."

"*You* just did, Mama."

Maggie gave him a withering look. She continued, "An' then that snake of a husband up and *kills* hisself to boot...I can't believe you'd even consider it, Mo."

"Margaret, it's an old house. It was a long time ago." I was mentally kicking myself for having stopped in to see her. She went on back to scaling her fish. Not getting anywhere with her, I turned to leave. Then without thinking about what I was doing, I said, "Your house is old, too, Maggie. You may have a body or two buried in *your* back yard!"

I heard her knife clatter to the table as George squealed, "*Cool!*"

# Chapter 9    *Summertime*

Over the summer, Joe Thickett came to visit me several times. I couldn't make him understand that I was not interested in a relationship. He never gave up asking me out, however. Mama invited him to supper a few times, trying to push me in his direction. I thought that before the summer was out, someone was going to have some feelings hurt. They were not going to be mine. Joe was nice enough, but there wasn't any attraction whatsoever on my part. It was sad in a way, too, because he was a nice man; I would have enjoyed his friendship, but I didn't want anything else.

One Sunday I was working at the Cork Street house. I wanted to prune the oak tree in the back yard. It was proving to be a difficult task.

"Hey, there!"

I looked in the direction of the voice, and there stood Joe Thickett. My heart sank. Wasn't it enough that I had to deal with him at Mama's?

"Hey, Joe," I responded, hoping my face didn't show the distress I was feeling. "How did you know where to find me?"

"I stopped by your mama's and she told me you was here. So this is the house you want to buy, huh? Ain't you skeered t' be here by yourself?"

By this time, he was standing right next to me. "Why should I be?" I asked, stepping back a pace or two.

"Don't you know this place is haunted?"

I sighed. "Joe, to be honest, I don't care. As long as I don't have to clean up after it, I really do not care."

Joe thought this was the funniest thing he'd ever heard, and he let out a boisterous laugh. I cringed, thinking, *Please go home now.*

"Well," I said, after he had sufficiently recovered, "I hate to be rude, but I really need to get back to work."

"What do you need done? I can hep ye."

"No, no, thank you, really, Joe. I can manage."

It wasn't that I thought I had to do it all by myself, but I knew that letting Joseph Thickett help me in any way would be like feeding a stray cat. Do it once, and you're stuck for life.

"Oh, I don't mind! Here, let me have them clippers." He took them right out of my hands and started pruning away. I protested and tried to retrieve the clippers, but he was much taller and avoided my reach.

"Joe, you don't have to do that."

"I know I don't *have* to. I *want* to. Why don't you just rest a spell and let me finish this?"

I was angry. I didn't want him thinking he could just come here and take over. I was angry at Mama for telling him where I was. Suddenly I turned on my heels and headed to the front yard, got in my car and left, leaving Joe pruning the tree.

"Ooo!" Mama exclaimed when I came through the front door. "Your face looks like thunder!"

"Mama, I am so upset with you right now I could bite a nail in half! Why in the world did you tell *Joe Thickett*, of all people, where I was today? He showed up over there! I don't want him coming over there when I'm trying to work! What were you *thinking*?"

Mama looked hurt, I had come down on her so hard. "He came by lookin' for you, and I didn't figure you would mind if he went over there to lend you a hand."

"Mama." I stopped for a second to calm myself. "I don't *want* Joe Thickett lending me a hand! Don't you understand? He wants more from me than I can give him. He's looking for a *girl*friend. I'm not looking for a *boy*friend! I haven't even been divorced a *year*! All I want to do is do my job at work, go over to the house to take care of it a little, and just mind my own business for the next four or so years. Because until then I don't have any business getting involved with *anyone* for *any reason*! Now you and Joe Thickett and Aunt Melba need to get that settled and leave me out of any future plans. Okay?"

"Okay," she said, and her voice sounded small. "I brought all this on, so I'll have a talk with Joe."

"Thank you. Now, I'm going to have some supper and go to bed early. I'm pooped."

"Uh, Mo..."

"Oh no. Mama. What."

"I told Joe to come back for supper."

I didn't reply. I went to the kitchen, collected the bread, peanut butter, and a spreading knife, and headed to my room. "Have a nice time," I said, and closed the door behind me.

**********

I could have screamed when Joe Thickett came through the office door the next day. I didn't see his name on our appointment list, so I knew he wasn't there on business.

"What can I do for you, Joe?" I asked, trying to pretend the day before had never happened.

"I'd like to talk to you if y' have a minute."

I let out a small laugh. *If I had a minute*? In *this* office?

"I can give you five. I can't be gone from my desk any longer than that." I wanted to get this over with. Whatever Mama had said to him the previous evening obviously wasn't enough.

"Mo," he started when we got outside, "why don't you like me?"

"I like you, Joe."

"Then why won't you go out with me? We're both single."

"I don't like you in that way, Joe. And to be honest? You aren't really single. Do you know that I know more about your ex-wife than I do about *you*? She's all you talk about. I know you need to talk about it— heaven knows I understand—but talking about all that to a woman you want to date? That's poison, Joe. You are *not* ready for a relationship, and to be frank, neither am I. I have a huge load on my back right now, and I cannot get involved with anyone. Even if I could, I'm just not ready. I haven't been divorced even a year yet. Can't you see? And I don't want to be with a man just because he's single, and I bet you'd feel the same way if you let yourself think about it. What do you and I have in common? Nothing. We're both nice people, but we don't belong together."

Joe remained quiet the entire time and let me talk. When I finished, he asked, "Are you sure?" I was relieved when he laughed.

"I just get so lonely," he said, "and I figured you did, too."

"I don't let myself think about it, Joe. I can't."

Joseph Thickett sighed. It made me feel sad. He said, "Well, I think you're a mighty nice gal, Maureen. I'm sorry we couldn't get together,"

I smiled. "You might be sorry now, but you'll thank me later when the right woman comes along and knocks the wind out of you."

**********

The summer moved on. It was August. George had finally tuned 15 in July and was now old enough to go to the boarding academy in Johnston, North Carolina. He was excited. Maggie said he was almost impossible to live with. We decided to all go because, as George said, it was a big deal.

Maggie and George and I sat in the back of the minivan and Mama sat up front with Wash. The back compartment was crammed with George's things, and there was still more to buy when we got to Johnston. He was not allowed to have a television in his room, which ticked him off, but he did have his phone, at least, and he could watch some things on that.

"What happened to the days when all a phone did was make calls?" Wash had asked. He was in shock over the price of the phone and what it cost for the service.

"Gone by the wayside, Bro-in-law," I said. "The wonders of technology."

"Why ain't you got one?"

"I can't afford one," I said, and honestly I couldn't. All I had to rely on was the house phone at Mama's and the phone on my desk at work. I lived in a small world.

George played with his new phone all the way to Asheville. Maggie kept telling him how ugly he was being, ignoring us, but he ignored her, as well. He was mesmerized by that tiny device. Wash announced he was stopping for some famous Biltmore ice cream, and that brought George around.

Over ice cream, Maggie said, "Mama, tell Wash and George that story you told us about Creeper Man. You know—when you was ironin' curtains that day?"

"Oh, they don't wanna hear *that*."

"Yeah we do," Wash said, eating his ice cream as though someone would be coming to take it away from him. "I like your stories, Mama. And George here will have stories to tell his *own* young'uns one day."

"Young'uns?" George burst out. "Fat chance!"

Mama smiled. "Well, in *that* case, I'll tell it!"

**********

Mama had a huge boiler iron that she used to iron the curtains. It was a professional-grade iron that Papa had scavenged out of the shell of a dry-cleaning shop. He worked on it and got it working fairly well. Mama loved it because the boiler tank was huge, and she only needed to fill it once. The iron was connected by a long hose that gave her plenty of room between her and the boiler. Its only flaw was the spray-steam setting; it didn't let out a gentle spray of hot water, but a gushing stream of boiling water that would remove wallpaper from 20 paces. Mama was fine with it; she was careful never to press that button.

When Mama needed to iron with it, she'd haul it out to the back porch. One spring day while we were at school, Mama washed the curtains and windows. Then she brought out the Beast, as she called it, filled it with water, and let it get hot while she waited for the curtains to finish spinning.

It was about noon, and she went in the kitchen to turn up the radio. She liked hearing the 12-o'clock news, and under no circumstances would she have missed the reading of the obituaries. "I want to make sure I don't hear my name," she'd always joke.

Mama had the freshly-washed curtains hanging over her arms when she went back out to the porch. The Beast was willing and able to get to work, so she smoothed the first curtain out and commenced ironing. She hummed while she ironed, but once the obituary announcements came on, she was quiet. The reader at the radio station liked to give dramatic pauses between each name directly after the age and cause of death. It was in one of these moments of silence that mama heard something shift over to the right of her, and as she lifted her head, she noticed that the screen at the door latch was ripped into a big, gaping hole. She caught a glimpse of something move. She snapped her head around in its direction, and she found herself looking into the face of Creeper Man. He had been sent to prison and had been gone a few years, but she recognized him. She dug her fingers into the ironing board, hoping her face didn't betray her terror.

"Can I he'p you with somethin'?" she managed to say, trying to look as nonchalant as possible.

"I know it was *you* what told the po-lice that I was abusin' my dog," he said in a low tone as he slowly walked over to her.

Mama didn't flinch. "Yep, you're right about that. I sure did. Know what else? I took your dog and give him to some *good* people. Yep. Sure did."

Creeper Man started undoing his belt, never taking his eyes off Mama's. "Well, that was unfortunate for *you*, then. I got sent to th' Big House 'cause of your nosiness. Now I'm fixin' to beat *you* like a *dog*."

With that, he raised the belt over his head. Mama was quicker. She had the iron in her hand and pressed the spray-steam button before Creeper Man had landed the first blow. The boiling water gushed right into his face, and he immediately began screaming and dropped to the floor.

Mama hit him with the water again. "Come on!" she yelled. "Show me what you gon' do! Come on, boy! I got more of the same waitin' for ya!"

Creeper Man was writhing on the floor in agony. "I'm gon' *kill* you!" he screamed.

"Yeah? Well, I'd like to see *that*." Mama released another boiling stream, this one going right in his ear. He screamed like a wild animal. "*That's* for *threatenin'* me, an' *this*," she said as she hosed him again, "is for what you done to *that dog*! If you think you gon' get th' best o' *me*, you too stupid t' *live*!"

Creeper Man by now was screaming non-stop and rolling around in the floor.

Papa came running around to the back porch from the outside, having heard the screams when he got out of the car. "What in heaven's name is goin' *on* here, Bess?"

"Brance, go get on the phone and tell Sheriff Delaney I got somethin' here he might be interested in. But tell him t' make it snappy or else I'm gonna to have to empty this whole tank of boilin' water out on this piece of *trash*!"

Hearing that made Creeper Man scream even more. "No! No!" he begged, "not no more o' that b'ilin' water! God, no! *Please, God, no!*"

\*\*\*\*\*\*\*\*\*\*

We all had tears in our eyes from laughing.

"Yeah," Mama said, drying her face with a paper napkin, "the sheriff come and got him. I don't remember all the charges now, but he had broken his parole on top o' all that, so he got sent up the river ag'in." She started chuckling again. "You shoulda seen his face. By the time the law had him cuffed, his face was a mess of blisters. I know it's ugly to laugh, but honey, he had it comin' to him."

\*\*\*\*\*\*\*\*\*\*

By late Sunday, we had George settled in his room. Maggie and I got the bed made and the curtains hung, and George and Wash helped by staying out of the way. Then before we realized, it was time for us to go. We all stood in a circle, holding hands, and Wash prayed.

"Lord, we want to thank you for makin' the way for us to have Georgie boy here to get a fine Christian education. We ask that You would keep him in Your care, watch over him for his mama and me, 'cause You know how much this boy means to us. He was a gift from You, Lord, and we thank You. Use him in Your service. For we ask this in Jesus' name. Amen."

We all said "Amen" together. There were hugs and kisses all around, and I noticed Georgie was dragging his feet a little and looking at the floor.

"You alright, boy?" I asked. He didn't look up and I realized his eyes were wet. I didn't want to embarrass him, so I quickly hugged him and told him how proud I was of him. He didn't walk out to the car with us, which was just as well, because Maggie was starting to lose her composure.

Once we got out of sight of the school, Maggie and Mama cut loose in tears. Maggie kept saying, "My little Stone!" Even Wash was sniffling. My eyes were moist, but I didn't feel like crying. In a way, I was envious of George; he had his whole life ahead of him, and he was about to embark on a great adventure.

# Chapter 10     *Another Autumn*

My year had come full circle. Fall arrived, and I had survived the first year of divorce. I was getting more involved with my church and New Ulster activities. In church, I joined the choir. I also joined a community choir that was headed up by the local Christian college. We already started rehearsing for the Christmas season.

I was still with Dr. Liske, who had actually given me a raise at the end of the summer. I certainly wasn't going to ask him why and give him the opportunity to change his mind. His finances were straightening out, as far as I could tell, so I simply expressed my gratitude for the raise and let it go.

Jean had met a new man, and she was hard to live with, talking about him at every turn. I was pleased for her, though. She had his pictures plastered all over her desk area. Dr. Liske looked around one morning and exclaimed, "What is all this, Jean? This place is starting to look like a shrine!"

"It's my beau, Dr. Liske, and I like havin' his pictures around."

Dr. Liske had given up on trying to make sense out of anything Jean did. He sighed deeply, unrolled the morning newspaper, and headed back to his office.

I was still working at the Cork Street house, which I had optimistically named the *Dearbháil*, pronounced Dearvahl, "Daughter of Ireland." I wanted to have a plaque made with the name on it, but I knew that had to wait. To celebrate fall, I dressed up the front porch with pumpkins and chrysanthemums. From the outside, it looked like someone lived there and loved the place.

*********

George seemed to be getting along fine at the academy. We had talked on the phone one evening, and he told me about a concert coming up in town. He really wanted to go, but he knew his parents were expecting him to come home for that weekend. I told him, "Just be honest and tell them what you want to do. They'll understand. It's just one weekend."

"Aunt Mo, really? I mean, this my mama, *your sister*, we're dealin' with!"

I couldn't help smiling. "Point taken," I said. "Well, if you aren't going to be honest with them, you'd better come on home, then."

I stopped by Wash and Maggie's on the way home from work one evening.

"George ain't comin' home on his long weekend. They're goin' into midterms and he wants to get some serious studyin' in." Maggie chuckled. "I'm glad he's serious about school, but I'll miss the ol' Stone." Break was from Thursday night to Sunday night, and she had been looking forward to his visit.

I felt a little uneasy. Was George up to something? I immediately dismissed it and didn't share that I had spoken to him. There was no need in putting ideas into her head.

I said, "Well, why don't you and Wash come over Saturday night and we'll have supper together? That'll keep you plenty of company."

So that's what we decided to do. Maggie and I cooked while Wash and Mama watched a true crime show on television. After we ate, we sat around the table for a long time just talking.

It was late when Maggie and Wash left. Just as I locked the door for the night, the telephone began ringing. I figured at that hour it had to be an emergency, so I snatched the receiver up and almost shouted, "Hello?"

The voice on the other end sounded young. "Miss MacKenzie?"

"Yes?"

"Hey, this is Sherry and I'm calling from Gilead Academy. We see you signed George out today and wondered when you'd be bringing him back in. When you signed him out, you forgot to put the return time. We just wanted to check because it's getting late."

I was completely flustered. Signed George out? Me? I wanted to panic, but I knew I needed a clear head. George's conversation came to mind and I began putting the pieces together. I realized I was probably speaking to a student aide and decided to lie. "Yes, I'm so sorry. I was in a hurry. We're having such a great time, I didn't realize how late it's getting. I'll have him there soon!"

When I hung up the phone, I was furious. I dialed his cell phone. "And you better pick up," I said between my teeth while it rang.

"Yo, Aunty Mo," he answered.

"Where are you, and you *better* not lie to me because *enough* lies have been told today. Just tell me where you are and don't you *dare move.*"

George didn't bother to argue because he knew he'd been caught. He learned a long time ago that I didn't put up with such foolishness.

"I'm in Asheville. I went to my concert like I told you I wanted to do."

"George, the school just called me and said that *I* had signed you out. What about *that*, fella? Listen, I don't have time to talk about this now. Just tell me where to pick you up, and you—better---*be* there."

It would take me maybe two hours to get to Asheville. I was rounding up my things when I spied a little leather pouch, and I stuck it in my jacket pocket. Mama was in the bathroom so I shouted through the door. "Hey, I have to go to the office. There's a problem with the alarm system, and I need to stay there till they get it fixed." I didn't give her time to respond. I immediately left and headed for the highway. I was boiling mad. That boy was in for some serious business.

I was blessed with good traffic and arrived in Asheville an hour and a half later. Now to find George. I had calmed down considerably by the time I arrived, which was good because I really didn't have the energy to get upset again while looking for an open car park. Finding one and feeling very relieved, I parked and headed out walking in the direction of the concert hall. It was further off than I expected.

"Aunt Mo!" I heard him call, and my heart felt nothing but relief. I didn't know whether to hug him or trounce him.

"Georgie!" I decided on the hug. "I could kill you," I said as I squeezed him. He laughed. "I'll decide later how. Let's go home."

"Not the school?"

"Oh, that's right. I'll need to get you back there. If I show up with you at home, your mama will have no end of questions."

We were walking down the sidewalk next to a busy four-lane. Speaking meant that we had to shout to one another. I asked him why he would tell such a lie about being signed out, and lying to his mother about why he wasn't coming home. Before he could answer me, he stopped and stuck his arm out in front of me. "Aunt Mo," he said, but I barely heard him. I looked in the direction he was looking, and right in front of us was a boy in ripped jeans and a running jacket. He had his hands in his pockets until he got a little closer when he drew out a knife.

"Give me your money," he growled, his eyes darting nervously around. I wasn't about to, and I said as much.

"You have to be kidding. *He's* a student without a dime, and I work hard for *my* money, so you needn't think I'm going to just hand it over to *you*."

I saw George out of the corner of my eye, and he was looking at me. "Mo!" he shouted.

"Be quiet, George. Now look," I said, not looking away from the thief, "you may as well get out of our way. I'm tired, thirsty, I have a long drive ahead of me, and I'm pretty ticked off at the moment as it is. So my advice to you is to go home to your mama and stay off the streets."

This seemed to make him angry. He brandished the knife around. "I will cut your head off."

I laughed. George's mouth fell open in disbelief. "Mo!" he shouted again, "Just give him your money!"

"I'll do no such a thing!"

The thug then stuck the knife out closer to me. I pulled the leather pouch out of my pocket. "This what you want? Really? Then go get it!" And with that, I flung it into the busy highway.

He called me an ugly name, and just when I thought no human could be crazier, he ran out into the traffic, darting around speeding cars, to try to retrieve the pouch. In the distance I could still hear him swearing.

I grabbed George's arm. "*Run!*"

At the corner of the block, I stopped, heart pounding and completely out of breath. There was an open Irish pub, and I headed in. "I need a drink," I said, and he responded, "Aunt Mo!"

"Of *water*, you ninny!"

We sat down at a booth and ordered a couple of sodas. I was exhausted.

"Aunt Mo, you're either very stupid or the bravest person I've ever met."

"I call it bravely stupid."

We laughed.

"How are you gonna to pay for this? You threw away your money!"

"No, I didn't. I threw away a pack of *Skip-Bo* cards, which were new, thank you very much."

George stirred his straw around in his soda. "So why in the world do you carry cards around in your pocket? That little deal saved our skins!"

"Oh, when I was getting ready to come up here, I felt really impressed to put them in my pocket."

"Impressed? By what?"

"The Holy Spirit," I replied.

George regarded me. "You don't really believe that, do you? All that Holy Spirit business?"

"Of course I do. You grew up in the church, George. You don't believe in the Holy Spirit?"

He threw his arm over the back of the booth seat. "I'm not so sure about all that stuff. To be honest, Aunt Mo? I think it's all a fairy tale."

I couldn't believe what I was hearing, but I tried to look nonchalant. "Nonsense? Why do you think that?"

He was considering his answer. "Well, if there is a God, why is He so quiet and uninterested in us? Why does he let bad things happen to good people?"

"Georgie, bad things happen to *everybody* at some point. This is a sin-sick world. But God sent Jesus here to be the cure, so to speak. Jesus willingly came and laid down His life for us. That's how much He loves us."

"So you believe that Jesus is the Son of God?"

"I do. And you don't?"

"Still out on that one, too. That virgin birth stuff...not very likely."

George was looking very smug. I felt sorry for him. He thought with all his education that he had the answers, but he was being fooled.

I weighed my words before I spoke. "Your Mama and Da are fine Christians. They have done their best to give you everything that we didn't have growing up. They have taught you the Gospel since the time you were born. You learned to pray when you were practically a baby. Why are you so willing to throw away the truth, the very basis of our existence? And if you don't believe any of it, why did you want to come to a *Christian* school?"

He thought for a minute. "I didn't *want* to go to a Christian school. But I came *here* to get away from home. As far as God," he said slowly, "He has never answered any of *my* prayers."

I regarded him for a moment, silently praying for the right words. "Have you ever stopped to listen long enough for an answer? Sometimes we flash off our prayers, say amen, and are up about our business without remembering to be still and know that He is God."

"Huh." George was scowling. "He can interrupt, can't He?"

"What is it that you prayed for that you think He didn't answer? He always answers; sometimes the answer is 'No' if it isn't in our best interest."

"What He didn't answer were my prayers about school. I thought I would be makin' friends here. I haven't. Why would He have me come to this place?"

George was upset; his face was red. I felt for him.

"Georgie," I said gently, "your Mama and Da only want the best for you. They saw a wonderful opportunity to send you to this Christian school. God opened the doors wide for you to be here without leaving your family in a lot of debt. Your school is known for its excellent scholastic program. You were so excited to be coming here to school! What happened?"

He wiped his face on his sleeve. "I *hate* it here! I don't have any friends. They're all back home havin' a good time, and I'm not there with them. And this stupid school doesn't even have *football*! I can't see any of this as bein' the best for me!"

"Only time will tell that, George. Sometimes we don't understand God's will until we see His purpose."

"What was His purpose in your *divorce*?" He said the word harshly, wanting it to hurt.

His words stung me, but I hid it. "Divorce is never His purpose, Georgie. It happened because my husband *chose* it to happen. But one thing I am sure about—God has been with me through all of this sadness, and He can take anything ugly and make it beautiful in His time. For whatever reason He has you here, it's a good one. God never asks anything of us that He doesn't give us the strength to go through. You may never see it in this lifetime. But you could, possibly. All God is requiring of you is that you trust Him. I know for certain, Georgie, that He will *never* let you down. Don't expect God to be Santa Clause, giving you everything you want just because you want it. He's much better than that."

I felt like I had preached enough. We were silent for a moment. But then I said, "And by the way, read the Old Testament if you want to know whether Jesus is the Son of God or not. Nothing is clearer."

I smiled at him, and to my surprise, he smiled back. "I don't want you to talk to Mama about any of this," he said. "I don't want her to know I'm miserable. I have to lie to her every time we talk on the phone. She worries enough as it is."

"In a lot of ways, you're growing into a man, George," I said, and he smiled again.

# Chapter 11     The Piper

The community choir was set to give its Christmas concert the second week in December. I was excited, because not only was I getting to sing with a great group, but I had auditioned for a solo and got it. I would be singing "Silent Night" in Irish. I had practiced "Oíche Chiúin" everyday starting in October. An added bonus would be a bagpipe. The director, Dr. Coleman, was shipping in a piper from Roanoke, Virginia. There were pipers in New Ulster, but this was a personal friend of his from his college days. The piper and I would be closing the concert with "Oíche Chiúin." I could hardly wait. Our first rehearsal together would be the night before the concert.

I went to the rehearsal hall early so I could warm up and be prepared. Dr. Coleman met me with a smile and said he appreciated all my hard work and conscientiousness. I felt myself blush, but I thanked him and went on to a warmup room. At the appointed time, I went onstage to join the rest of the choir. We had a short warm-up, and then plowed right into the program as though it were concert night. The music was glorious. We opened with a number called "Arise, Shine!" and followed with hymns and songs that told the Christmas story.

After the last song, the piper came in from behind the curtain. "I'm sorry I was running a little late," he said. "Traffic was terrible."

"That's alright!" Dr. Coleman beamed. "We're just happy you arrived safely! Choir, I'd like you to meet my old friend and our piper, Brendan Fitzgerald."

The choir applauded, and Brendan gave a little bow and a big smile. Dr. Coleman waved me off the riser.

"Come down, Maureen, and let's do this closing number. I can hardly wait to hear you two together!" When I reached the floor, Brendan shook my hand as Dr. Coleman introduced me. "Brendan, this is Maureen MacKenzie, our soprano soloist."

His handshake was firm but not bone-crushing. I liked that. His dark hair was just getting grey at the temples. He had a prominent nose, but it didn't detract from his looks. As a matter of fact, it made him all the more striking. Against the green of his pullover sweater, his green eyes looked huge.

"It's my pleasure," he said, and I suddenly felt funny in my legs. Whatever I was thinking, I dismissed it to take my place on stage.

We were side-by-side, Brendan sitting with his Uillean pipe and I, standing. On Dr. Coleman's cue, this man named Brendan Fitzgerald began playing. I could feel the sound down to my soul. He played one verse, the Uillean pipe sounding so sweet. He held the last note, and then faded out so I could begin. I just stood there. The choir began snickering.

I could feel my face turning red, and I exclaimed, "I'm sorry! I was so fascinated by your playing that I forgot I had to sing!" Both men laughed. We started over. On Brendan's last note, I began singing in Irish. As I held my last note, the pipes came in again, and we performed it together. When we finished, I was breathless. Not from singing, but from the beauty of the music and Brendan's playing. The entire hall was quiet.

Then Dr. Coleman said, "Well done!" and the choir applauded.

I looked over at Brendan to shake his hand. He took it, leaned in and said, "You have an extraordinary voice," and I could feel my face getting red again. He smelled wonderful.

I went to bed that night thinking of Brendan Fitzgerald. I scolded myself, though, because I knew nothing could come of it, and I needed to stop being so foolish. And then I felt tears come to my eyes, which surprised me because I hadn't allowed myself to cry in such a long time. I gave in and cried into my pillow so Mama wouldn't hear. Then sleep finally came.

**********

The next evening, I took my time getting dressed. We were wearing concert black, which I loved, and I had made my dress myself years ago when I sang with other choirs. It was holding up pretty well.

"How do I look, Mama?" I asked, and twirled around in front of her.

"Like a diva," she said. "Just don't start *actin'* like one." We laughed. I drove her over to Maggie's and left her to go with them. I had to be at the concert hall early for warm-up.

I was standing in the hallway downstairs from the auditorium with most of the other singers while we were waiting to go up for some last-minute spot checks. I looked up when the back door opened, and in walked Brendan Fitzgerald in full Irish kilt. I think I stopped breathing. He gave his greetings to all those standing around, and then he made his way straight to me.

"Hello," he said. "Do we have time for a run-through before we go up?" I said we did, but in all honesty I had no idea whether we did or not. I figured Dr. Coleman would find us. We went into a rehearsal room.

"Your kilt is beautiful," I said when he'd closed the door.

"Thank you," he replied, smiling. "I play with a group in Roanoke, and we all wear kilts. You look very nice tonight."

"Oh, thanks. I...thanks." I was flustered and couldn't think of anything to say that wouldn't sound stupid. "So...shall we?"

Brendan began to tune up. He said, "You know what 'Uillean' means, don't you?"

"No," I said.

"It's Irish for 'out of tune.'" He went on tuning, and I laughed. I wanted to look at him, but I didn't want him to think I was staring. But I really wanted to look. I really wanted to stare. Before I could sing, Dr. Coleman burst in and said we needed to be upstairs.

The concert was flawless. We had a full house. Everyone was given a candle, and during "Oíche Chiúin," the candles were lit, one by one, each one by the next, until they were all lit. The concert hall looked amazing. It was a very moving evening.

Dr. Liske was there, and so were Jean and her beau. I didn't get to speak to them, but I did wave from on stage when the crowd was breaking up.

I was about to go downstairs to get my coat when I felt someone take my arm. It was Brendan. "Maureen, you sang beautifully tonight. It was an honor playing music with you."

"Thank you, Brendan! It was honor playing with *you*." There went my face again, turning three shades of red.

"Listen, I know you must be tired, but would you like to go out for a bite to eat? Or maybe just a coffee?"

*Absolutely not, I thought. I can't go out with you. I would make a complete fool of myself. No, I cannot, will not, even consider heading into something that has no future!*

"I'd love to," I said.

The only place in New Ulster that was still open was the Waffle World. I didn't mind; I had a secret passion for their pecan waffles. I rarely allowed myself one, so I considered this a treat.

"I don't like to eat before I perform," Brendan said as he looked over the menu.

"Ooo, I don't either," I agreed. "Too hard to keep breath control, not to mention just feeling so heavy, even if it's a light meal."

Brendan looked at me. He smiled. "I know exactly what you mean. So now I'm starved! Any idea what you want?"

"A pecan waffle, dark, please."

"Ah, a waffle connoisseur, I see," Brendan teased. "A woman who knows what she wants."

"Well, at least when it comes to food!" I laughed. "Actually, I'm a vegetarian, so this is one of the few things I can have here. A salad, yes, but how boring!"

Brendan looked curious. "Vegetarian? How long have you been a vegetarian?"

"About 20 years."

He stared. "Really? So why vegetarian?"

"I just think it's the healthy way to go."

"Well, now I feel terrible. I was going to order the steak and eggs!"

We laughed. "You go ahead and order whatever you want, Mr. Fitzgerald. And don't feel terrible."

I was halfway through my waffle when I thought, *Don't eat this whole thing. He'll think you're a hog!* I looked over at his plate, however, and he was really putting it away. I couldn't help smiling.

"What?" he asked.

"Nothing."

"No, what?"

"Well, Brendan, I was just admiring your appetite. Now I don't feel bad for going ahead and eating this entire waffle!"

"You'd better," he said, amused. "You never know when we could turn into a couple of starving musicians."

So the evening went. We had delightful conversation over absolutely nothing. I told him I'd been born in New Ulster and had lived most of my life there. He was born in Arlington, Virginia. After college he moved to Roanoke for a job.

"What's the most boring job you can imagine?" he asked.

"Shoe salesman!"

"Oh, now, shoe salesmen get a pretty bad rap! Imagine having a job where you get to put your hands on ladies' ankles all day."

"Not for me!" I said. "So please tell me you're not a shoe salesman. My ankles would feel mighty exposed."

"No," he said and smiled. "I'm an accountant."

I had heard my entire life that accountants were boring people.

"Really? How fascinating!"

"Maureen, you're a terrible liar. Now I know what's racing through that bright mind of yours. *Accounting is boring, so accountants must be boring.* Am I right?"

I giggled and nodded.

"Do you find me boring?"

"Absolutely not!"

"Well, there you go, then. Actually, accounting is very interesting work. I always liked math, and I just felt drawn to accounting because of my fascination with money."

"I have a fascination with money, but I never felt compelled to be an accountant. Of course, math was not one of my strong points."

"So what is your fascination with money?" he asked.

"I think it's fascinating how quickly it disappears! Just like vapor!"

Brendan laughed. I told him about my sisters and mother, my job, about Dr. Liske and Jean. His mother had originally been from Ireland, and after her husband died, she decided to move back there.

"I have a younger brother, Andrew. We've been, well, estranged, since Dad died. He lives up in DC, so I haven't seen him for a while."

"What about your mother?" I asked. "When have you seen her last?"

Brendan looked down at his plate. "That's a story for another time," he said, and then looked at me. Something passed between us, and I understood.

He told me that he'd been married before, but it ended in divorce.

"Actually, it ended *before* the divorce. She left me for another man. The two of them were on a skiing trip, and she had an accident and died later that evening. We were still legally married, so I had to take care of all that."

"That must have been really hard."

"Yes. But it was a long time ago. I had a great struggle, but with God's help, I healed and have moved on. Actually, my life is like a romantic comedy."

"Oh?"

"Yes, only minus the romance and just me laughing at my own jokes," he said, and I laughed. "What about you?" he continued. "Ever been married?"

"Yes. But it ended in divorce, too. Last fall."

"How are you coping?" He seemed genuinely concerned.

"Like you, I have moved on."

"Well Maureen, I've had a wonderful time tonight. I'd like to see you again, if I may."

I felt my heart begin to pound. What could I say? "I thought you lived in Virginia."

"I do. I'm going back tomorrow, but I'd like to have breakfast with you before I leave." He smiled and looked so handsome that it took my breath. "Besides, Roanoke is only four hours away."

I knew I should say no, but I didn't. I enjoyed his company, and it was so refreshing being with a man who had his head on his shoulders. I just hoped that I did, too.

"Alright. I'll meet you in town. Seven o'clock sound good?"

"Sure! What's a good place around here to get breakfast?"

"You're sitting in it," I said.

"No complaints here, if it's okay with you."

He walked me out to my car. I wanted him to kiss me, but I was afraid he might. I was a bundle of nerves. Instead, though, he took my hands in his and said, "Let's have prayer together." And his prayer was one of thanksgiving for a good concert and a nice evening out. He also prayed for my safe-keeping as I made my way home. When he finished, he lifted my right hand and kissed it.

"Good night, Maureen. I'm already looking forward to the morning."

**********

Mama was waiting up. "You're awful late," she said, not looking up from her crocheting.

"I went out for supper with the piper."

She looked at me. "Well?"

"Well?"

Mama rolled her eyes. "Are you gon' tell me about it, or do we hafta play *20 Questions*?"

I sat down on the sofa opposite Mama and smiled. "Mama." That's all I could say for the moment. She waited.

"His name is Brendan."

"Yeah. I got *that* much out of the bulletin. Tell me the good stuff."

"Well, he invited me to supper, and I should have said no, but I didn't. I couldn't. I wanted to go out with him."

"Girl, what's wrong with *that*?"

"Oh, Mama, you know how it is. I can't let myself get involved with anyone to *any* degree." I felt my eyes stinging.

"Look, Mo. I know you got the shaft in this divorce. I *know* that. But you cain't put your whole life on hold because of it. You go to work, you work at your house, you come home. This is your whole life. And I'll be honest with you, girl. Your life is *borin'*."

"Gee, thanks."

"Now you know what I'm sayin's th' truth. It ain't meant to hurt you. I'm just tryin' to get you to see that hidin' yourself away ain't good for you. When the time comes and you ain't got to pay no more alimony, what then? You'll have all these years behind you, but they'll be empty years. Maybe you'll get that house; maybe you won't. We cain't see down the road that far. But Mo, life is more than an empty house. I don't want you to wind up empty because all the life got drained out of you."

I was trying not to cry. I'd been so happy over supper, having such a good time, that I forgot all about my problems.

Mama continued. "Did you even tell him about your divorce?"

"Just that I was divorced. Nothing more."

"Why not?"

"Well, Mama, look. We're talking as if this man is going to be my future. We just met yesterday and had supper once. I can't let my guard down for something so new and uncertain."

"You're talkin' like you're tryin' to convince *yourself,* not me."

We looked at each other. Mama's face was so sweet, so full of kindness. No wonder Papa loved her.

"I hate to see you sad," she said.

"Me, too."

"So tell me. What do you think of this piper Brendan?" She was smiling as though she and I shared a secret.

"Well, Mama, he's so nice. A gentleman. Very smart. And on top of all that, he's *Presbyterian*!" We laughed.

Mama said, "But *you're* not."

"I *know* that, Mama, but I thought it would please *you*. He lives in Roanoke, Virginia, and works as an accountant."

"An *accountant*? Mo, talk about *borin'*!"

"Oh, no, Mama, there's not a *thing* boring about *him*! He has a wonderful sense of humor, and he's interested in everything."

"Do you think that includes you?"

My face flushed. "He's taking me to breakfast in the morning," I said shyly.

Mama sat back in her chair and looked at me, smiling. "Whatcha gon' wear?"

"Well, everything will pale in the light of *this* dress," I said, running my hand down the sleeve. "Just whatever I'd wear to work."

"Maybe he'll wear his kilt again. He looked delicious." Before I could say anything, she said, "Well, I tell ya, if *you* don't want him, *I'll* take him! There's something about a man in a kilt!" We laughed.

We were quiet for a moment. I figured it was time for her to get nosy.

"I take it he's divorced."

"Sort of."

She looked shocked.

"Mama, you'd die if I told you."

Her mouth fell open. "You better tell me, girl. I'll die if you *don't*."

"He and his wife were in the middle of a divorce when she was killed in a skiing accident." Mama's mouth fell open again. "She was with another man."

"*Then* what happened?"

"He had to handle her affairs and bury her. That's all I know."

"Well," Mama snorted. "He got off lucky. At least *he's* not payin' alimony! Does Ol' Thang ever go skiin'?"

"*Mama!*"

**********

Brendan and I met up again at the Waffle World the next morning. I pretended I hadn't had one the night before and ordered a dark pecan waffle. He decided to have one as well.

"I'm open to trying new things," he said and smiled into his coffee.

I smiled back even though I wasn't sure why. He just made me want to smile.

"And something I'm open to trying, that I've been unwilling to do till now, is a long-distance relationship. Maureen, I'd like to see you again, and I don't want to have to wait till next year's Christmas concert." He was looking at me so intently that I thought surely he could read my thoughts.

"Brendan, I really don't know what to say."

"I was hoping it would be 'yes,' but maybe I misread you. I had the feeling last night that something was happening between us, and I certainly wanted to pursue it if it's there."

I was quiet for a moment.

"I'm sorry if I've made you uncomfortable," he said.

"You haven't," I finally replied. "I am honored that you see something in me that you'd like to know better. I think you're a wonderful man, Brendan."

"But?"

"I don't think I'm ready for a relationship. I have a lot of baggage. I don't want to burden anyone else with that right now. It wouldn't be fair to you, Brendan. I hope you understand."

It was his turn to be quiet. Then he said, "I *do* understand, Maureen. I felt the same way after all that business I went through. I should have thought of that. I'm sorry if I made you feel pressured or put on the spot."

"You didn't. You have been a gentleman, Brendan, something rare these days. And if this were a different time....oh, my, I'd be the luckiest woman in the world. I mean that."

He looked at me for what felt like a long time. "You really are an extraordinary woman, Maureen. Pardon my saying, but your husband was a fool."

**********

Christmas Eve came. There in the mail was a card addressed to me, and the return address was Roanoke. It was a beautiful card from Brendan. The front was a painting of a farm in Ireland, featuring a cottage with a thatched roof. The front door was adorned by a simple wreath. Inside was a hand-written letter.

*Dear Maureen,*

*I hope this finds you well. I've thought about you and our last conversation, and I want you to know that you are in my prayers every day. I feel you deserve the very best in life, and I know that in time, your life will come back together, and you'll feel whole again.*

*I hope you don't mind my writing to you this way. I would hope that we can be friends, in spite of the distance and your present circumstances. We all need good friends, and I would like to be yours and have you as mine. If you'd rather not, I'll certainly understand. I know the last thing you need right now is more confusion and entanglements, and I certainly don't want to bring either of those.*

*I really enjoyed the brief time we spent together, the laughter, the music. If you ever want to talk about what is going on in your life, I'm more than willing to listen. Sometimes just having a good listening ear makes troubles seem a little less bothersome.*

*Merry Christmas, Maureen! I hope this is the best one ever.*
*All the best,*
*Brendan.*

The paper smelled faintly of his cologne. I breathed it in deeply, and remembered what he looked like, his voice, the sound of his laughter. I was so happy to hear from him, but at the same time, I could feel some distant pain.

# Chapter 12    A Man of Letters

Dear Brendan,
    Happy New Year! I hope you enjoyed your Christmas. I really appreciate the card you sent, and especially the message it contained. I would like us to be friends, as well.

    Did you do anything special for Christmas? Our family got together, as usual, and my oldest sister, Rose, was able to make it from New Mexico. The three of us girls had a really fun time together. Rose will be with us a few more days, so Mama is happy about that.

    I guess I should tell you up front that I live with my mother. I came back home after my divorce, and she graciously took me in, po' little chil' in a basket that I was. Haha. I know I laugh now, but I am really grateful to Mama for helping me out in such a big way.

    Please do write again when you can. I enjoy getting mail, especially in this age of email. A hand-written letter is something to cherish.
Have a blessed New Year,
Maureen

                    **********

Dear Maureen,
    Happy Martin Luther King Day!
    Let me tell you right off that there is absolutely nothing wrong with your living with your mother. That shows the great love she has for you. She's helping you get back on your feet after a great loss, and I admire her for that! I know this has been hard for you, but you seem to me to be a strong woman, so I have no doubt that you'll do fine.

    I was glad to receive your letter. Good to hear that Rose made it for Christmas. Your other sister is Maggie. So you're the baby, right? I'm 39, by the way. What about you? I should warn you that when I want to know something, I come right out and ask.

    Another thing I need to warn you about—I love corny jokes and puns. It's a weakness. If you don't care for such humor, I'll try to be on my best behavior.
May God bless you,

Brendan

**********

Happy Valentine's Day, Brendan!

I hope you are well and rosy! I enjoyed reading your letter. I'm 38, so I can commiserate. Hard to believe we're staring 40 in the face!

Yes...I'm "the baby," as Mama still calls me.

Rose teaches at a college in New Mexico and loves it out there. We see her at least once a year. Sometimes Christmas, sometimes summer. When she isn't teaching, she keeps the road hot, going on adventures.

Dr. Liske hired a new nurse who has the personality of diaper rash, so Jean and I call her Ol' Soggy Bottom. Not to her face, of course! Ha! (The last one quit after only several months. Honestly—just when you get used to someone.) All in all, we all work well together, and I enjoy what I do. But I'm still hoping to hit the big time so I can leave this job and open an antiques store. I love restoring furniture. But it's hard to win the lottery if you don't play!

Well, I hope you have a nice Valentine's Day. If you get any candy, save me a piece.

Maureen

PS Why did the rubber chicken cross the road?

**********

Happy Valentine's Day to you, Maureen! I wanted to send you a Valentine greeting and let you know that I am thinking of you and praying for you, my friend. I hope your day is beautiful and special. Enjoy this little gift!

Yours in Christ,

Brendan

PS To stretch her legs?

**********

Dear Brendan,

Thank you so much for the box of Valentine candy! I love coconut and chocolate! How very dear of you, friend. I shared it with my family, and they now think you hung the moon.

I was thinking this morning about Valentine's Day when I was in the first grade. I had the biggest crush on a little boy named Jimmy Patterson. He sat one row over and a desk up from me. I used to stare at his head and wish he'd turn around and smile at me. Oh, he was a beautiful boy. He had black hair and big blue eyes, and just seeing him get off the bus made my heart go pitter-pat, pitter-patter, pitter-*patterson*! Ha! Well, during the week of Valentine's Day, we were coloring our little bags for our party. I wanted to put a big red heart on the front of my valentine bag, but I didn't have a red crayon. I noticed that Jimmy Patterson had a red crayon. I kept one eye peeled on the teacher, because she had said NO TALKING, and when she said that, she meant it! So I cautiously leaned over and whispered, "May I borrow your red crayon?" The words were hardly out of my mouth when Miss Campbell called my name: "MAUREEN MACKENZIE!"

I looked at her in perfect horror. She was looking at me with disgust, and told me to get up to her desk IMMEDIATELY. Oh, my, I was terrified. Miss Campbell was a dragon with a beehive hairdo. So I left my desk, trembling, and went up front. I'll never forget, either, that I was wearing a navy blue dress with a white bib on the front. When she said my name, the poof went right out of my sleeves. She seemed to love any opportunity to make a point. I was her point that morning. She said, "Didn't you hear me say that there should be no talking?" I expected flames to come out of her nostrils. I said, "I'm sorry, Ma'am." Then she motioned me to lean over the trashcan so I could take my punishment. I leaned over the little round can, and she popped me on the behind with a stick. I was so humiliated, but I was determined I would NOT cry in front of her or the class. I stood up and bravely went back to my desk. Some of the children were looking at me, but I pretended I was not bothered in the least by her popping me, and I started coloring again—a PINK heart, at that. At lunch I decided that because I had been publically humiliated by Miss Campbell, how much worse could it get, so

I asked Jimmy Patterson if he would sit with me in the lunch room. Do you know what that beautiful boy said to me? "You're ugly."

Well, forget pride! I ran to the bathroom in tears! Haha, I've never forgotten that day OR that dress!

Thinking of you,
Maureen

**********

Dear Maureen,

Happy St. Paddy's Day to you! I hope you have some exciting plans!

Guess what I'll be doing? Our group, Piping Hot, will be playing in the St. Patrick's parade in Abbeygrove, a little town near Roanoke. This will be the first time we've played there, and I'm really looking forward to it because we've been working on some really awesome tunes this winter.

Please tell me you weren't kidding about antiques. I enjoy going antiquing on the weekends! We'll have to plan to go sometime when the weather is nice, if you'd like to. What do you think?

Where would you open your store? Are you serious about that? I think that's amazing, and I wish you the best with it. Write and tell me more!

I think this Jimmy Patterson must have been quite the churl. If you had asked me to sit with you at lunch, I not only would have accepted, but I would have shared my sandwich with you--AND carried your books!

I don't have a Valentine story, but I do recall when I was 13 and playing bagpipes in a parade for the first time ever. I had been playing for years with my father and brother, so he and Andrew and I decided to get together with a couple of other musicians and play in the parade. It had been threatening rain and was cold, but we were already committed. My father always said that no Fitzgerald was ever a quitter. So out we go down Main Street. I'll never forget we were playing "Steam Train to Mallaig." I was having a mighty time! In spite of the cold, my fingers were feeling nimble, and our playing all came together so wonderfully. And then it happened. We were passing a group of high school girls, and one of them yelled, "Show us what's under your skirt!" Well, I was 13, and easily embarrassed. I was mortified by what she'd said, and then the laughter that followed it, so I lost my concentration and my playing went right out the window. Father gave me a stern look, so I tried playing again, but it sounded awful. All that discipline destroyed by the likes of a snotty high school punk.

She and Jimmy Patterson are probably still in night school together.
All the Best,
Brendan

**********

Dear Brendan,

Hey there!

I'm very serious about antiques and having a store. I have my eye on a house in town that has a building on the property that would be just perfect for a little store. Of course, I don't know what the zoning laws are like, but if I couldn't have it there, it would make a great shop to do my restorations in. I even have a name—"Prim and Proper"!

I would love to go antiquing with you sometime. There are some great places around the Saluda, NC area.

I hope your St. Paddy's parade went well. I screamed when I read your story! I'm glad that didn't mark you for life and that you still play. I wish I could have been there. We had a good time here. After the parade downtown, Mama, Maggie, and her husband Wash and I got together with some of our extended family and had a nice dinner and celebration. Maggie and Wash have a son, George, who is away at boarding academy, and he couldn't make it, but he said he spent the afternoon listening to bagpipes on a CD. Smart boy!
Blessings,
Maureen

**********

Dear Maureen,

It came to me today that I should tell you about my divorce. You're my friend, and I know I'm yours, so I feel that I need to tell you about it so you will know what happened, in case you ever had any questions. I normally don't say a lot about it, because I don't need to, but I want you to know who I am.

I've been divorced six years, or widowed, however you want to look at it. I was married for 10 years when my wife took up with a coworker. She kept it well hidden. I never suspected anything even though she was becoming a little distant. I just chalked it up to our busy schedules because she was spending so much more time at work. Finally she and her paramour wanted a life together, so she left me and he left his wife. Two families were torn apart. I'd like to say it was an amicable parting, but it was anything but that. I was so blind-sided by the whole affair that I just could not believe this was happening. I fought against the divorce.

A week before our court appointment, they went for a weekend ski trip. At some point in the afternoon, she lost control while skiing and slammed into a stand of trees. She suffered severe brain damage and died that evening. Maureen, the whole divorce ordeal was unbelievable to begin with, but this nearly destroyed me.

I handled the funeral arrangements because we were still legally married, and it had to be done. It was very difficult, to say the least. You see, in the process of tending to her affairs, I found out that she had already changed the beneficiary of her insurance over to her lover. Because I was still legally her husband, it was my duty to see that she was buried. My friends said I should just walk away. But when all was said and done, I knew I had to do what was right, even if she hadn't. I was absolutely grief-stricken. I took care of her funeral and other business and then tried to get on with my life. Over time, I became very bitter. I found out that her lover had reconciled with his wife. He not only had the insurance money, he had robbed me of my wife, and he still had his to go back to. I didn't care about the money, but I was dumbfounded that things had taken such a turn. Bitter isn't a strong enough word.

One day in church, the pastor was speaking on forgiveness. He said that we need to forgive more for ourselves than for the other person. It really hit my heart, and though I was bitter and angry, I asked God to help me forgive my wife and this man. I asked Him to take away the bitterness because I didn't want it coming between Him and me. And I wanted, needed desperately, to heal. I wanted to be better, not bitter.

I began changing. I had moments of real happiness. I held on to God because I know He has all the answers. I will never understand why things happened the way they did, but He knows all things, and I am certain that my future is safe in His hands.

Years have passed, and I feel that life is good.

So there you have it. If there is anything more you'd like to know, please feel free to ask.

Have a good night, dear friend, and I hope to hear from you soon. All the best,

Brendan


**********


Dear Brendan,

Thank you for sharing your story with me. It means a lot that you trust me that much. I have been wanting to tell you some of my circumstances, but I didn't want to come off as a bitter old shrew who lost her husband and now hates the world. It has been difficult. There have been days when I didn't think I would make it. But I have worked at rebuilding my life, and I am much happier now, but there are circumstances that keep me from being totally free.

I was married 14 years, now divorced almost two. My husband was evidently living a secret life, at least that's my guess, because he had no reason, on the surface, to want a divorce. Everyone thought we were happy because we kept our problems to ourselves. But he would be absent from me for long stretches. Not in body, but in his attitude and his relationship with me. I thought it was a phase he was going through. Then one day he told me it was over. I insisted on counseling, which we went to, but he was such a smooth talker that the counselor ended up siding with him and acting as if I were the sole problem. Talk about a mess! I was beginning to believe I was the clingy shrew he accused me of being! But I hung on because we were married. That meant something to me. So I worked harder to make him happier. I kept my distance more so he could have his time. But one day he told me to get out; he'd had enough. I knew he meant it. I packed my things and left. Like you, I was blind-sided.

Living with my mother has been a blessing most times, but I know it's been a big adjustment for her. She always said that the empty nest was a beautiful thing, and there I was coming back home. But she's never made me feel that I'm imposing on her space. Well, there was an incident involving some toothpaste, but that's a story for another time.

The house I told you about? I have been keeping the yard clean and going over there a lot, dreaming. In my head, I'm already living in it. Insane I know, because I can't buy it just yet. It's said to be haunted, so I hope that works in my favor and keeps potential buyers away. HAHA! Anyway, that house and I have needed each other, and working on the exterior has helped me heal, I think, because when I found it, it was broken down, too.

There is more to tell you, but I just don't think I can go there right now. I hope you understand.

Easter is coming up! I love the hymns! Do you have any plans? Whatever they are, I hope you have a beautiful Easter season.
He is risen!
Maureen

\*\*\*\*\*\*\*\*\*\*

Dear Maureen,

My Easter plans involve coming to New Ulster to play the pipes at the college chapel service. Any chance I can see you while I'm in town?
Hopefully,
Brendan

# Chapter 13    *The Whole Wide World*

The *Dearbháil* was all decked out for Easter. I put flowers everywhere and hung a dogwood wreath on the front door. It looked happy, and I smiled as I admired it from the street. It was Sabbath, and I drove by there on my way home from church. I had a little more than three years to go now, and I could buy it. I was still saving for the down payment. To be honest, I could have used some new clothes, but I wanted to save instead. I didn't have that much to put by, so I hated to dip into my savings for much of anything.

I was happy as I drove home, humming the last hymn of the service.

Mama met me at the door, smiling. "You got a card from Brendan, *and* a call. He wants you to call him back."

"Is he in town?"

"He didn't say."

I was a little nervous dialing his number because I felt that maybe he wasn't coming after all.

"Maureen! I'm glad you called! How are you?" he said, sounding as though he were grinning.

"Just fine, Brendan. Everything all right with you?"

"Chip as a cricket," he said. "I'm in town, and if you haven't eaten yet, I'd like to take you to lunch."

"No, I haven't eaten yet," I said, feeling relieved. My heart was jumping. "But look, I have lunch all ready here, so why don't you come have lunch with us?"

Mama was waving her hands, making a big silent "NO" with her mouth.

"I'd love to!" he said. "Give me directions and I can be right on out."

When I hung up the phone, I said, "Mama! What in the world is wrong with you?"

She said, "What's wrong with *you*? Here you've invited this man over and I look a *sight*! I'm wearing a' old housedress, on top of my *hair* not bein' fixed!"

"Well, you have plenty of time to change and do a little something to your hair."

"Them's mighty big words comin' from somebody who just got in from *church*! You're *already* dolled up!" She flounced off to her room.

**********

There was a knock at the door, and I jumped a foot. I was nervous.

Mama said, "Do you want me to get it?" And I said, "No, I will." But I just stood there, looking at the door.

"Maureen!" Mama whispered fiercely, "Open the door!"

I put my hand on the knob, took a deep breath, and swung the door open. Brendan was standing on the porch, smiling, holding a bouquet of flowers. "Hi!"

"Hello!" I answered. "Come in!"

He breezed past me, and I could faintly smell his cologne. "These are for you," he said, handing me the flowers.

"Thank you, Brendan. How sweet of you!"

I heard Mama clear her throat.

"Brendan, this is my mother, Elizabeth MacKenzie. Mama, this is Brendan Fitzgerald."

"Mrs. MacKenzie, I'm so pleased to meet you. I've heard a lot of nice things about you from Maureen." He took Mama's hand and gently held it with both of his while he spoke. I could see her flush red.

"Well, I, I," she stammered, "I'm happy to meet *you*, Brendan. And call me Bess, do."

I couldn't help smiling. Mama looked like she just met a movie star or something. Suddenly she said, "I thought you'd-a worn your kilt."

Brendan laughed. "I'll have it on tomorrow for the Easter services. I hope I'll see you there."

Mama blushed again. I wanted to laugh.

We sat down to eat lunch. It was a vegetarian meal, which Mama always shared with me on Sabbath, because it meant she didn't have to cook. I always had everything prepared on Friday. Mama would set things to warming while I was at church.

"So you went to church today?" Brendan asked. "Something special going on?"

"Oh no. I go every Saturday," I said.

"I'm sorry!" He looked embarrassed. "I remember your telling me that."

"I think she's a Jew," Mama threw in. I shot her a look.

"Oh, I see," Brendan said, "you observe the seventh-day Sabbath. But you're a Christian, right?"

"Absolutely!"

"She *used* to be *Presbyterian*," Mama added, stuffing part of a roll in her mouth.

"Mama's never forgiven me," I said, smiling. "She acts the same way *her* parents acted when she left the Catholic church and became a Protestant."

"Now, Mo, it ain't the same thing."

Mama and I could never come to an agreement on religious matters, so I quickly changed the subject. "How do you like the casserole, Brendan?"

"It's delicious. And it's vegetarian?"

"It is. I hope you don't mind."

"Oh, no," he said. "A good home cooked meal makes a nice change. I eat out or have sandwiches a lot." He smiled and drank some sweet tea.

"Well, save some room for dessert. I have a nice apple crisp. Mama put the apples up last fall. They came off our own trees."

I looked at Mama and she looked proud. I guess she was over my having cut her off at the pass earlier.

"Them's the best apples," she agreed. "Mo's Da planted them over time. We've enjoyed our apples for many a year. As a matter of fact, the crisp we're havin' today is made from *Mo's* apples."

"Mo's apples?" Brendan asked.

"I'll explain later," I replied.

"So Bess," Brendan said to Mama, "you were raised in the Catholic church?"

"Yeah, I was."

Brendan wiped his mouth off with his napkin, folded it, and put it neatly on the table. "Then I suppose," he said, "you know how to make holy water?"

**********

Later that afternoon, Brendan and I drove into town so he could see the *Dearbháil*. On the way he said, "So your mother calls you 'Mo'?"

"Yes. Or 'Moze' or 'Mozie'. I've been called one of those for as long as I can remember. We hardly call Maggie 'Margaret.' But Rose? Rose can't stand nicknames for herself. She is and always has been just *Rose*." I gave a little laugh. "Some poor boy in the fifth grade learned *that* lesson really quick."

"What happened?" he asked.

"He called her 'Rosey-Posey'. She clobbered him with her English book. At least that's the story I heard."

Brendan laughed. "My family used to call me 'Bren' or 'Brendy.'"

I smiled. "Ok, Brendy, turn on the next street and we're almost there."

He looked at me and smiled. "'Mo'," he said. "I like that. And you can call me whatever you want. You can even call me collect."

"Here we are," I said, laughing. "This is the *Dearbháil*."

"Wow." He pulled into the driveway and we just sat there for a moment. "She's a beauty, Mo. Can we get inside?"

"Unfortunately not. But we can peek through the windows. I came over with the real estate agent and had a look inside. It needs work, of course, but it could be done and end up a showplace. Let's look around."

Brendan was impressed with what I had done to the grounds. On the front porch he said, "You know what this porch needs? A swing. A nice oak swing hanging right...*here*." And he moved to the place at the end of the porch. We looked up, and there had indeed been a porch swing at some point. The ceiling hooks were still there.

"That's one of the first things I'll do," I said, grinning. "I love a good porch swing. I can come out here in the mornings with my coffee. Wouldn't that be fun?"

"Yes, I can see that. Now...tell me about this place being haunted."

As we sat on the steps, I told him the whole story of the murder, and all the supposed things that had gone on in the house after that. His eyes were wide when I finished.

"And you want to *live* here?" he asked.

"Oh, Brendan, of course I do. I don't believe all that trash. Oh! Let me show you the other building where I want my shop!"

We walked to the side of the house. The other structure was set back just a little further from the main house. It also had a long front porch but no railing. "It's wood," I said, "and I think with some work, I could make it look more like a cabin. Put a rail on the porch, a cute screen door, some flower boxes. It would just make you want to stop and go in!" I was happy just talking about it.

Brendan regarded me with a faint smile. "You are quite a woman," he finally said, and I could feel myself blush.

**********

We went to the chapel together that afternoon for his rehearsal for the Easter service next day. I never attempted to play any type of bagpipe because I found the instruments too intimidating, but Brendan was flawless. He wasn't playing the instrument; he became the instrument. I watched and listened in awe as he made "Let All Mortal Flesh Keep Silence" come to life. There were several more pieces that he played with other pipers, ending with "Crown Him with Many Crowns."

As he drove me home, he asked if I would be at the service in the morning. I assured him I would. We arrived at the house and he walked me to the door. "Come in for a light supper?" I asked.

"As much as I'd love to, I don't want to wear out my welcome."

"Bren, how silly! I wouldn't have asked if I hadn't meant it," I protested.

"I know you mean it, Mo, but I'm afraid if I stay here with you any longer, I'm not going to be able to fight the temptation."

"Temptation?" I was puzzled.

"To kiss you."

I couldn't say anything. I simply looked at my feet. I could feel tears stinging my eyes.

"I'll see you in the morning," he said quietly, and kissed me on my forehead. Then he was gone.

**********

"I don't *believe* you didn't invite him to supper!" Mama chided me when she saw that I came in alone.

"I did, but he declined."

"Why?"

I was all shades of red. "He wanted to kiss me."

Mama's eyes widened. "An' you didn't *let* him?" Her hands went to her hips. "Girl, I woulda been on that boy like a dog on a bone!"

"Mama, I don't believe you're saying that!"

"Well, I woulda! He's obviously interested in *you*, girl, so what's the problem? And don't tell me it has to do with your *divorce*."

"Oh, Mama," I said as I put my face in my hands. "I think I'm falling in love with him!"

Mama put her arms around me. "Now there, baby girl," she soothed. "Don't it feel better to have that out in the open? You cain't spend the rest of your life denyin' your feelin's. I know you don't want a new relationship to start while you're still tangled up with Ol' Thang, but Brendan is a carin' man. Look at all them nice letters he sent you. He'll understand if you told him the whole story."

I wiped my eyes and tried to pull myself back together. Maybe Mama was right.

"I just can't," I said.

"An' why not?"

"I guess I'm afraid if I tell him I'm stuck paying alimony, he'll decide it's too much trouble, and I'll never see him again."

Mama frowned and looked at me with a serious face. "Where do you get off judgin' that boy like that? You don't know what he's gon' do! And if he *is* the kind that would just up and leave, wouldn't you want to know it *now*? Instead of time down the road?"

I sat down at the kitchen table and put my head down.

Mama continued. "If you have feelin's for this boy, an' I really think y'do, don't you think you need to be upfront and honest, the same way you'd want *him* to be with *you*?"

"I hate it when you're logical, Mama," I sniffled, blowing my nose, "because you're always right."

"So you'll tell him?"

"I'll tell him," I said quietly.

Mama slapped her hands together and it made me jump. *"That's* m' girl!" she beamed. "Lawsey, I believe we need some coffee!"

\*\*\*\*\*\*\*\*\*

The next morning, I headed to the chapel for the early Easter service. Mama was going to her church, so I was going alone. I asked her to come with me, but she refused, saying she hadn't missed an Easter service at her church since she'd married Papa, and she wasn't about to start now.

"Besides," she added, "I don't want to be in the way when you talk to Cutie Pie."

The chapel was already filling up when I got there. Brendan was nowhere to be seen, but once the service started, the pipers came in from the back with Brendan playing the first verse of "Let All Mortal Flesh Keep Silence" as a solo. The other pipers were following, and by the time they took their places up front, they were all playing. The harmonies took my breath away.

I couldn't help staring at Brendan. When the playing stopped, his eyes scanned the room and stopped when they reached mine. He smiled broadly. I smiled back.

I hardly heard a word of the sermon. All I could think about was Brendan Fitzgerald, how he was in the same room with me, and I'd get to see him again after the service. I felt like a school girl, and it embarrassed me. Here I was 38 years old and going goofy over a man. I also considered what I would say to him, and I began to worry again. *I'll ask him to lunch and then tell him. Never give a man with an empty stomach bad news.* I figured I'd have my speech all set by the time we'd finished the meal.

After the service, the pipers led the recessional, going out as they had come in, and finishing their playing out on the front lawn. I was listening in wonder. When they finished, Brendan looked for me and made his way over.

"That was a blessing," I said.

"To God be the glory," was his reply, and he was smiling almost shyly.

Before I could even think, before I had time to consider the consequences, I took a step closer to him, right up next to his body, and I said, "Kiss me, Brendan Fitzgerald."

Later that day when I told Mama about it, she said, "An' he *kissed* ya? Right there in front of the *whole wide world*?" Her eyes looked like dinner plates.

"In front of the whole wide world," I said

.

**********

That afternoon, Brendan had dinner with us. He helped clean the kitchen and then regaled Georgie with the wonders of math. Afterwards we went for a walk together. We went down to my favorite childhood spot. We made our way through the woods behind the house, out past where the old outhouse had been, and stopped just short of where the ground fell away to a dry creek bed below. I loved this place as a child. Once after a terrible wind storm, I discovered a downed tree over the cliff, as I called it, and made my home there many afternoons after school. The tree was long gone, and the ground grown over, but we managed to find a clearing and sat down in the pine needles.

"I have something to tell you, Bren," I said. I had so built the alimony problem up in my head over the last two years, that it had grown larger than life, and I was preparing myself to be left behind by this man.

"Shoot," he said, smiling. "I'm all ears." He leaned back on his elbows and looked at me, waiting.

I signed. "Well, when I got divorced, I didn't really get set free, or whatever you want to call it. There were some issues to work out."

"You had to sell your house?"

"No, no, not that. There were some...entanglements." I stopped for a moment, trying to pull my thoughts together. I had rehearsed in my head what I was going to say, but now that the time was here, I felt like I was sinking. I sighed again and decided to just plunge ahead. "When the divorce was granted, the judge also granted my ex maintenance. Alimony. He was granted alimony."

"You must be kidding me."

I didn't look at him. "No, I'm not kidding you. I was ordered to pay alimony for five years so he could get an education or training to earn a living for himself."

Brendan sat up straight. "Five *years*? Are you serious? And it's been how long now, two years?"

"In the fall," I said.

112

"I can't believe this. Well, no *wonder* you're living with your mother! What kind of man is this jerk?"

"A big one," I said.

He was quiet for a moment. Then he did something totally unforeseen. He leaned over, put his arms around me, and kissed my hair. Quietly he said, "I am so sorry, Mo. I had no idea. Never in this lifetime would I have guessed."

"I didn't want to tell you because I figured you would just disappear from my life. I'm sorry for being so selfish. But I didn't want to see that happen."

"So you were going to leave me hanging for a few more years?" He smiled at me.

"Well, if you stopped seeing me, I'd want it to be for any reason other than my ex-husband and all my baggage."

"Mo," he said, and he softly kissed my face. "I'm glad you told me. I don't want anything between us. And I don't care about the alimony—I see it as *his* being a letch, not as baggage of *yours*." And then he asked, "Do you ever think about him, miss him?"

"Goodness, no."

"Well, that's good. I wouldn't want a third party involved. And I'll wait for as long as it takes."

"Wait?"

He was smiling, his eyes sparkling. "Well, the way I look at it, Miss MacKenzie, is this: you're telling me this news because you feel something for me that's more than friendship. After all, if all I am to you is a friend, why would you think this would make a difference in our relationship?"

I blinked and stammered for something to say. Brendan was having a good time with me. He continued. "I feel, too, especially after that kiss this afternoon, that you and I share the same feelings, and it's definitely more than friendship. Am I right?"

"You—you should have been a lawyer instead of an accountant." I looked down in my lap and felt my cheeks grow even hotter.

"You're changing the subject. But that's okay. As I said earlier, I can wait." I could feel his breath on my face. "I can wait for you to tell me how you feel, but I can't wait to tell *you* how *I* feel."

"Oh?" I was feeling breathless.

"Oh, yes. See, I've fallen for you. Head over heels." He took my face in his hands and looked at me. "I love you, Maureen MacKenzie."

# Chapter 14    *Nobbling*

Independence Day came, and Rose made it home for a visit. We were having a party at Mama's, and the four of us and Aunt Melba were in the kitchen making the food. I was expecting Brendan that afternoon, so I was a little more excited than usual.

"What time is your beau coming?" Rose asked as she made potato salad.

"About two. I told him we'd eat around three," I replied, wiping tears from my eyes from chopping onions.

"Well, I can't wait to meet him," she said. "I just hope he doesn't turn out to be a deadbeat like Ol' Thang was."

"No, not hardly." I smiled and began humming. One would think chopping onions was the most fun job in the world, I was going at it so.

"Mo," Mama said, "you don't have to chop the whole ten pounds. Just a coupla onions will do."

I looked at the result of my work, and I had a pile of onions that would put a sand dune to shame. "Good grief, I hadn't even noticed."

Maggie was grating cabbage for coleslaw and never looked up. "I swannee, all this *love* business is makin' me *sick*."

"You hush up," Aunt Melba chided her. "It's about time she found some happiness. You and Wash could stand some of *that* y'self."

"Aunt Melba, for your information, me and Wash are happy as clams at high tide. We just don't gush all over the place about it."

"Well," Rose remarked, "if I recall correctly, and I know I do, you and Wash used to carry on like a couple of dogs in heat. And don't say a word, because you *know* it's the truth."

Maggie was silent, but only for a minute. "That was uncalled for, Rose."

Mama laughed. "If y'all gals don't hush up and get to work, I'm gon' throw all of you out! I heard enough of that stuff when you was growin' up. Get back to work before I get out th' wooden spoon!"

We all laughed at her hollow threat.

"Y'all remember when we went to Uncle William's that year and Cud'din Willie caught the boat on fire?" I asked.

Maggie hooted. "Law' have mercy! Who could forget that! When it was all over, I was hopin' Uncle William was gonna throw Cud'din Willie in the river, but we couldn't *get* that lucky."

"Maggie, that was mean," Mama said, but she was laughing.

There was a knock at the front door. We all froze. There we were in the midst of cooking and slaving over a hot stove, and someone was at the door.

"That ain't Wash, 'cause he would just walk in," Maggie said.

"If it's Brendan, I'm going to kill you," Rose said to me. "My first time meeting him and I look like a skank!"

Mama wiped her hands on a towel. "Girl, we *all* look like skanks. If it's Brendan, don't worry about it. He's so crazy for me that he won't notice any of *ya'll* lice."

Mama had this game going where she pretended that Brendan was absolutely besotted with her. She and I would go on something awful.

"Oh, Lawsey, that good-lookin' thang's comin' in here and I look a *sight!*" Aunt Melba couldn't tolerate being disheveled in front of company. She made an attempt to straighten her hair.

"Brendan!" we heard her Mama say from the front room, "You're early! Come on in!"

Rose shot me a look that said she could kill me, but she was getting ready to die instead.

"Yes, and I'm sorry. But I left home this morning and couldn't wait to get here."

"That's alright!" she was saying as they came into the kitchen.

"Hey, Brendan," Maggie and Aunt Melba said, and he returned their greeting. Then he kissed my cheek and gave me a squeeze.

"Bren, this is our sister, Rose," I said. "Rose, Brendan Fitzgerald."

She was wiping her hands and apologizing for being such a mess. He took her hand in both of his and said, "Rose, I'm so honored to meet you. I've heard nothing but good things from your sisters! I'm sorry for coming so early and catching you on the hop."

"That's quite alright, Brendan," Rose said, and the smile on her face was sickening, as Maggie said later. "Have a seat--please. Would you like some sweet tea?"

"Yes, thank you." He sat down with me and held my hand under the table. "That might pep me up."

"You tired?" I asked.

"Yes! Listen, this morning at three o'clock, my neighbor came banging on my door! Luckily I was still up playing my bagpipes."

I laughed but I heard Aunt Melba say, "Have murdah!" She never knew when Brendan was kidding.

"We were just reminiscing about a previous Fourth of July," I said.

Rose came and set his tea down and looked at me with a "get your own tea" look. I smiled.

"Oh? I'd love to hear about it," he said.

The Fourth of July after the Christmas of the Deadfall, as it had come to be known, we all gathered together in Greenville County to celebrate at Uncle William's place. It was unusual because we were never invited there. I heard Aunt Melba tell Mama once, "Doris needs to get that stick out of her bum and stop actin' like a gobdaw."

As I got older, I had Aunt Doris figured out for myself. Aunt Doris, in plain language, thought she was better than the rest of us. Her family came from money. Her family didn't work in the cotton mill. Her family had their noses so far in the air, it was scandalous, Mama had said. Why she married Uncle William, no one could figure out. My mother's family made a living in the cotton mills of South Carolina. Aunt Doris looked down her nose at anyone who was a "lint head," as she put it.

Aunt Melba said Uncle William somehow got tangled up with Aunt Doris when he went away to college. "Doris reckoned that William was so handsome an' smart that he was a prize she didn't want anyone else havin'. It made her Da mad when he found out William's family was cotton mill workers, and he told Doris she'd better get shed of him. Ol' Doris, she liked it that it made her Da mad, and she dug her nails into William, alright. That boy couldn't make a move without her. Shoot, he couldn't break wind but what she didn't smell it first."

Aunt Melba gave us the low-down on Uncle William marrying Aunt Doris, saying that they eloped in the dead of night. "Her Da 'bout killed William, thinkin' he musta got his little girl into trouble, but Doris promised he hadn't. It was years before they ever had Willie. Shoot, I think she was just too blame *lazy* to get pregnant."

So the end of it all was that Aunt Doris's father wrote her off for marrying Uncle William. All she had left was William and his family, and as much as they tried to be good to her, she never accepted the fact that she was now a Doyle. Her parents finally came around when Cud'din Willie was born, but by then too much water had gone over the dam. Mama, who hardly ever spoke against her brother, said, "I'm surprised Doris didn't make Will change his name to Keatley."

"Why we goin' to Unka William's this year, Mama? Why ain't we gon' have our party here?" I asked.

"Uncle William," Mama said, "done got hisself a boat, and I reckon he wants to show it off."

"Make sure you wipe your feet off 'fore you get in that boat, little girl," Papa said and patted me on the head.

They rounded us three girls up in the car, and we headed off to Greenville County. It was a big adventure to us. We'd never been to Greenville, so we were excited about that. Of course, the excitement wore off when we realized that Cud'din Willie was part of the deal.

We got to their house, and there was that new boat, sitting under a brand-new shed that Uncle William had had built for it. It was a beauty; on the stern was painted the Irish and American flags intertwined with the name *Innisfree* under them.

The plan was that we would have our barbeque at the house. Then afterward we'd haul the *Innisfree* to the river and spend the rest of the day tooling about on the water. I could hardly wait. Cud'din Willie kept fussing about why didn't we eat on the boat. Rose, Maggie, and I simply kept our distance. "Ol' Fussbudget," Rose hissed.

It was incredibly hot that day, and the mosquitoes were rampant. Aunt Doris had decided early on that we would eat inside to get out of the heat. "She just wants to show off her air conditionin'," Aunt Melba complained. "Whoever heard of a barbeque *inside*?" Her reckoning was probably correct as no one else in the family had air conditioning.

But, oh, I have to say that it was nice. That dining room was as cool as could be, and I actually had goosebumps on my naked arms. And there was not a mosquito in sight. In perfect peace, we feasted on burgers and hotdogs, coleslaw, potato salad, baked beans, and gallons of sweet tea. I nearly forgot all about the boat ride that was to come.

Aunt Doris was just about to serve apple pie when someone came banging on the front door, accompanied by shouting. Uncle William jumped up like he'd been shot out of a cannon.

"Mr. Doyle," the voice said when he opened the door, "your boat's on fire!"

Everyone at the table shouted, *"Fire?"* in unison and jumped up to go outside. Aunt Doris was actually knocked down in the melee, and as I was being pushed along by the crowd, I looked back to see her in the floor, covered with homemade apple pie.

Once we got outside, the scene was one of pure chaos. The neighbors had come out and were running around screaming to put water on it. Uncle William was trying to get the hose out but it wasn't quite long enough to reach. The boatshed by now had caught on fire. The flames were licking up toward the roof.

Finally we heard the fire trucks coming. They came screaming around the corner and stopped in front of Uncle William's house. The firemen jumped into action and soon had the blaze extinguished. The boat and shed were a total loss. In all the confusion, Aunt Doris had the clarity of mind to offer the firemen some barbeque. I couldn't help wondering what they must have thought of this woman whose face was smeared with apples and bits of crust.

Uncle William realized that Cud'din Willie was nowhere to be found. Aunt Doris started screaming, "Oh, William! He was playing in the boat all morning! You don't think...." And she let out a blood-curdling scream and started running for the charred remains of the *Innisfree*. Uncle William caught her by the hair and they both tumbled to the ground. Some of the firemen headed to the shed to take a look around. Then in all the noise, Uncle Clive was shouting, "I found Willie! I found Willie!" Cud'din Willie's clothes were charred in places.

The fire chief was a tall, imposing-looking man, and he soon had the story from Cud'din Willie. It seemed that Cud'din Willie was so bound and determined to eat on the boat that he had taken a pan, piled some charcoal briquettes on it, and lit it on fire with some kerosene. It quickly got out of hand and spread all over the interior of the *Innisfree*. The fire's rapid spreading scared Cud'din Willie so terribly that instead of running in to confess what he'd done, he'd hidden in the bushes.

We all stood around taking in the carnage. Uncle William's yard was a mess. The boat shed was a trembling pile of charred beams, and the fire chief put up several "keep out" signs. Papa and the other men started cleaning up in the aftermath, and with all of them, they managed to get some kind of order back to the place. All this time, Cud'din Willie was nowhere to be seen.

**********

The cooking went on as scheduled, and even Brendan rolled up his sleeves and began helping. Aunt Melba put him to whisking eggs for meringue. He surprised us all by being quite fast with a whisk.

"I guess playin' the pipes gives you muscles, huh?" Aunt Melba asked, poking his arm with her finger.

"I guess so, Ma'am!" Brendan looked red in the face, but I think it was more from whisking than embarrassment. He seemed to be enjoying himself. I stood looking at him from across the room, thinking how proud I was that he was my beau, and how I narrowly missed out on him.

**********

After dinner on that Independence Day, we all took a rest so we'd be ready for the fireworks in the evening. I was sitting on the porch glider, and Brendan, with his head in my lap, was all curled up for a snooze. I could barely keep my eyes open.

As I dozed in and out of sleep, my ex-husband kept coming into my dreams. I forced myself to stay awake, and I felt troubled. I couldn't shake the feeling. Memories of our courtship and marriage kept going through my head. All the time I lived with him, I really didn't know who he was, though on the surface, I thought I did. He kept himself hidden from me for some reason. It was all over now, behind me, and I was happy, but there was still that something in the back of my head that kept nobbling the contentment that I had worked so hard to regain.

That evening, we had a spectacular fireworks display. As usual, Uncle Russ had outdone himself. The night was a multi-colored firestorm. Brendan and I were standing next to one another, and I felt his arm slide around my waist.

"Your uncle really puts on a good show!" he shouted. I nodded in return.

I looked over at Uncle Russ, who was watching the fireworks very carefully, smiling the entire time, and I wondered how much longer he would be with us. He looked so small this July Fourth.

I felt Brendan lean in to me. I thought he was about to say something, so I strained to listen over all the noise.

"Maureen, will you marry me?"

# Chapter 15    Summer's End

Jean and her beau broke up over the July 4th holiday. She was in a sour mood when we went back to work. When Dr. Liske informed us that he was going to be in Germany for two weeks, and we would have to man the office phone, she turned absolutely rancid.

"If you think," Jean said in a tone something like simmering rage, "that we're gonna come into this office for two weeks and deal with *that phone* when we could be catchin' up on stuff, you have lost your flippin' mind!" She flounced into the restroom.

With his mouth hanging open, Dr. Liske watched Jean disappear down the hall.

"What has gotten into that woman?" he demanded to know, and all I could tell him was that she was going through a personal crisis and probably had no idea she was being rude. Dr. Liske had gotten used to Jean's eccentricities, as he called them, but this was behavior beyond his scope of understanding.

I felt sorry for Jean, but all I could think of was the terrible timing. Brendan Fitzgerald had asked me to marry him, and I couldn't share it at work because I didn't want Jean feeling worse than she already was. I kept my news, and my answer, to myself.

To my surprise and annoyance, Joe Thickett walked in that morning. He had a genuine medical complaint, however. Although he didn't have an appointment, he needed to be seen right away, so Jean took him to a room. He had cut himself that morning and decided to bypass the emergency room so he wouldn't bleed to death. I was glad to see he was going to be fine, but I was even happier that he didn't stop to chat with me. I didn't think I could handle it.

Jean came back to the desk, humming and wearing a smirk on her face.

"Joe and I have a date," she said, and plopped down in her chair.

"Oh?" I asked, totally shocked.

"You don't mind, do you? I won't go if you mind." Jean considered me her friend, so I knew she meant it.

"I absolutely don't mind," I said. "I'm just a bit surprised that you'd go out with anyone right now, given you just had a break-up."

"Well," she said, and she began snapping charts around, "I can't go the rest of my life grievin' for one man. Life is too short. Joe seems like a nice guy, so when he asked, I figured *why not*? Are you sure you don't mind? I mean, y'all used to go out and all."

"Jean, Joe Thickett and I *never* went out. *Never.* He came to Mama's a couple of times, but we were never an item in any shape or form. So please, go and have a good time. He *is* a nice man."

Later when Joe came out of the patient room, his hand was wrapped, and underneath the bandages were five stitches. "I hate to sound mean," he said, looking over his shoulder, "but that nurse o' yourn, she's got the personality of a dead carp. I think her face woulda fell off if she'd-a smiled."

Jean and I tried not to laugh.

**********

The next morning, Jean came to work with a scowl on her face. "Have you ever," she said slowly, "seen anybody eat pigs' feet?"

"No, thank goodness."

"Well, *I* won't be seein' it again, either. Joe took me out to a barbeque pit, and what does he order? Pigs' feet. That was about the grossest sight I've ever witnessed. I nearly threw up in my coleslaw. I sat there thinkin', *Buddy, there is a reason you are single.*"

"So I take it you won't be going out with him again?" I tried to be serious, because I knew she was, but it was difficult keeping a straight face.

"Heck no! I can put up with a lot of things, but a guy gnawin' on some pig's ankles is *not* one of 'em!"

**********

That evening on the way home, I thought about Brendan's proposal. When he asked me, I said, "What?" There was so much noise that I wasn't sure of what I was hearing.

He said in a louder voice, "I'm asking if you'll marry me!"

At that moment fireworks exploded above us, and they lit up his face as bright as daylight. I looked into his eyes and there was something there. Love. I had seen that look before from him, but I had ignored it because of my fear. But this—this was something I could no longer ignore. Brendan Fitzgerald really loved me. He had told me, and now he was showing me.

"Maureen, do you love me?" I could now see worry in his face, and he looked like such a little boy that I laughed.

"Yes, Bren, I love you! I love you! And yes, I'll marry you!"

**********

It was almost time for George to go back to school. He'd had a good summer with his friends, much to Maggie's dismay. They weren't the kind of friends she wanted for her son, and he knew that, but he was bull-headed and was determined to have his own way while he was on vacation. I witnessed an ugly exchange between George and his mother on the day before he left for school.

"You're not joyridin' with those boys tonight, and that's *that*!" Maggie said, and turned her back to him and began washing dishes.

"Why do you think you have to tell me ever' move to make, Mama?" he shouted at her. "I'm almost old enough to *drive*! You treat me like a baby! All fall an' winter I'm by myself at school, so you'd think I could spend time with my friends in the summer!" His face was as red as his hair.

"Listen, George, I've let you hang out with those idiots all summer, but you're not tonight, do you hear? You're goin' back to academy tomorrow, and I want you *home* tonight! That's all I'm gonna *say* about it, and I don't wanna *hear* any more about it!"

"So my friends are idiots, is it? Well, what does that make *me*?" He was almost screaming.

I could feel things escalating, so I said, "Hey, George, why don't we go out for one last hurrah at the ice cream parlor?"

"I don't want no *d* ice cream!" he snapped at me.

"Oh, yes you *do*, Son," Maggie said, turning around from the sink with a wooden spoon in her hand. "You blamed *right* you do!"

I took George by the shoulders and led him out the front door. My ears were ringing from all the shouting. In the car, he was sullen and didn't want to speak. When we pulled up to the ice cream parlor, I saw out of the corner of my eye that he was wiping his face.

"I don't know about you," I said, pretending I hadn't seen, "but I'm going to splurge and have a banana split!" I cheerfully got out of the car and hoped he would follow. He did.

We both had banana splits and ate them in silence. After a while I said quietly, "Georgie, your mama didn't tell you, but she's throwing a going-away party for you tonight. She couldn't do that and let you go with your friends, too. I wasn't supposed to say, because it would spoil the surprise, so I'd appreciate it if you didn't give me away."

George was playing with his ice cream in between spoonfulls. "I won't say," he said. "But boy, she really makes me mad."

"I can tell. But George, put yourself in her place. It's hard for her to see you go. She gets upset. No matter how old you get, you'll always be her little boy. She never thought she'd have children, and then you came along. You were her miracle baby. So it's hard for her to see you grow up and grow away from her."

"Well, I'm *goin'* to, and *nothin'* can stop that."

"I know. And *she* knows. She also knows once you're 18 and out of school, she has done all she can, and she'll have to let you go. Can't you just, maybe, go along with her and keep the peace? It breaks my heart to see you two go at it like you do. You used to be so close."

George looked like he was thinking. "She called my friends 'idiots.'"

"I know, and I'll bet she's sorry she said that. She was upset, George, and we *all* say things we wish we hadn't at some time or other. Can you overlook it—this time?"

He was silent for a moment. I could tell he was considering what I'd said, and I could also see a pain in his eyes. He hated it when they fought, too, and that seemed to happen a lot lately.

"Do you think she'll let me invite some of my friends over to the party?" he asked.

"I'd bet anything on it. Your mama isn't unreasonable, Georgie."

He began eating his banana split with renewed zeal. "Ok. Well, this party might not be so bad after all!"

**********

It turned out to be an evening with mostly family. Some of the young people from church came, but George's joyriding friends decided to go joyriding instead of accepting his invitation. This crushed him. That would have been his last time to see them. Although he was sullen, I couldn't help noticing one of the church girls was giving him the eye. When he looked in her direction, she quickly looked away, her face blushing.

Lydia, the blushing girl, went to Sunday school with George. She was a pretty little thing with blonde hair and huge brown eyes. I could tell by the way she was dressed that her parents weren't well off, but her clothing was immaculate. She kept herself very neat. I noticed she wasn't brash like some of the other girls were; Lydia kept seated, her back straight, and her dinner plate balanced perfectly on her knee. She never talked with her mouth full like the other young people did. I went and sat next to her.

"Enjoying yourself, Lydia?" I asked.

"Yes ma'am, thank you. I'm happy to be here." Lydia's voice was sweet.

"We're happy to have you! Now there is plenty of food, so help yourself to whatever you want."

"Thank you, ma'am." She blushed again, and I noticed that she stole a glance at George. He was looking at her, and she quickly dropped her eyes. I decided to be nosy.

Leaning in towards her, I said quietly, "So what do you think of our George?"

"Oh, he's very nice," she said, smiling and blushing even harder. "He doesn't say much in Sunday school. As a matter of fact, I don't think he wants to be there at *all*." Then she quickly put her hand up to her mouth as though she'd let a secret slip. "I'm sorry. I didn't mean to gossip."

I smiled and patted her arm, "Lydia, you aren't telling me a thing I didn't already know. He's questioning a lot of spiritual things right now. It's a shame he's leaving tomorrow. Maybe you could have talked with him."

"Oh, I'm leaving tomorrow, *too*," Lydia said, smiling broadly. "I'm going to Gilead Academy." Her eyes were shining. "I won a full scholarship."

"Lydia! I didn't know! I'm so proud of you!" I hugged her so suddenly that I knocked her plate right off into the grass.

We laughed about it while we cleaned up. I couldn't help wondering why Georgie hadn't mentioned it, or if he even knew. I would corner him later.

"Till now I've been home-schooled," Lydia said. "This will actually be my second year of academy. I'm sorry to be leavin' my family, but I'm so happy! I want to go on to college. My Da has borrowed a truck and is taking me." She was more animated than I'd seen her all evening. "Mama can't go 'cause she has to stay with my brothers. There's not enough room for all of us."

"And you're excited?"

"Oh, *yes* ma'am! This is an answer to prayer! I really didn't think I'd get a scholarship, but they said my grades were some of the best they'd seen!" Then she looked shocked, and I got the impression she didn't talk about herself too often.

"Well, Lydia," I said, "I think that's wonderful! You have every reason to be excited. I'm so happy for you!"

George, who had been looking at us the whole time, decided to come over. "What are y'all gabbin' about?" he asked.

**********

For two families in New Ulster, the summer did not end well. Three of the joyriding boys had been caught trying to break into a convenience store and were sent to Big Ridge Home for Delinquent Boys. As it turned out, this was not the first trouble they'd gotten into. The judge decided a slap on the wrist was not enough.

Maggie was breathless over the phone. "Just *think*, Mo! What if George had been caught up in all that? I'm so thankful to God that he was home that night!"

I agreed. I hope George agreed, too, because not only would he have lost his scholarship, he probably would have been kicked out of school as well. He may have been unhappy at the academy, but when all was said and done, it beat the socks off reform school.

**********

Jean was waiting for me the Tuesday after Labor Day. She had big news. She and her beau had gotten back together. He had even proposed, and she accepted. The girl was over the moon while putting his pictures up all over her work area.

When Dr. Liske came in, he stopped cold in his tracks. He looked around at all the photos, muttered something in German, and went back to the kitchen for his coffee.

Mama called me at work that morning with her own news. She'd heard through her grapevine that Joe Thickett had gotten married. He'd met a dancer at a bar, and in two weeks' time they'd tied the knot. I imagined they must have served pigs' feet at the reception.

# Chapter 16    Second Wind

Brendan and I planned to marry in January. After a long discussion, ironing out the logistics of the matter, we decided that I should make the move to Roanoke. His business was there, and he had a large clientele that he felt he couldn't leave in the lurch, especially at tax time. It would be very easy to find a job there, he told me, or if I wanted I could refinish antiques and work from home. All the way around, it seemed the best thing to do. As much as I hated leaving home again, I wanted to be where Brendan was.

It was October, and the air in the evenings was getting crisp. One evening out of the blue, Mama asked, "Will you to take me to the highway department tomorrow? I want to get my license renewed."

My mouth fell open so quickly that it made a smacking sound. "Your license? You mean your *driver's* license?"

Mama looked irritated. "Close your mouth, honey. You look like a walleyed pike. Can you take me or not?"

I regained my composure. "Well, of course I can. I'll take you on my lunch break tomorrow."

Mama's face brightened. "Good! And maybe on the way home I can do the drivin', you know, to get the feel of it again. Why don't we stop at the Ice House and celebrate with an ice cream?"

Mama hadn't driven for years, but she'd kept her car, and Wash always made sure it was in tip-top shape. Sometimes he would take her driving around the countryside in it just to keep the carburetor clean. She'd say, "Come on, Wash! Peel rubber!" They didn't go as often now that Aunt Melba lived in town, but Wash or I would still take the old Delta 88 out for a spin now and again.

The next day I went home for lunch to pick up Mama, as I had promised, and she was waiting at the door. "I didn't think you'd *ever* get here," she said, giving me a big grin. "I'm excited to *go!*"

"Well, let's get going," I replied, feeling grumblings in my stomach. It wanted to eat. I told it that it would have to wait for ice cream. I would get it a doozy, too.

We hit it just right time-wise at the DMV; there was only one person ahead of us. Mama went through and took her test, which was required since her license had lapsed. She looked relieved when she was told she passed. "Some o' them questions was stupid," she whispered to me, "and I was afraid they was *trick* questions."

She also passed her driving test, although the instructor who took her out looked a little shaken when they got back. "I guess I got a bit of a lead foot," she explained, "but I promised him I would slow down. To be honest," and she looked around and drew in closer to me, "I think he only give it to me 'cause he saw my cross hanging around the mirror. He must be a Christian hisself."

After a jerky beginning, Mama sailed down Main Street in her Delta 88, her cup of ice cream between her knees. "How'm I doin'?" she asked, beaming.

"Great, Mama," but I sounded irritated. It wasn't at her, however; I hated the seat belt on the passenger side because it had no give to it and was constantly sawing into my neck. "Hold this, please, Mama," and I gave her my ice cream cone. I undid the seatbelt and reclicked it, keeping my arm through it so it wouldn't be near my neck. I took my cone from Mama and held it in my right hand where the belt was. That seemed to work beautifully. I could eat my ice cream in comfort.

"Really, Mama, it's like you've been driving every day," I said, my irritation gone since having dispensed with the seat belt problem.

"Well, I guess there are some things you just don't forget." She hummed between bites of ice cream.

"So why do you want to drive again?"

"I'm not gettin' any younger, Mo, and you gon' be married soon, so—I want to be able to drive myself around again. I don't want to have to bother Melba or Maggie so much."

"Mama, you're not a bother! They'd do anything for you, and you know that. So would I." I looked into my ice cream, a double-dip chocolate fudge in a fresh waffle cone. I took a couple of licks.

"I know y'all would, Mo, but---*Lawsey murdah!*" she screamed, slamming on brakes. My seat belt snapped up tight, I lunged forward, and my face went down into the ice cream.

"*Mercy me!*" she wailed as the car jolted to a stop. "That fool woman pulled *right out in front of me!*"

There was chocolate fudge ice cream up my nose and all over my face. I dropped the cone in my lap. "Mama," I said. There was a moment of stunned silence on her part when she looked at me. Then she began to scream with laughter.

**********

Brendan was coming for the weekend, and I could hardly wait. Mama was excited, too, because she wanted to show off her driving. She was even talking about buying a new car.

"A new *car*? Mama! What for?" Maggie asked, putting food on the table. We had gone to her house for Thursday supper. "Your car is in excellent shape."

"It shore is," Wash said. "I keep it tight."

"Yeah, you do, and I've appreciated it. But I'm thinkin' it might be time for a change," Mama remarked, loading her plate with mashed potatoes, not paying attention to what she was doing.

"If you get a new car, maybe George could drive your old one," I offered. Maggie looked at me as if I'd lost my mind.

"Girl. Can you honestly see Georgie drivin' that big old car? No offence, Mama. But you know how young people are."

"Oh, I know," Mama said. "I'd thought about Georgie myself, but I figured he'd be too embarrassed t' be seen in it."

"Huh," Wash sputtered. "He'd be dang lucky to have that car. It's a cream puff."

I looked at Wash and smiled. He was trying to grow a beard, but it wasn't happening. His hair was blond and fine but grew in thick, but as for growing a beard, his face wasn't cooperating.

"If you aim to get a car, Mama, I'll buy your 88. An' I'll take you to the car lot too, so they won't try to fob off a lemon on you."

"I'm obliged, Wash," Mama replied.

Going home that night, I asked Mama what all the fuss was about.

"What fuss?" she asked innocently.

"Getting your license and now talking about a new car. Mama, you've always been so...so..." I was trying to think of the word.

"Predictable?" she finished for me.

"Well....yes."

"I know. But I feel like I'm gettin' my second wind in life, girl, so I want to make the best while I've got life left in me."

"So what else do you have in mind?" I asked, feeling like I was on the cusp of some secret truth.

"You worry about yourself," she said, and looked out the passenger window.

**********

Brendan knocked on the door that next afternoon. We'd both gotten off early so we could have a little extra time together and also to be able to bring in the Sabbath. He respected my beliefs, and I his, so it pleased me when he wanted to be with me during such a special time.

At sunset, I lit candles around the front room. I read from the Bible, and then had prayer while holding hands. Mama used to sit in front of the TV on Friday nights, but lately with Brendan coming almost every weekend, she didn't think it was fit for him to be in my bedroom with me, which is where I usually brought in Sabbath alone. She suggested I move my "ritual" into the front room. The days were getting shorter, and to my surprise, she joined us on Friday evenings. Sometimes she even chose the scripture to read.

Brendan and I had discussed the differences in our denominations, and we came to the agreement that he would go to church with me on Sabbath and I would go with him on Sunday. He had been going with me on the weekends he was in New Ulster, and then we would go to church with Mama the next day.

"Girl, I've always been a staunch Presbyterian, but since I met you, I've had a whole lotta churchin'!" He was also beginning to pick up a little of the local dialect.

After Sabbath began, Mama went into the kitchen to make a little snack and some coffee.

I whispered to Brendan, "She's up to something."

"What do you mean?" he whispered back.

"Well, I told you she got her license renewed."

"Um-hum."

"Now she's talking about buying a new car."

Brendan's brow wrinkled. "But her car is the bomb! Why does she want to get something else?"

"She said she wants to start 'living again,' but what she means by that, I haven't figured out."

"You don't think she'll get something crazy like a sports car, do you?" He seemed concerned.

"Mercy, I hope not."

"I swannee," he said, "the road wouldn't be safe with her *and* Aunt Melba in high gear."

Mama came back, chewing on a Wheat Thin. She had a bowl of them in her hand and placed it down on the coffee table. "Coffee'll be ready in a minute," she said. "I made enough for all of us, and yes, it's decaf."

"Mama," Brendan said, "Why don't you go to church with Mo and me in the morning?"

"Oh, nooooo," she answered. "I got thangs to do."

When she went back into the kitchen, he and I looked at each other.

"She *is* up to something," he said.

**********

When Brendan was at the house, I bunked in with Mama, and he took my room. That morning when I woke up, Mama was already up and banging around in the kitchen. Usually she was slow getting up, especially with the mornings getting chilly.

"I'm makin' pancakes this mornin'," she told me when I went into the kitchen. Then she looked at me. "Maureen! Go put on some clothes! Brendan will be up any minute and here you are in y' gown tail!"

I went back to her room and slid into the jeans and t-shirt I had on the night before.

"This better?"

"Yeah, it is. Now let me go get that boy up."

"Mama, it's still early. He has time to sleep in a little. He had that long drive yesterday."

"Well, y'all don't want to be late for church. I'm getting' his motor started."

She went to the bedroom door and pounded. "Brendan! Time to get up! And put some clothes on!"

From the other side of the door I could hear him mutter, "Whaa?" I could tell he was just as confused as I was over her behavior. Usually she pampered him and cooed over him like he was a baby. This morning she sounded like a drill sergeant.

When we were dressed for church, she practically pushed us out the door. "Y'all have a good time!" she shouted, and I heard the door slam and lock behind us.

Brendan and I stood in the yard, staring at each other with our mouths hanging open.

"*Girl*," he finally said.

"I *know* it."

\*\*\*\*\*\*\*\*\*\*

After church, we drove by the *Dearbháil*. "I'll miss this house," I said to Brendan as we looked at it from the car. "It's been my friend."

"I'm sorry to be whisking you away from home," he said, truly sounding remorseful.

"Brendy, home is where *you* are."

\*\*\*\*\*\*\*\*\*\*

When we got to Mama's, the kitchen was as cold as a rock. Mama had not put our dinner in the oven to heat. I started to worry.

"Mama?" I shouted. We went to her door and tried to get in, but it was locked. "*Mama?*" I shouted again.

"I'm in here. Just hold your horses." She sounded irritated. "Is Brendan with you?"

"I'm here, Mama," he said, a look of relief on his face that she was alive.

"Well, you go get dinner to warmin'. I need to talk to Maureen by myself."

He looked at me, puzzled, but said, "Yes, ma'am," to the voice behind the door and went dutifully into the kitchen.

"Alright, Mama, it's just me."

I heard her unlock the door but not open it. "Come on in," she said.

Not knowing what I would find, I slowly opened the door and crept in. Mama was sitting on the bed with her hair in a towel. "Anything the matter, Mama?" I asked cautiously.

"No. Well, yeah. Oh, I'm a *mess*."

She took the towel off her head and I gasped. Mama's head looked like a dandelion gone to seed.

"Oh, *Mama*. What did you *do*?"

"I give myself one of them home perms." She wouldn't look at me.

"But you cut your *hair*! Mama! What were you *thinking*?"

"Now, look, Mo. I feel bad enough without you scoldin' me on top of it!" I could tell she was ready for a fight.

"I'm not scolding you, Mama. I'm just so shocked! You never said anything about wanting a haircut, much less a perm. Why didn't you tell me, and we could have gone to a salon?"

Mama sighed. "I don't know. I guess I'm just crazy."

I sat down on the bed with her and took her hand. "Tell me what's going on with you, Mama. You've been different lately, and you know I'm all for change, if it's good, but I declare, you have me confused."

I could see her eyes well up. "Well, you know since your Da passed, I've tried getting' on with life. It's hard. I miss him, still."

"I know you do, Mama." I wiped a tear off her cheek.

"Well, lately I've felt like I could, you know, start over. I don't mean to be unfaithful to your Da's memory, but I....I feel..." Her voice trailed off.

"Are you trying to tell me that you're interested in a man?" My voice was practically a whisper.

"Well....yeah...I guess that's it." She was blushing profusely.

"So that's why the license and the talk of a new car?"

She nodded.

"Well, Mama, I think that's a *fine* idea. Everybody needs somebody. And I don't think you're being unfaithful to Papa's memory. He'd *want* you to be happy. Don't you think so?"

"I'd like to think so, yeah. Oh, Mozie, do you think I'm bein' a' old fool?"

I put my arms around her and squeezed. "Not in the least. Well, as long as he's a *decent* man. Who is he? Do I know him?"

She was silent, looking as if she were weighing whether to tell me or not. Finally she said, "Do you remember Sheriff Delaney?"

Sheriff Delaney came to our house that day Mama and I had rescued the dog from Creeper Man.

"Oh, my word. Mama, please don't tell me you were sweet on him all those years ago!"

"Girl! Hush your mouth! Certainly *not*! We were both married then, and I never looked at any man other than your Da!" She seemed insulted, and rightfully so.

"I'm sorry, Mama. Go ahead and tell me everything."

She sighed again. "His wife died a year after Brance. A couple o' weeks ago, we ran into each other at the grocery store and got to talkin'. He asked if he could call on me sometime. I told him I'd have to think about it. But I think I've thought about it enough."

I smiled at her. "Well, we need to do something about your hair. Oh, Mama."

"I cut it off in a ponytail, so I still have it."

"Well, it can't be glued back on, Mama. Tomorrow we'll find a salon that will take care of your hair for you. They can...do something with it. It'll be alright, Mama."

I went to bed that night smiling and thinking to myself that my Mama was sweet on old Sheriff Delaney. Second wind, indeed.

# Chapter 17    *What Happens in Vegas...*

I had survived divorce and was going to marry again.  I was excited, but at the same time, I was having moments of worry.  "That's 'cause you been burned," Mama would tell me.  "Brendan and Ol' Thang are as different as night and day.  And just remember what the Bible says: 'Perfect love casts out fear.'"  I knew she was right on that score, so I wanted to get rid of this feeling once and for all.

Because I would be moving to Roanoke, I began making weekend trips there to get used to the area and make plans for Brendan's house.  It would be our house now, he said, and he wanted me to make it my home.  The last weekend I spent there was wonderful; we picked out paint colors and fabrics for drapes, and we even looked for a new washer and dryer.

"Not exactly hot romance," he said as we looked at the new machines, "but practicality goes a long way!"  I laughed, though I knew he was right.

It was Sunday afternoon by now, and I needed to be heading home.  I made one more check of my room to make sure I hadn't forgotten anything, and then closed the door.  I left it spotless, but he preferred the doors to stay closed.  I had never been in his room before, but it made me wonder if it was actually a tip.

"Brendan," said as I put my travel bag by the door, "Could I see your room?"

"My room?" he asked, looking amused and puzzled at the same time.  "Alright, if you really want to."

I followed him down the hall, and he opened his bedroom door.  I gasped.  It was perfect.  As a matter of fact, it could have been in a magazine.

"It's beautiful!" I said.

"Why are you so shocked?  Did you think it was a pig sty or something?"  He tried to look hurt, but he couldn't stop smiling.

"Well, I just didn't know.  You always keep the doors closed."

"I guess that's a habit I developed in college.  I shared a suite with three other guys, and they were hogs.  I kept the doors closed because their rooms were garbage piles. I couldn't stand looking at them. I kept my room closed off because I didn't want them in there dragging in their food and drinks. And they tried a couple of times, because their rooms had gotten so bad there was no place to sit down. As a matter of fact," he chuckled, "I ended up putting a lock on my door when I came in one evening and there was one of my suite-mates sprawled across my bed in a dead sleep! But anyway, we can keep the door open if you like. You need to see this room anyway, because it will eventually be our room."

We both blushed.

Brendan said, "I have to confess, though, that I have a woman come in once a week to clean. I keep the place picked up, but I can't stand dusting. I'm willing to pay someone else to do it, I hate it that much."

I laughed. I hated dusting, too. I didn't want him to think he'd be stuck living in the Dust Bowl, so I said nothing.

We had prayer together, he walked me to my car, and I drove away. I was exhausted by the time I got home, but I was so happy.

My happiness continued into the week, even though things at the office were as crazy as usual. Jean was getting married in November, and she talked of nothing but her plans. She asked me to sing at her wedding, and I felt honored. Dr. Liske came in day after day to a room filled with wedding books and fabric samples. "*Mein Gott!*" he exclaimed one morning. "What are we running here? An office for sick people, or a bridal salon? Honestly, Jean, I think you need to elope or something!"

She pooh-poohed his comment and ignored him. I was amazed at her, though. In spite of all her excitement over her wedding, she still did her job and never missed a detail. I looked at her and smiled.

"Jean, you are something else," I said.

"Oh, I know. I'm da bomb." She never even looked up from her magazine.

I was missing Brendan, of course, but I kept having to remind myself that I wouldn't be seeing him that coming weekend. He had a conference to go to in Richmond. He would leave Thursday night and be back Sunday night. I tried to imagine a hotel full of accountants and couldn't quite wrap my head around it. But the thought made me smile.

On Friday afternoon, John Hobrick left me a message to return his call. It was urgent. Anytime he called was with unpleasant news, and

I couldn't understand his calling now. My divorce had been final for some two years.

"John, this is Maureen. What's going on?"

"How are you, Maureen?" He was sounding very upbeat.

"I'm fine. Curious, though."

"Well, when I finish telling you my news, you'll be feeling fantastic."

I decided to sit down. Mama turned the TV off so I could hear. John Hobrick jumped right in. "Your ex-husband has been arrested," he said.

"Wait, wait, wait." Then to Mama I said, "Could you let me take this call? I won't be a minute, but if you could go in the kitchen or something..."

"Sure," she said. "I hear some ice cream callin' me anyway."

When she left and I was sure she wasn't eaves-dropping, I told him to go ahead.

"As I said, he was arrested today, in Las Vegas, in a sting operation."

I could feel the blood drain from my scalp. "What are the charges?"

"Solicitation of a minor." John went on to tell me that an internet sting operation had been set up in Vegas. My ex was vacationing there at the time, and, using the screen name "Brian," he spent most of his time holed away in his room, on his computer, visiting a teen chat room. He set up a meeting with a "teen girl" decoy. When he walked in the house, he was nabbed. He had all kinds of excuses, John said, but he was caught, no doubt about it. He went on to tell me that more likely as not he could get the alimony reversed.

I was hearing his words but not really listening. My heart was pounding so hard that I could hardly think beyond the sound. All that was in my head was that I had lived with this man for 14 years and didn't really know who he was. I had spent a large piece of my life with a total stranger.

John told me to sit tight, and he would get back in touch with me as soon as he had any further details.

My first thought was to call Brendan. I needed to hear his voice. I called his house. The voice on the other end wasn't his. It was a woman. I said, "I'm sorry! I dialed the wrong number," and promptly hung up. I shook my head as I dialed again, this time more carefully because my eyes were full of tears. The voice on the other end was the same woman's that I had just heard. She sounded a little irritated that time, and I simply hung up.

I kept thinking my head was going to explode, I was so upset by this point. I dialed Brendan's cell phone next, but it went straight to voice mail. He had it turned off.

I put the receiver in the cradle. Then I burst into tears. My Brendan, the man I was going to marry, was with another woman. And on top of that, I remembered that he'd told me he was going to be out of town. I wanted to lash out at something. Grabbing a pillow from the sofa, I hurled it across the room just as Mama was coming back in.

"Lawsey mercy, girl!" she exclaimed. "What in the world did Mr. Hobrick have to say?"

I couldn't answer her. I was furious. I had been taken for a fool. Again.

**********

I didn't tell Mama about my ex. I was too stunned, and I thought of the talk if word got out around town. But what was really pressing on my heart was Brendan. I told her what had happened, and she listened in silence. I saw her wipe her eyes a few times. When I'd finished talking, she asked several times was I sure that was Brendan's number. Maybe I'd made a mistake, she said. I could see she was disappointed in him but didn't want to believe it. She was also sad for me; she knew I'd been so happy.

The next morning, I sat at the kitchen table, eyes red and puffy from not sleeping.

Mama tiptoed around me as she made breakfast. "Honey, you want some fig preserves on your toast?"

"No, Mama. I'm not hungry, I'll just have coffee."

"Pish-tosh!" she said. "You gotta eat somethin'. You can't sit in the Lord's house with your stomach growlin' and carryin' on."

"I don't think I'll go to church. My head is pounding with a headache."

Mama regarded me. Then she asked gently, "Did you talk to Brendan?"

"No."

"He didn't call?"

"I don't know. The phone rang, but I ignored it. I didn't think I could handle talking to him last night."

I could tell Mama was weighing her words. She said, "Mo, let me ask you to consider this. If Brendan was seein' another woman, do you think he would have called you last night? I mean, that would be a little awkward, don't you think, with her right there?"

I didn't answer her. I was rubbing my head and staring into the finish on the table. Tears were dropping down, making little puddles.

"I don't know what to think, Mama," I finally said, and then I got up and went back to my room. I pulled the blankets over my head and wished for sleep.

In a little while, Mama was tapping on the door. "Mo, honey? Brendan's on the phone. He really wants to talk to you."

"Tell him I joined the army," I said, feeling foolish even as I said it. "I don't want to talk to him right now. I'm trying to get rid of my headache."

"Mo, he's waitin' on the line! It's *long distance!*"

I thought, *Tough luck!* but said nothing. I heard her move away from the door and go back into the front room. I closed my eyes and eventually went to sleep.

When I woke up later, my head was feeling better. I decided I needed to pull myself together and try to make sense of things. First I wanted to eat. I felt as if I hadn't eaten in a week. Mama was gone but had left a note on the table.

"Mo, I've gone to town to take Melba some of these fig preserves. I'll be back soon. Love, Mama. PS. Please call Brendan, please."

I ate a bite of lunch. It was warm potato soup, and it felt good on my stomach, but I could feel a hard edge forming around my heart. I decided that I had survived divorce, from a pervert at that, and I would most certainly survive being jilted by some piper-man. Taking a sandwich in one hand and my jacket in the other, I headed out into the woods. I would spend the afternoon in my favorite childhood spot.

I lay in the autumn sun and thought about my situation. I realized what was bothering me on the Fourth of July. My confidence had been nobbled; it was fake, and it had been put to the test. I hadn't had a relationship with anyone but Brendan, and it was easy to shove the truth behind me and pretend I was alright. The hard truth was that I had not faced being betrayed by my former husband. I had had no reason to face it till now. I was happy with Brendan, but the second trouble with him arose, I was ready to flee. Another thing that came to mind was how insanely jealous I was feeling. Until that point, I had never realized that about myself, and I found it ugly.

As I lay in the pine needles, I kept praying, "Lord, please see me through this." I didn't know what else to say. I felt myself drifting off, and I soon fell asleep. When I woke up, it was to the sound of feet crunching the leaves and pine needles. Shielding my eyes with my hand, I looked up and saw Brendan.

"Mo," he said, and I could see he was distressed.

"What are you doing here? How did you know where to find me?" I sat up.

"Mama told me why you wouldn't come to the phone and speak with me," he said, sitting down across from me. "I couldn't believe what I was hearing, so I left my conference and drove straight here. You weren't in the house, and I figured you might be here. Mo, you can't believe that I would be cheating on you."

I could feel my anger and hurt rising all over again. "I called your house and a *woman* answered the phone! How do you explain *that*?"

His face held a look of surprise. "Oh, *Maureen*! That was my partner's *daughter*! She's in *high school*! She has a research paper to finish up and needed someplace quiet, so I told her she could work at my house while I was away. I *told* you I'd be in Richmond."

I knew instantly that he was telling the truth, and I felt like an idiot. I burst into tears.

He moved to my side and put his arms around me. "Don't cry, Mo. It's alright! If I had known you were going to call the house, I would have told you in advance that she was going to be there. I'm so sorry I've caused you such grief!"

It broke my heart even more to have him being so kind to me. I felt beyond stupid.

"Please don't cry," he said, almost pleading. "I hate to see you like this."

I snuggled into the depths of his sweater. He smelled so good, and for a moment I was comforted. I didn't know what to say.

We sat together in silence as it began getting dark. He was stroking my hair. "I love you, Maureen," he said. "I want you to know you can trust me, and that I would never, *ever* do anything that would hurt you. Please believe me."

"Oh, Brendy, I'm sorry. I do believe you. I do. But..." I pulled away and looked at him.

"But what?"

I then told him all about my ex and what he'd done to be arrested. I told him every detail I knew, and as I spoke, some things about our marriage came into my remembrance, things that didn't make sense then, but did in light of the truth that I now knew about him.

"Wow! What a story!" he exclaimed. "No wonder you were upset! Oh, Maureen, I'm so sorry I wasn't there for you."

"Well, Brendan, I guess it doesn't matter. I mean, I'm glad you came here today. I've acted like a fool. But at the same time, I have learned something about myself that you should know."

"What's that, love?"

And the words killed me to say them. "I can't marry you. This weekend has proved that I'm not ready. I thought the baggage was behind me, but it isn't. Look how quickly I jumped to conclusions when that girl answered your phone! Do you honestly want to live like that, with me questioning your every move? *I* can't."

"Mo, you don't mean it."

"I'm sorry, Brendan. But you will be so much better off without me and my craziness."

I got up, and avoiding the look on his face, I made my way home in the moonlight.

**********

Mama insisted Brendan spend the night. It was too late to drive all the way back to Roanoke. As usual, I bunked in with her and he took my room. Mama talked half the night.

"I swannee, girl, I don't know what you're thinkin'. Brendan *loves* you! He ain't *Ol' Thang*! He's decent and hard-workin' and would walk over hot coals for you. I see it in his face ever' time he looks at you."

I just lay in the dark, silent.

"Mo, talk to me. I know you ain't asleep. Open up."

Finally I raised up on one elbow and turned my head in her direction. "What do you want me to say, Mama? What?"

"You got that edge to your voice, Maureen. They ain't no need for that."

"Oh, don't be so precious, Mama. You're keeping me awake, and you want me to be all sweetness and light. Look, I made my decision not to marry Brendan, and that's that. I won't marry him and make his life hell, and that's exactly what I'd be doing with my insane jealousy and suspicion."

This time Mama sat up. "What you really sayin' is that you're gonna punish Brendan because you can't punish Ol' Thang. *He's* the one who divorced you! Not *Brendan.*"

"I am *not*! Mama, you don't know what you're *talking* about!"

"That, my dear girl, is *exactly* what you doin'."

"Well, you're wrong, Mama, and frankly I think you should mind your own business." With that, I flopped back down and inched closer to the edge of the bed. I was angry. I was also glad I hadn't told her about the arrest; I would never have any peace.

By her silence, I knew I had hurt Mama's feelings. She just sat there in the dark.

"Well," she finally said, her voice small, "if that's what you want, I'll mind my own business. Excuse me for carin' about your happiness. If you don't want Brendan, I'll take him. He's a catch, and I ain't one for lettin' him go."

I sighed. "Mama."

"What?"

"Just go to sleep."

"I ain't tired now. I think I'll go see if Brendan wants to play *Skip-Bo.*" She tossed the covers back.

"Mama," I hissed in the dark, "if you get out of this bed or say one more word, I'm going to a hotel."

She lay back down. I could feel the wheels turning in her head. The silence was heavy and thick.

"Humph," she huffed, and flipped over with her back to mine.

**********

We all got up late the next morning. Mama got up before I did, but I was awake. I could hear her mumbling as she put her house dress on, "Gonna go to church today lookin' like death warmed up." I pretended to be asleep.

When she closed the door behind her, I heard her knocking on Brendan's door. "You awake, Brendan? You want some breakfast?" I could hear him say something, but I couldn't make out what it was.

I decided to stay in bed until they both left. I didn't want to face either of them. I was physically and emotionally spent.

I could hear Mama rattling around in the kitchen as I dozed in and out of sleep. I smelled coffee and dreamed about it. At some point, Maggie came in, and I could hear low voices. She and Mama were talking about me; I could feel the hair stand up on the back of my neck. Then Brendan was up, and there were more voices. Somewhere between sleep and wakefulness, I heard Mama say, "Brendan, it ain't *decent*!" Then the bedroom door flew open and Brendan was standing over me.

"Girl," he said, "we're going to *talk*!" I knew he meant it. I was beyond embarrassed with him standing there, I in my nightgown and hair all tangled.

Mama and Maggie came to the open door. Before they could say a word, Brendan turned his head sharply and looked at them, and Mama silently closed the door with her Maggie on the other side. I sat up in the bed and pulled the blankets up around my chin.

"Now, listen, Mo. I'm about to go home, but I'm not going until you've heard everything I came in here to say. First of all, I am *not* your ex-husband! I can't help what he did to you nor what he's sitting in jail for now. I am *not him*. I won't pay for his crimes, and I think you're wrong to think I can. Second, you either love me or you don't. I think you do, but only *you* know the truth."

"Brendy," I began.

"Don't speak!" he said angrily. "I'm not finished. Third, no one said we have to get married *this* January or *next* January. If you still want to get married, I'll wait as long as you need to. I'll wait, but don't think for *one minute* that I'll be waiting around just for you to take out your fear and suspicion on *me*. I won't have it."

I just sat there, not looking at him because I had never seen him like this, and it shook me up.

"The last thing I want to say is that I hope you know I would never step out on you with another woman. You're the one I love; you're the one I want to grow old with. There could never be anyone else, Maureen." He paused, taking a deep breath. "I'm finished now, if you want to say anything," he said, his voice calmer.

"I *do* love you, Brendan. I do. I don't want to make you miserable. Right now I feel like a wreck, damaged and suspicious of everything. I just wanted to do the right thing by you."

"I appreciate that, but I think you should let *me* have a say in it." He sat down on the bed, facing me. "You don't have to answer me now, but if you still want to marry me, I'll let you set the date. I'll wait. But I *won't* take his punishment."

"Fair play," I said. Before I could say more or protest, he leaned in and kissed me, more passionately than he ever had. Then as quickly, he was up and the door was closing behind him.

# Chapter 18    Reuben

November rolled in, and Jean's wedding day came and went. The days following were all a flurry because I had to do my job and hers while she was on her honeymoon. Dr. Liske had dragged his feet on finding a temp, so it was just me on the phones and desk and Katje coming in to do filing.

On that Wednesday, I took my lunch break to make some phone calls. My last call was to Mrs. Kennedy. I had been thinking about it and came to the conclusion that because I had decided to wait another year to marry Brendan, I would go ahead and buy the *Dearbháil*. It was time I moved out. I had the down payment, and I wasn't making alimony payments anymore, so I didn't see any reason why I shouldn't have my own home until I married.

"Mrs. Kennedy," I said, "I'm ready to buy the Cork Street house!"

The other end of the line was silent for a second. "Well, I declare, I hate to tell you, honey, but it's been sold. Bought a week or so ago."

"Sold? But it's *haunted*!"

"I didn't think you believed in all that," she replied.

"I don't, but I was hoping the story was still around so nobody else would want it."

"I thought you weren't interested anymore because you were movin'."

My heart sank. I *had* told her that. I assumed that the house would still be there, given its history. "Well, I'm just sick over that, Mrs. Kennedy. I still *am* moving, but not for a year or so. I was hoping to have that place."

"I know, honey, and I'm just as sorry as I can be."

When I hung up the phone, I felt a wave of sadness. It would have been a beautiful house when I finished with it. I hoped that whoever bought it loved it as much as I did.

**********

"Well, Mama, I guess you're stuck with me, unless I can find an apartment," I told her over supper.

"Nonsense!" she snorted. "Nobody's askin' you to leave, Mo. You can stay here till you and Bren marry. *If* you marry," she threw in.

"What's that supposed to mean?"

She shrugged and tried to look nonchalant, saying nothing.

Brendan hadn't been coming down every weekend like he had before. I assumed he was trying not to crowd me. This annoyed Mama to no end. She thought we should go ahead with our plans to marry in January and be done with it. I couldn't make her understand that there was no rush.

"You gon' *'not rush'* him right into the arms o' some other woman, somebody what *wants* to get married."

"Oh, Mama, could we just not go over this again? Brendan and I talked about it and he said he'd do whatever I thought was right. If it's okay with him, why should it bother you? Right now all I want to do is eat my pot pie before it gets cold."

She got up and began fussing around in the kitchen. "Brendan loves pot pie," she said. "You'll need to learn how to make 'em."

"So when are you seeing Mr. Delaney again?" I asked, changing the subject.

"He's comin' for dinner on Saturday, if you don't have any plans."

Finally! I was going to see old Sheriff Delaney after all these years. Mama had kept him away from me since they'd starting courting. She always had some excuse to ride into town now. I smiled around my spoon. I imagined the two of them, Mama holding his hand to keep him from stumbling. I figured he must be 80 at least. I'll bet she spoon-fed him like a baby.

"What are you smilin' at, girl?" she wanted to know as she sat back down.

"Just you and old Sheriff Delaney. Has he taken you skating yet? Has he given you his skate key?"

"Oh, you're just a panic, *you* are." She was clearly not as amused as I was at my kidding her.

\*\*\*\*\*\*\*\*\*\*

Sabbath came, and I was sitting in church alone again. Brendan had not come that weekend. I tried focusing on the sermon, but my mind kept wandering. Sitting in the choir, I felt dislocated from everyone. We sang "For All the Saints," one of my favorites, but I still felt no connection. I prayed about it because I hated feeling that way. I didn't want anything to come between God and me.

I remembered that Reuben Delaney was having dinner at our house, so I hurried home after the service. My jaw dropped when I walked in the door. As usual, Mama had the dinner warmed, but she had put on the dog. There were flowers on the table, a lace cloth, linen napkins. Just like Aunt Melba, she had put on the *whole* dog. She'd even fried some chicken in case old Sheriff Delaney didn't take to vegetarian food. And Mama herself was dressed to the nines.

"Mama, you look like a picture," I said, kissing her on the cheek.

She blushed. "Go on with ya," she said. I thought she looked like a young girl, and I smiled. Since she'd cut her hair, she had been keeping it short, and it was a style that suited her. I thought she looked snazzy.

"He'll be here any time," she said.

I could hardly wait. When I heard the car pull into the driveway, I went to the front room window and looked out. There was a blue pick-up truck, extended cab, all shined up like a new penny. The door opened and I let out a gasp. *That* was old Sheriff Delaney? He was tall, lean and muscular. He walked toward the house with a confident stride.

"*Moze*, get away from that winda 'fore he *sees* you!" Mama ordered, her hand on the door knob. "Do you want him to think you're rude?"

I stepped back and stood behind her.

"Reuben! Come in!"

This tall, strong man stepped in and handed Mama a box that had a flower in it. He then, right in front of me, kissed her on the cheek.

"You might not remember Maureen, she's all growed up. Maureen, you remember Mr. Delaney?" Her face was flushed.

He extended his large hand and took mine. "I remember you as a little thang," he said.

"It's good to see you again, Sheriff," I said weakly. I meant it, but I was still in shock.

"Oh, just call me Reuben," he said, and his smile was broad. "I hadn't been Sheriff in a long time!"

"Well, dinner's ready, so we may as well eat." Mama ushered us into the kitchen, and she and I got the food on the table. We all sat together and had the blessing.

Reuben Delaney was a nice man, a talker, and a real story-teller. He entertained Mama and me all through dinner. At one point, I was laughing so hard at one of his stories that I nearly got choked. I wiped the tears from my eyes with my napkin, one of the linen ones that she only used for company.

"Oh, murduh, Reuben, that was a good'un!" Mama laughed. "You sure had an interestin' life as a sheriff!" She got up to get out the apple pie.

"Indeed I did," he boomed. "Folks tell me I ought to write a book, but I'm not so good with paper and pencil."

I studied his face. It was kind, with bright blue eyes that seemed to take on a life of their own when he was laughing. His white hair was curly and worn right above his collar. He was flawlessly clean-shaven.

"What do you do now?" I asked.

"When I give up sheriffin', I went back to farmin'. My daddy had left me his farm, and I've carried it on like he did. Not on a grand a scale, though, but it keeps me busy."

That would explain his muscles and tan. He was old-school from the start. I wondered if he even had a mule.

"How old are you, Reuben?"

"Maureen!" Mama dropped a whole piece of pie to the floor.

Reuben Delaney threw back his head and laughed. "I'm 70, girl! Most people seem shocked by that, like you do now, but I just tell 'em it's good livin'!"

**********

Reuben stayed with us all afternoon. I enjoyed his company tremendously. I could see why Mama liked him; he was like Papa in so many ways. Mama walked out to his truck with him, and he gave her a little kiss that I found so endearing. It made me miss Brendan.

Mama came back in after Reuben had left. "I guess you saw that," she said. I smiled. "That boy's built like a brick house," she said as she closed the door. Then she and I looked at each other and giggled like little girls.

# Chapter 19    Home Again

It had been three weekends since I'd seen Brendan. We spoke on the phone, but he seemed very vague about how he'd been doing. I wasn't sure what to think. It was nearly Thanksgiving, and I was hoping he'd come for dinner with us.

It was Sunday, and Mama was gone to church. I had the house to myself, so I decided to call Brendan. I knew he'd be in church, but I would leave a voice mail. My stomach felt knotted while the phone rang.

"Hello?" he said, and I could tell he was in the car.

"Hey, Brendy," I said, trying to sound normal, but I was surprised that he wasn't in church. "What are you up to today?"

"Hey, Mo! I'm on my way to pick up a friend to go antiquing. What are *you* doing?"

I felt jealous. *I* should have been with him.

"Not much. I just wanted to tell you...well, I haven't seen you in a while...I was hoping you could come for dinner on Thanksgiving."

"I'm sorry, Mo, you're breaking up. What was that?"

"I said I was wondering...oh *never mind*. Brendan, am I ever going to see you again? I've missed you something terrible." I could feel my face flush red.

"About to miss my turn! Gotta go!" And the line went dead.

I stood there, looking at the receiver in my hand. Then I hung up. Maybe Mama was right. Maybe I had "not rushed" him into another woman's arms. He did say he was on his way to pick up a friend. "I'll *bet* a *friend*," I muttered. "And skipping out on church?"

I immediately felt ugly for letting my jealousy surface.

Sighing, I went into the kitchen. I'd surprise Mama by taking her to lunch when she got home. She'd like that. I needed to do something to keep my mind occupied.

I thought about calling Maggie, but she'd be at church, too. So would Rose. Left with nothing to do, I decided to go for a walk. I went to my room to get my coat. As I bundled up, there was a loud banging on the door.

"What in the world...?" I made my way into the front room, suddenly very irritated that someone would be banging on my door like a common thug. I slung it open, and there stood Brendan Fitzgerald.

I jumped into his arms. He hugged me and kissed my face and told me he'd missed me. We went in and sat in the front room.

"You said you were on your way to pick up a friend!" I exclaimed.

"I was! I was on my way to pick up *you!*" He laughed and squeezed my hand.

I decided to get right to the point. "Well, where in tarnation have you been all these weeks?"

"Well, a lot's been going on, girl. Mighty big stuff!" He was smiling broadly, and his eyes were sparkling as he teased me. "But I'll get to all that later. Right now I want to go antiquing. Up for an adventure?"

"How can I say no to *that*?" I asked.

"Great. Oh, where's Mama? Maybe she'd like to come along."

"She's at church, but she should be along home any time now." Suddenly I was struck with a brilliant idea. "Oh, Brendan," I said and snickered. "I have a plan."

\*\*\*\*\*\*\*\*\*\*

I was hiding behind the kitchen door when Mama rolled up at half-past 12. She came in the front door saying, "Brendan? I declare I'm glad to see you! Where's Mo?"

Brendan had stood up when she walked in. "She's in her room. She's all busted up."

"Busted up? What do you mean?" Mama sounded concerned.

"She broke it off with me."

"What? She did *what*?"

"It's alright, though, Bess." He took a step toward her. "Bess, I can't go on denying my feelings."

"*What* feelin's?"

"For you. *You're* the one I love. I'm so crazy about you, Bess, you're all I can think about!"

I would have given anything to see Mama's face, but her back was to me.

"What? Brendan Fitzgerald, you have *lost your mind!*"

He walked toward her, and she backed up.

"No, I haven't, love. And I know you feel the same way about me. Maureen told me you wanted me."

He took another step and Mama went running into the kitchen.

"She's crazy! She knew I was teasin' with her! Get away from me!" She put her hand on the back door and shrieked, "Mo! *Maureen!*"

I came from behind the door. I was laughing so hard I could barely see her. Brendan was doubled over and holding his stomach.

"Oh, y'all are just a couple of riots, ain't ye? Hooligans! Get outta my kitchen!"

She was visibly upset. Through my tears I tried to apologize, but she would have none of it. Brendan said, "I'm really sorry, Mama, really, but the look on your face!"

"If y'all don't get outta here right now, I'm callin' the po-lice!"

"But, Mama," I gasped, "I was going to take you to lunch!"

"Lunch, nothin'! You ain't suckin' up to me like that to get back in my good graces. Get outta here, the both of ye, and take your fool jokes with ye!" She was flustered, but I could tell she was recovering.

"I think that means," I said to Brendan, "Reuben is coming over!"

Mama actually swatted me with a dish towel. Brendan stole a quick kiss on the cheek from her, and then he and I ran outside.

"Do you think she'll stay mad at us?" he asked as we walked to the car.

"Mercy no," I said, "She thinks you hung the moon!"

He said, "Before you get in, let me show you something! I brought you a surprise!"

He made me close my eyes and then led me to the back of the SUV. I could hear the back open and he said, "Ta-da!"

I was looking at a beautiful oak porch swing. "Oh, Brendy."

"I thought we could go over there and put it up," he said, beaming.

"Dang, Bren, I guess I didn't tell you. The house is gone. Sold, I mean." I suddenly felt terrible that I hadn't told him, but we hadn't exactly had any in-depth conversations lately.

He just stood looking at me for a minute. "Well, shoot, Mo." He shrugged. "I'm not about to drag it all the way back to Virginia. Let's go put it up anyway. It'll make someone a nice house-warming gift."

We drove into town, and I felt so happy. It started to rain a little, but I didn't care. My Brendan was here with me.

The house was still unoccupied. I was relieved, because I figured we'd have to knock on the door and tell total strangers that we'd brought them a gift. After we'd hung the swing, we sat in it.

"This is nice," I said. "That was so thoughtful of you, Bren."

"Well, you can't have a porch like this and not have a swing. It's just not Southern." He smiled at me and kissed my hand.

We sat in silence for a while and enjoyed the sound of the rain. It was cold, so sitting close together had an extra benefit to it. Finally I said, "I'm so glad you're here today. I can't tell you how much I've missed you."

"You know, when you told me that on the phone, I *knew* I had made the right decision in coming down. I needed to hear that."

"Brendy, will you marry me?"

"Sure."

"No, I'm serious. Well, January, like we'd planned."

His face lit up. "Do you mean it? *Mo!*"

And he grabbed me with such force that the swing nearly flipped us out of it.

He pulled himself together after a bit and asked, "What brought this on?"

"I just suddenly realized that I don't want to spend another day away from you. I can't worry about the past anymore. I can see now that the divorce was nothing I could have ever stopped, because it was all on him. He has his own demons to wrestle with that have nothing to do with me. And as far as trusting you, Brendan, well, I don't think there is another man on earth I could trust more. I'm sorry I ever doubted you. I want to marry you and go to Roanoke and be your wife forever."

"Maureen, I've hated being away from you, too. These last few weeks have been meaningless. I have prayed every day that God would help you see the truth, and to help me be the man He wants me to be. I can't tell you what it means to me to hear you say that your past is just that—the *past*. Your ex can never do anything else that can hurt you. I'm here now, and I promise you will never have to worry about anything ever again." He kissed me.

I held onto him, not letting him go. Finally he pulled me away from him and looked at me. "Well now, though, I have some news, love. That mighty stuff I was referring to earlier."

"Okay. Let's hear it."

"Well, I decided that I was willing to do anything to win your complete trust," he began. "So I sold my part of the business to my partner, and I'm going into business for myself."

"Oh?"

"Yes. I'm leaving Roanoke. I'm putting down roots here in New Ulster."

"Don't tease me!"

Brendan continued. "The way I see it, you have family here, and I have none in Roanoke. Why uproot you from the only family you have? I want nothing more than for you to be happy, Moze. I know you'd be okay with me in Roanoke, but *this* is where you belong. And I've come to see that it's where *I* belong, too. So, over the next several weeks, I'll apply for my license here and start setting up shop."

"How are you going to do that from Virginia?"

Brendan smiled. "Girl, I'll be doing it from *here*. My house is on the market already and the sale of the business is final. I'll be looking for an apartment in New Ulster. That's why I haven't said much to you lately. I didn't want to spill the beans. There was no reason on earth to be away from you any longer."

Suddenly I began to cry. I doubted my own hearing. "You mean you're not leaving today or tomorrow? You're staying here *for good*?"

He nodded as he wiped the tears from my face. "And I already have you a wedding gift," he whispered in my ear.

"What?" I asked.

"You're sitting on it."

I looked down at the swing.

He said, "I bought us the *Dearbháil*. The swing was just a place to sit down while I told you my news."

"Brendan!"

"I was going to buy it after we married, but I was so afraid someone else would take it. You have it looking so nice on the outside, after all. So, after I settled with my partner, I bought it outright, cash money. This is our home now, and you'll never be without a roof over your head. I promise to give you the best life I can, Mo."

My arms were around him again.

"Welcome home, love," he said.

**********

December came in in a mad rush. There were plans for the wedding that seemed never-ending. The ceremony was to be simple, but every day it seemed to grow larger until I would have sworn it would walk by itself. I told Brendan we ought to elope.

"And miss out on all the great food?" he asked. "Never! Mo, I think you're getting worried over nothing. Just let Mama and Aunt Melba handle things, and you sit back and relax. All you need to do is show up, and I'll be there with a smile on my face."

We were sitting at the kitchen table having coffee, waiting on Mama to come home from church. Maggie and Aunt Melba were coming later, and we'd all work on wedding plans.

"As far as the honeymoon," Brendan said, "leave that to me." He smiled and went back to his travel magazine.

"Bren, I've been wanting to tell you something." He gave me his attention. "I want to spend our wedding night at the *Dearbháil*. I know it still needs fixing up, but it has lights and water now. It'll just be for one night, and then we can leave on our honeymoon trip. What do you think?"

"I think that's a beautiful idea, Mo. We have several more weeks. We could get a bedroom painted or wallpapered—whatever you want! And furnish it! A good excuse to go antiquing. Let's do it!"

Brendan was staying with us for the time being. I had moved into Mama's room, and he took mine. Mama would not hear of him getting an apartment. "A waste o' money," she said. It would have been logical for him to stay at our house while we were working on it, but he told me he didn't want to move in until we did together as man and wife. He spent the day getting his new office ready, advertising and interviewing for a secretary ("Slim pickings," he'd groaned after a particularly long afternoon), and then in the evenings, he and I worked on the *Dearbháil*. We would come home destroyed, but Mama always had a hot supper waiting for us. She had forgiven us for our practical joke, and even laughed about it now. She petted and fussed over Brendan. "Sick'nin'," Maggie would say.

Mama came home with Reuben in tow, and we all had lunch together. As I was washing dishes, Brendan decided to give his brother Andrew a call to make sure he'd gotten his invitation to the wedding because he'd heard nothing from him. After a few minutes, he came into the kitchen and sat down.

"Andrew won't be coming," he said, and sounded a bit upset. I stopped washing dishes and looked at him. He looked shaken.

"Why not?" Mama asked, putting a cup of coffee down in front of him.

Before he could answer, we heard Aunt Melba barrel up the driveway. Maggie was with her, and I could see the terrified look on her face even from the kitchen window. She hated the way Aunt Melba drove.

"Here goes nothin'!" Mama shouted as she flung open the front door.

It was a flurry of absolute madness. Reuben called us the Irish Hurricanes. He and Brendan retreated to the front room and turned on the TV.

Aunt Melba brought out her menu for the reception. "Girl, does all this food have to be *vegetarian*?" She said it like it was a disease.

"Not everything, no. I was thinking half-and-half. But no pork or shellfish."

"What? I was plannin' on makin' shrimp kabobs and slicin' up a ham!"

I sighed. "Aunt Melba, no. No. I won't even go into this with you again. Just no. Make some kind of chicken or beef, even lamb. No pork, no shellfish. We've already been over this."

Aunt Melba made a clucking sound and went back to her recipe books. By the look on her face, she was not pleased. I heard her mumbling under her breath, "Ain't no call not to have *ham*."

I felt myself rolling my eyes, but I found myself smiling, thinking that I hoped Brendan knew what he was getting into.

# Chapter 20    *Certainly*

Rose was coming in from New Mexico. "Do you think I'd miss your wedding with Cutie Pie?" she asked one night on the phone. I laughed. "What about school?"

"What about it?" was her reply. "You let *me* worry about that. I get paid the big bucks to figure stuff out. I'll see you on Saturday, girl."

I was excited about the coming wedding day, and it was difficult keeping my thoughts straight. I was so grateful that Mama, Aunt Melba, and Maggie were lining everything up, because I was a wreck. As Brendan had said earlier, "Just relax and show up." I was trying to do just that, but this wedding was taking on a life of its own. With Rose coming in, I was feeling a little better. Rose was not given to high emotions and falling apart. She would have a calming effect on us all.

When I had initially postponed the wedding, Maggie was behind me. She liked Brendan very much, but she loved me more. She didn't want me to jump into anything. "I jumped into it, you know. No point in rushin'," she'd said.

Maggie had been 16 and Wash was 18 when they married. Mama and Papa had put their foot down about it, so the young couple up and eloped. I thought Mama had gotten news of a death in the family, the way she carried on. I was 11 at the time and looked on Rose and Maggie as adults because they were in high school and dressed like grown ladies. I couldn't imagine why Maggie's marriage had hurt Mama so, and nothing I said would comfort her. The greatest comfort I could think of was to reason, "Mama, we won't have to wait so long to get in the bathroom now." From her bed where she was sobbing, she reached out and pulled me to her and cried all the more.

Wash had done well for himself. He had worked at some kind of job ever since he was 12, so when they married, he put down his savings on a little house in town. Wash was very mature for his age, and he went into marriage with wide-eyed seriousness. Sometimes he worked two jobs so they could put by money for when they had a baby, but a baby didn't seem to be coming any time soon. After 10 years of marriage, they had given up any hopes of having children.

One July evening during supper Maggie was complaining that her back hurt. "Good golly," she said, "I feel like I'm passin' a kidney stone."

Wash drove her to the emergency room when the pain became unbearable. Within 15 minutes, Maggie had given birth to a six pound baby boy. She had never known she was pregnant, and now here she was going home with her little Stone. Wash was beside himself with excitement. He built onto their house so Georgie could have his own room.

The Friday before the wedding, I was in the kitchen preparing lunch for the next day. Maggie was with me.

"So you're really sure this time?" she asked.

"Yes, no doubt," I replied. "I think Brendan and I will have a great life together."

"Well, you know I only want what's best for you, Mo."

"I know that, Maggs."

"I think we got everything in order," she said, brightening. "Should be smooth sailin' come Sunday!"

"I hope so. I'm so frazzled, I may show up in my nightgown. 'Ready or not!'" And she laughed with me.

Brendan came home early from the office. He decided he'd close at noon on Friday. The office was shaping up and he had gathered in some clients. He'd finally had some success in hiring a secretary. Mrs. Clanahan, he said, was a bit scary to look at, but she was cracker-jack at her job. Her hair was teased up foot high, and she wore orange lipstick and big glasses. Brendan had reported that the day she came in for the interview, he thought someone was playing a prank on him. But Mrs. Clanahan turned out to be the real deal. He was happy with her.

"Seems like she got the best end of the deal," Maggie had said. "She got eye candy and you got Halloween!"

Brendan kissed me on the cheek. "So what's for lunch tomorrow?"

"Fifteen-bean soup and corn bread. Only the soup is only about 8 beans."

"I've been gypped!"

"Ready for Sunday, Brendan?" Maggie asked him.

"You bet! I can hardly sleep a wink."

Mama would not allow Brendan to ever give her money for his keep, so he would slip it into her purse or coat pocket whenever she wasn't looking. This day I saw him put a wad of bills in Mama's stash she kept in one of the cupboards.

"You know she's going to find it and *know* it was you," I said, stirring the soup.

"She'll have to prove it," he said and closed the cupboard door. He smiled at me, and I loved him more.

**********

"So why ain't Brendan's Mama comin' to see her boy get married?" Mama wanted to know that Friday night when she and I were alone in the kitchen.

I was taken aback at her sudden questioning. "Well, Mama, she *does* live in Ireland. Maybe she can't afford the trip." I was guessing, because Brendan was estranged from his family. That's all I knew, and I didn't feel it was my place to share that with Mama.

"An' how 'bout that brother?"

"I don't *know*, Mama," I said.

She put her hands squarely on the table and stood up. I knew that could only mean thing. "Oh, Mama, no," I began, but she was already out of the room.

Mama stood over Brendan, who had fallen asleep in Papa's recliner, a book across his chest. "Brendan," she said rather loudly. It startled him, and he looked confused as he came out of the fog.

"What's wrong, Mama?" he asked.

"That's what *I* wanna to know," she replied, hands on her hips.

"Mama, please," I said, but she ignored me. I knew my mama, and she was on a mission.

"What's wrong is why your mama-- and your brother, while I'm at it-- ain't comin' to this weddin'."

The look of embarrassment on Brendan's face pained me. But Mama was plain-spoken, and when she wanted to know something, she threw tact out of the window. She sat down on the sofa and waited for his answer. I just stood there, wringing my hands, until she finally said, "For goodness' sake, Mo. Sit down and stop lookin' like you're three shades from a ruptured kidney." I obeyed and sat beside her. My face must have borne an expression of horror, shame, and disbelief, but

Brendan and I made eye contact, and I knew that he wasn't angry at her intrusion.

Mama said, "I don't need to know right now, if ever. But if there's something that needs to be told, Maureen here should be the first to hear it. The worse thing between a couple is secrets. I'm gon' make some coffee and leave you be." With that, she got up and went into the kitchen.

"Bren, you don't need to explain anything," I said.

"Yes, I do," he said. After a few minutes of quiet, Brendan began. "My mother hasn't said much to me since my father died. Hardly anything, really. Our relationship was distant at best before he died, but after that..." He searched for words. Then he continued after taking a deep breath.

"We were always a close family when I was growing up. Dad had told us all about our ancestors and how they'd come from Ireland. Mother had been born in Ireland, and so she was familiar with all the places Dad mentioned. When I was in high school, we were studying genetics in biology. It fascinated me. Our class project was to go back several generations and trace our characteristics. Well, with all I knew about our family, this was going to be a breeze.

"The more I poured over family pictures, even the black and white ones, I could see that everyone in my family had light eyes, on Mother's side and Dad's. I remember my teacher telling the class that there was almost a zero possibility of two blue-eyed people producing a child with dark eyes. He said that blue was a recessive gene, while brown was dominant. In order to have dark eyes, either the mother or father would have to have dark eyes."

He paused, looking at his hands folded in his lap, and I resisted the urge to ask him what on earth he was getting at. He had green eyes. I didn't understand where he was going with this lesson in genetics, but I kept silent.

"As I said, I went back several generations. No one had dark eyes." He finally looked up at me. "My brother Andrew has dark eyes. Dark. Almost black."

It was finally beginning to dawn on me what he was trying to tell me.

"Oh, but Bren...Bren, with genetics, there are possibilities of mutations and...well, I'm no scientist; I don't recall the right words. But that doesn't mean anything. What are you saying? You think your mother had an *affair*?"

"Well, you know how it is when you're a teenager. You learn a little something, and you think you're so smart. One night during dinner—I was way into my school project by then—Andrew picked a fight with me at the table about the Super Bowl. How stupid. One thing led to another, and I blurted out, 'Yeah, well, at least I know who both my parents are!' You know, trying to be funny and get his goat. I heard silverware clatter to the table. Mother and Dad were both staring at me in disbelief. Mother actually swung her arm, shoving her plate and water glass off the table, and they went crashing into the dining room door. Then she got up and shouted at Dad, '*Go dtachta an diabhal thú!*' Then she stormed from the room."

Brendan ran his hand over his face. He seemed to be reliving the moment.

I said, "Bren, you don't have to go on."

"Yes, I do. Mama is right. No secrets. *Ever.*" He sighed then began again.

"Things at our house were tense, to say the very least. I didn't know what I'd said that was so wrong, and neither did Andrew, and he and I talked about it at great length. He said he knew I was horsing around and that I was a big jerk, and he laughed it off. So things were okay between us. But Mother and Dad...quite a different story. Mother wore an angry expression all the time—all the time—and Dad looked so downcast. I don't know what he was like at work, but when he came home, he made his own supper, went in his den and ate alone. The times that I went in to talk to him, he seemed so depressed. He'd help me with my homework when I asked, but it was like he and I weren't even in the same room. He didn't seem angry with me, just depressed and distant.

"I would say, 'Thank you, Sir,' when we were finished. He'd pat my hand and try to smile, and then he went back behind his cloud.

"After some time, things seemed to be normal between him and me. We started playing the pipes together again. Mother even started cooking supper for all of us after not doing it for what seemed like such a long time, I mean including Dad, and we went back to eating at the table like a family. But I could feel that pall over us. It never really left.

"Well, after a couple of years, I went away to college. I called home a lot and Dad and I kept in touch. Mother never seemed to be around or was too busy to talk. Andrew would get on the phone and talk with me till Dad finally had to take the phone away." Brendan smiled. "I can still hear him, 'Hand me that phone, Son. It's long distance!'

"Then that summer Dad collapsed at work and died on the way to the hospital. Massive stroke. I was crushed. Dad had been everything to me. He was the greatest man I'd ever known, and I wanted nothing more than for him to be proud of me and what I would make of my life. Given my mother's cool attitude with me, I actually felt like an orphan.

"And then—the day of the funeral. Oh, Maureen—that was the day it all came out and hit the fan. The service was over, and Mother and Andrew and I went home. Just as I reached my bedroom door to go in and change, she was suddenly behind me, pushing me in the room and slamming the door behind us. Oh, her face—I'll never forget the look of absolute hatred on her face as she spit out the accusations."

"Accusations?"

"I won't repeat everything she said, Maureen, because it's far too painful, even now. But the end was that she *had* had an affair. She'd been unfaithful to Dad. She got pregnant as a result. I can only assume that she wanted to leave and marry this man, because I vaguely remember her being gone, and Dad saying she'd gone away to take care of her sister. I don't know what happened, but after a while, she came home again. Dad welcomed her back, nothing was wrong, announced to me that I was going to soon be a big brother. He was such a good, godly man, my father. He must have forgiven her. And when Andrew came, Dad announced to everyone that a new Fitzgerald son had been born. And Andrew was a Fitzgerald. I never noticed any difference in the way he treated my brother. And then that night at the supper table when I'd said what I did about not knowing who his parents were...that hit the nerve that had been buried for 14 years.

"Mother just lost her mind that night. She assumed that Dad had confided to me about her affair and about Andrew, but I swear, Maureen, he had never said a word to me. He and I were very close, but that was something that never passed between us. She called me a liar, and said she never wanted to see me again. Then she stormed out and slammed the door so hard that the frame cracked.

"You know, I could have lived with what happened. I thought it over, and she was my mother, and in spite of the distance she'd put between us over the last few years, I still loved her. But she felt betrayed, and there was nothing but ice after that.

"Then she told Andrew the truth. She convinced him that Dad and I were both in on the secret. She turned him against me. When I went back to school that fall, she said I should plan on staying on the campus the next summer. Maureen, she never looked me in the eyes. Andrew wouldn't even come tell me goodbye.

"I cried all the way to the airport. I could not believe that in the course of the summer, I had lost my entire family. Two weeks later I got a package in the mail from Dad's attorney. It was Dad's bagpipes and a check. My entire inheritance. No letter from Mother. Nothing.

"I found out later that after Andrew graduated, she moved back to Ireland. After several years, I tried connecting to Andrew again. I finally found his phone number. That first call was awkward, but I convinced him to see me. Oh, Maureen. He was so changed. Mother had filled him with so much hate and bitterness. He had a chip on his shoulder, acting like the world owed him some kind of restitution. We've seen each other a few times over the years, but it's been strained, even now. He's a total stranger.

"When I called him about our wedding, I told you he wasn't coming."

"Yes, I remember," I said.

"The reason is that Mother is with him. She has been in the States since before Christmas. Mo, I was absolutely floored. And I really don't understand why I feel this way. She never contacted me when I married the first time, nor when my wife died, so why should she now? I just can't explain to you how...." His voice trailed off.

"Well, that's my story," he muttered. "You truly are my only family."

I put my arms around him. I could feel the tears rolling down my cheeks.

**********

On Sabbath, snow began to fall. What a treat, I thought. Snow for our wedding! We stood out in it for a few minutes as we were leaving church. I felt like a child again and wanted to run and play in it. I figured it wouldn't amount to much, but I would enjoy it while it was here.

On the way home from church, we stopped by the *Dearbháil* to make sure the heat was on so the pipes wouldn't freeze. Although it only had one room finished, it felt like home. Soon we would be moving in.

As he was closing the door on our way out, Brendan stopped and said, "You're almost my wife."

"No regrets?" I teased.

"Never, girl."

The rest of the day went just as we'd wanted; quiet and calm. Rose was in and staying at Maggie's house, and so any last-minute details about the wedding were being taken care of over there. All I had to do was show up. I liked that idea more and more. It would be a restful, quiet Sabbath, and then a beautiful snowy day for our wedding. In less than 24 hours, I would be Mrs. Brendan Fitzgerald!

**********

That evening Mama turned on the TV. There was a new true crime show coming on that she wanted to see, so she went in the front room with her bowl of ice cream and cozied into her chair in front of the television.

Brendan and I stayed in the kitchen and had hot chamomile tea. Suddenly we heard Mama shout my name as her bowl of ice cream clattered to the floor. We got up and ran to the front room.

"MO! You gotta see this! I think I just saw *Ol' Thang* on TV!"

"What??" I stood transfixed in front of the picture tube. Sure enough, there was my ex-husband on the screen, having been caught in a sting operation that John Hobrick had told me about months earlier. I thought my heart would stop. Just then the phone rang. "Here we go," I said, and before I could even get the receiver up to my ear, I heard Maggie screaming on the other end of the line, "Turn on the TV! *Turn on the TV!*"

**********

"Mo, why didn't you tell us?" Rose wanted to know. She, Mama, and Maggie were all piled into the kitchen with Brendan and me as soon as the program had gone off. The phone was ringing constantly from people calling. Brendan took the receiver off the hook.

"I didn't want y'all to know because it was humiliating knowing I'd been married to a pervert all those years! Don't you think *I* was shocked? I had no idea! I didn't want people knowing and have to deal with that humiliation every time I saw them on the street!"

"Well, the cat's outta the bag *now*," Maggie said. "I had people from my church callin' and askin' wadn't that my old brother-in-law what was picked up by the Vegas po-lice. 'Ain't he the husband of that one what goes to church on Saturday?' I had to unplug my phone! Moze, if you'd a-told us, we coulda all been ready with a' answer. The whole family's been scandalized!"

"Now look," I said, "I had no idea he'd be on national television. All I knew was he'd been arrested, and I thought that was that."

"Well," Mama said, "people gon' be comin' to the church tomorrow just to ask nosy questions. I may stay home. Maggie, you and your crowd might wanna do the same. We'll get our churchin' at the weddin' tomorrow afternoon."

I stood up and made for the bedroom. "This is a *disaster*! We may as well call everything off!"

I slammed the bedroom door behind me and lay across the bed. I heard a light knock on the door, and Brendan walked in. "Mo?"

I grunted an acknowledgement but didn't look at him.

He sat down on the bed and gently rubbed my shoulder. "I'm sorry, love. I guess you feel this is never going away."

"That's how it feels, yes."

He lay down behind me and put his arm around me. "Well, I'm planning to be at the church tomorrow to marry you and be your husband. I was hoping you were still planning the same thing."

I sighed. "You're marrying a scandalized woman," I said.

"No, you aren't. It's not your fault what he's done. If people can't accept that, then it's no big loss to see them go."

"People are going to be talking about this for a long time."

"Let them talk. It leaves some other poor soul alone."

"Brendan, I don't ever want you to be sorry you married me. You have a business you're trying to start up. What if this spoils your chances?"

"I'm willing to take that chance. I don't care what people say. You've done nothing wrong, love."

I brought his hand up to my face and kissed it.

"Do you know," he asked, "why I fell in love with you?"

"No."

"When I first saw you, I was immediately interested. I know that sounds shallow. But I was. I thought you were beautiful. But in the back of my mind were my mother and my ex-wife, and I thought, 'What if she's like that, too?' The next night, I was terrified about asking you out."

"You didn't act terrified," I said.

"I was, though. I know I was looking all like Mr. Cool."

I giggled.

"But I had prayed about it. Kept praying. I was nervous, but I wanted to get to know you better. I knew I couldn't run from relationships forever. When I had dinner with you, I realized there was something about you that I'd never had."

"What?"

"You were so genuine. Nothing fake about you. Truly a godly woman. I could see it in your face, and I heard it in your voice. I realized that that was what I was looking for in a wife. I wanted to get married again, but I had not met anyone who made me feel as safe as you did. I saw right away that you didn't play games. There's something about you, Maureen, that is so...earnest. It was almost as if the Lord were telling me, 'Ok, Brendan, pay attention to this one'."

"Really?"

"Um-hum. I didn't even feel bothered by the fact that we lived so far apart. I was willing to step out in faith and see what the future held. I already knew *Who* held it."

"God will work this out, won't He?" I asked, but it was more of a statement.

"Yes, He will. He didn't bring us this far just to abandon us, Mo."

I felt so safe, so reassured. I felt myself smiling.

Just then Mama knocked on the door. "Y'all ain't doin' nothin' shameful in there?"

We giggled. Brendan said, "Yeah, Mama, your daughter is in here bein' mighty wicked! She's tryin' to steal my innocence!"

I could feel Mama thinking on the other side of the door. "Y'all full of it. Come on out here. I got pie and coffee."

**\*\*\*\*\*\*\*\*\*\***

During the night, I kept hearing thunder and seeing lightning flash. I'd never seen such a thing in the snow. The wind was howling as well. Several times Mama got up and went to the window and looked out. "Lawsey mercy, you should see how that snow's comin' down. I ain't never seen the like in all my borned days!"

I finally got up and looked out. When the lightening flashed, I could hardly believe my eyes. The bird bath that was in the side yard was nearly completely covered.

"Mama! We're having a *blizzard!*" The trees were creaking in the wind.

"Murdah, I sure hope one o' them trees don't decide to come down on our roof!"

"What about tomorrow?" I began to feel panic setting in.

"Don't you worry none, girl," Mama said, patting my arm. "This'll probably be over by mornin'. Now I'm goin' back to bed. My bum's *freezin'*!"

I couldn't believe how calm she was. In all my life, I had never heard of a blizzard in South Carolina.

It was all over the news in the morning. Many people were without power. The wind had died down, but lines were still coming down from the heavy snowfall, a record-breaker. We were blessed to have power at Mama's house.

Everyone was up and looking out the windows.

"I've never seen such a sight," Brendan said. "I've seen some heavy snow, but *nothing* like this." He pulled his sweater up around him closer. The house was warm, but there was something about seeing all that snow that made us all feel a bit colder.

"Well," Mama said, sounding cheerful, "my coffee'll take the edge off that snow, alright."

"Mama, do you think we ought to put the phone back on the hook just in case?" I asked.

"In case of what?" she asked.

"Maggie or Rose might be trying to get us this morning."

"I guess so."

I went into the front room and put the receiver in the cradle. It immediately rang. Mama and Brendan came in and we all three stood there looking at the ringing phone.

"Let me get it," Brendan finally said. "Hello? Yes, it is. Good morning. What? Well, what happens now?"

Mama and I were motioning to him to tell us what was going on, but he turned away and covered up his free ear. Finally he said, "We'll get back to you, Pastor Yates."

The two of us stared at him.

"I'm sorry if I acted rude, but there was a lot of crackling on the line and it was difficult to hear."

"What's the matter?" I asked, starting to feel sick.

"There's no power out at the church."

Mama and I looked at each other. I wanted to burst into tears but I didn't want to have a swollen face by that afternoon. I told myself to be calm.

"We'll fix this," Mama said. "Let's put our heads together an' come up with *somethin'*."

The phone began ringing again. Brendan picked it up. Before he could say hello, the voice on the other end began talking. He handed the phone to Mama.

"That's Maggie," he said to me as he took my arm and led me into the kitchen. "It's my sole job today to keep you as calm as possible. I would hate to have to go chasing you into the woods to bring you back."

"No, love, I've been praying. I'm going to keep a cool head today. We'll get through this. A blizzard in South Carolina will have people buzzing for weeks, and they'll forget all about that mess with my ex. In a few hours, we're going to be husband and wife, come snow or high water!"

**********

After a clan gathering by phone, we decided to have the wedding at Aunt Melba's. No one loved a party more. She said to just come on, everything would be ready. I spent a good part of the morning on the phone, trying to let people know, but I also knew hardly anyone could come because of the weather.

I watched from the window as Brendan was digging the car out, and it occurred to me that the road into town would be impassable. I told Mama what I was thinking. She said nothing in return, but got on the phone.

"Reuben? I got a favor t' ask."

When she hung up, she had a smug look on her face. "Problem solved."

"What can *he* do? He's not sheriff anymore. He can't tell the snowplows where to go first."

"Nope, but he *is* a farmer, and I know for a fact he's got a' old snowplow he uses out at his place. He's gon' bring it here and cut us a path clear into town!"

**********

That afternoon, Aunt Melba's house was alive with candles and laughing and the smell of hot food. Maggie, Wash, George, and Rose had made it the few blocks over. There was such a festive atmosphere in the house that I didn't even care that the guests would be only family, and few at that. I was feeling happier than I'd ever felt in my life.

Aunt Melba made me stay upstairs until time for the wedding to start because she didn't want Brendan seeing me. All the women were gathered in the bedroom where I was and cooing over me as they helped me get ready. Maggie did my hair in an up-do with a few curls hanging around my face. I thought it was just lovely. They all stood back and admired it.

Mama began crying, and then Aunt Melba, and finally Maggie. Rose stood firm. "You look beautiful, Mozie," she said, "but forget crying. I'm not showing up in your wedding photos with my face looking like a swollen carp."

I had chosen to wear the MacKenzie tartan skirt and a white blouse with a sash. Mama said I looked like one of our ancestors, and that made me feel proud. I was missing Papa, but I swallowed back the tears.

The time came. The women went downstairs, and Uncle Clive came in.

"Ready, my girl?" he asked. I could see his eyes were a little red.

"Yes, Sir, I am."

"Well. Let's be off, then." He took my elbow and we stepped into the hallway. I could hear Brendan playing the Bach-Gounod "Ave Maria" on his bagpipe. Aunt Melba was accompanying him on the piano.

Uncle Clive leaned into my ear and said quietly, I have a poem I've been waiting all day to recite to you."

Uncle Clive was a romantic at heart, and given to much reading, and he had a wonderful voice for recitation.

"I'd love to hear it," I said, smiling at this kind man I had come to love all the more since he and Aunt Melba had returned to New Ulster.

He paused, catching his breath so he wouldn't become emotional. Guiding me down the stairs, he began:

*A Man and a Maid stood hand in hand*
*bound by a tiny wedding band.*
*Before them lay the uncertain years*
*that promised joy, maybe tears.*
*"Is she afraid?" thought the Man of the Maid.*
*"Darling," he said in a tender voice,*
*"tell me--do you regret your choice?*
*We know not where the road may wind*
*or what strange byways we may find.*
*Are you afraid?" said the Man to the Maid.*
*She raised her eyes and spoke at last.*
*"My dear," she said, "the die is cast,*
*the vows have been spoken, the rice has been thrown.*
*Into the future we will travel alone.*
*With you," said the Maid, "I am not afraid."*

I looked at Uncle Clive as tears stung my eyes. "That was beautiful," I said. "Did you write it?"

"Mercy, no. As much as I love poetry, I couldn't write my way out of a wet paper bag." He sounded so serious, wiping his nose at the same time, that I giggled. He held on to me tighter.

We reached the bottom of the staircase, and I could hear sniffling from the front room. The music had stopped. "In we go, dear," Uncle Clive whispered. We walked through the French doors, and I saw Brendan for the first time since we'd arrived. He was dressed in full Fitzgerald kilt. The tears began falling down my face. I could see him catch his breath, and he smiled broadly when he saw me. By this time,

Uncle Clive was audibly sniffling. He pulled out his handkerchief and wiped his nose again. We carried on toward Brendan and Pastor Yates.

Uncle Clive and I stood with Brendan. Pastor Yates asked who was giving this woman, and Uncle Clive answered, put my hand in Brendan's, and then stepped back. It all seemed to me to be a dream.

As Pastor Yates began speaking, the power snapped off. I heard Aunt Melba gasp, "*Law' murdah!*" Other than that, no one moved. The pastor went on as if nothing had happened, a pillar of calm.

Before long, I heard, "Do you, Brendan Timothy Fitzgerald, take this woman, Maureen Siobhán MacKenzie, to be your lawfully wedded wife?"

"I certainly do," he answered. Then facing me, Brendan continued, "By the power that Christ brought from heaven, mayst thou love me. As the sun follows its course, mayst thou follow me. As light to the eye, as bread to the hungry, as joy to the heart, mayst thy presence be with me, O one that I love, 'til death comes to part us asunder."

"Do you, Maureen Siobhán MacKenzie, take this man, Brendan Timothy Fitzgerald, to be your lawfully wedded husband?" Pastor Yates then asked me.

"I do," I answered, speaking barely above a whisper. I turned to Brendan. "By the power that Christ brought from heaven, mayst thou love me. As the sun follows its course, mayst thou follow me. As light to the eye, as bread to the hungry, as joy to the heart, mayst thy presence be with me, O one that I love, 'til death comes to part us asunder."

Pastor Yates smiled at us. "Brendan and Maureen, you have entered this covenant of marriage in front of God and these witnesses. This is not a covenant to be taken lightly. Do you solemnly promise your true faith to one another?"

Brendan and I spoke together, "We swear by peace and love to stand--heart to heart and hand in hand. Mark, O Spirit, and hear us now, confirming this, our sacred vow."

**********

The power had gone off at the *Dearbháil*, but we were staying there on our wedding night in spite of it. We had plenty of wood for the fireplaces, and Mama and Aunt Melba had sent us off with a load of food.

We walked in the front door and were greeted by the dark, cold house, but it was home.

"Any regrets?" Brendan asked, smiling.

I shook my head and smiled. Tears were pooling in my eyes. I whispered, "'With you,' said the Maid, 'I am not afraid.'"

Leaving everything by the front door, Brendan took my hand gently and led me upstairs in the frozen quiet.

# Chapter 21    *Snow Haven*

I awoke, and Brendan was not in bed. When I raised up, I saw that he was stoking the fire. Other than the light from the fireplace, the room was dark.

"You're up early," I said, rubbing my eyes.

"I woke up and the room felt a little cool, so I put some wood on the fire. Know what? There's a wood stove in the basement. I checked out the pipe and it seemed clear, so I got a fire started down there. We don't have to worry about the water pipes freezing."

I looked at my new husband. His hair was tousled, silhouetted in the firelight. It made me smile.

"Come back to bed, Bren," I said, and turned the covers back. He put the poker back in the stand and did as I requested. His body felt warm from the fire. I snuggled next to him.

"Guess what else I did?"

"Washed and waxed the car."

"No, I thought I'd leave that for tomorrow. I put the food in the kitchen."

"How long have you been up?" I asked, surprised because of the hour.

"For some time. I woke up and couldn't go back to sleep. You were sleeping so soundly, I didn't want to wake you. After I stirred the fire here, I thought about checking the water pipes when I remembered about the wood stove. It just kind of snowballed."

"You're a wonderful husband," I said.

He kissed my hair. "I hope I you always think that."

"I will. Do you know why I fell in love with you?"

"My stunning good looks."

I laughed. "Well, I did notice right away that you were handsome. But as I got to know you, and as you shared your past with me, I felt so comfortable. And not one time did you ever make me feel threatened."

"Threatened?"

"You know--that you would never act in any way but as the Christian man you claimed to be."

Brendan kissed my cheek. "Well, I knew I couldn't say one thing and act a different way. I knew that if God were leading me in your direction, I needed to follow His instructions. You were so comfortable to be around. There was no way I wanted to do anything that would dishonor God or you. I knew that if you were the Christian *you* claimed to be, you would show it in your character. And you did. You were just what God knew I needed. Last fall when you told me you wouldn't marry me, I was crushed. After you left me in the woods that night, I knew I needed to pray. And did I ever pray! And when God and I finished talking, I knew it would be alright in the end. I didn't know how or when, but I knew it would."

I couldn't help giggling, "When you came in my bedroom that next morning, you seemed so angry! Your face looked like thunder!"

"Well, I had built up a head of steam. I knew I didn't want to leave without talking to you. I guess I lost control of myself there for a few minutes! Mama kept telling me that I couldn't see you, and I lost my cool. I was sorry about that later."

"All was forgiven. Mama could never get mad at you."

"And see? It's all worked out in the end. And now we have a new beginning." He put his arms around me tighter. "Are you alright?" he asked, and I could feel his warm breath on my face.

"Oh, yes," I said.

\*\*\*\*\*\*\*\*\*\*

The next time I opened my eyes, it was daylight. Brendan was still sleeping. Quietly, I reached for my dressing gown and got out of bed. The fire had died down, and the room was chilly again. I put more wood on and got it really flaming. The heat felt good. I dashed back to bed to get my feet warm.

Brendan stirred. "What time is it, love?" he mumbled.

"Right about eight o'clock."

He groaned. "What's it like outside?"

"Still white," I said, pulling the blankets tighter around us.

"Umm. I dreamed it was summer."

"That was just the sunshine in my face," I said, and he opened one eye and looked at me.

"I love you," he murmured.

"I love you, too. Let's have prayer and get up. I don't know why, but let's get up anyway."

We had prayer together, which we would do every morning. I remembered a sign once that said, "Let your prayer be the lock of the evening and the key of the morning." It would be as important to us as breathing, especially in the coming year.

"I'm sorry we can't leave on our honeymoon today like we'd planned," Brendan said.

"We *are* on our honeymoon." I replied. "We don't have to be anywhere special. Just being with you as your wife is special enough."

**********

When we were up and dressed, I figured out that I could warm the food on the woodstove in the basement. We had brought a few pots and pans and dinnerware, so with the wedding food and breakfast makings we'd been sent off with the day before, we'd do well for ourselves. We still had water, for which I was grateful, so I got a kettle heating so we would have water to wash with and for drinking.

"This is a bit like camping," Brendan remarked as he poured water for our tea.

"Yes, but without having to sleep on the rocky ground."

"I'm glad you can see all this as an adventure," he said.

"*Life* is an adventure! Well, it's easier to take the hard parts if you look at it that way."

"Mrs. Fitzgerald, I'm happy to have you as my adventure partner."

"Same here, love. Food's ready!"

We were ravenous.

Afterwards, we carried the dishes up to the sink and I ran the water to clean them. Brendan came up behind me and said, "You're not going to believe this."

"What happened?"

"I just realized that our hot water tank is gas, so we've had hot water all along."

My mouth dropped opened. I turned on the hot water tap, and within seconds, I could feel warm water. "The boiler is gas. So why don't we have heat?"

"That takes electricity to run the thermostat."

"So we spent all morning heating water for nothing?"

He nodded. I thought for a second, turned the water off, and dropped the dish rag into the sink. I slowly backed up and eased toward the door. Then I burst into a run, bolting for the stairs.

"I got dibs on the shower!" I shouted.

"We'll see about that, girl!" he said, racing after me.

**********

Later in the afternoon, we decided to go to Mama's. Because she still had her electricity, I knew there would be hot coffee. I gave her a call to let her know we were coming out for a visit.

"What y'all comin' out *here* for? Y'all on your *honeymoon*! Didn't have a spat already, did ya?"

"No, Mama, we just couldn't leave on our trip, so we thought we'd get out of the house for a while."

"Anything wrong?" she asked, almost whispering.

"No. What do you mean?"

"Well, if I was freshly married to the likes of Brendan, you'd never get *me* outta the *house*."

"Mama!" I took a deep breath. She was being outrageous again, just trying to embarrass me. "Do you want a visit or not?"

"Yeah, y'all come on. I'll have food and coffee ready for ya."

I hung up the cell phone and handed it back to Brendan. "That woman."

"What is it now?"

"Oh. She just.... Never mind. Maybe she won't pull anything if you're there."

I should have known better.

When we got there, Maggie's car was in the driveway. I had a sinking feeling. Sure enough, Mama, Rose, and Maggie were all at the kitchen table, waiting like a band of snipers. Wash and George were in the front room watching television.

Brendan greeted everyone and started to sit at the table.

"Bren," Mama said, "fix yourself a plate! I got hot vegetable stew and cornbread and lots o' coffee. Take it on in the front with the boys and watch some TV."

I started making meals for both of us, and as he stood with me at the stove, I hissed, "Don't leave me alone with them," but he didn't hear me. He just kissed my cheek, thanked me for the food, and made his way out of the kitchen. I stood with a bowl of hot stew in my hand, watching him disappear into the next room. I could feel all the MacKenzie eyes on me.

I sat down at the table and didn't look at anyone. "This smells great, Mama. Nothing like hot stew on a snowy day."

"Oh, yeah there *is*!" Mama said, and she and Maggie laughed. I looked at Rose, who was not laughing, but she was wearing a big grin.

They were all quiet for a minute, and then Mama said, "I'll bet that boy never made it out of his kilt."

"*Mama!*"

Maggie suppressed her laughter. "When y'all pulled in the drive, Mama started singin' 'The Wreck of the **Brendan** *Fitzgerald.*'"

"Leave Moze alone," Rose said. "That's a personal thing to be teasing someone about, especially your sister or daughter."

"Thank you, Rose," I said.

"But," she continued, "if you want to share anything with us, we'll be glad to listen!"

"Y'all are *diseased*," I said, getting up from the table.

Mama put her hand on my arm. "Now, Mo, sit down. We'll behave, I promise. That was ugly of us."

"I think you're turning into a dirty old woman, Mama."

At this, Maggie and Rose hooted. "We just got through tellin' her that right before you got here," Maggie laughed.

"Sit and eat your stew," Rose said. "You still without power?"

"Yes, but we have hot water. The fireplace is nice, and there's a wood-burning stove in the basement that I can cook on."

"My little pioneer gal," Mama said, pouring me a cup of coffee.

Rose got up to check on "the boys." Mama and Maggie jumped on the opportunity.

"I think Rose's got a beau!" Maggie whispered.

"What makes you think that?" I asked.

Mama said, "She keeps talkin' about Professor-Somethin'. I can't remember his name, but it's Italian, if you can believe that. It's 'Professor *this*,' an' 'Professor *that*.'"

"*And*," Maggie said, "she blushes when she says it!"

I considered the possibility. Why shouldn't Rose have a beau? She had everything to offer the right gentleman. This blushing business, however, was not a lot to go on.

"Why don't you do what you usually do and just come out and ask her?"

Mama looked at me as though my head had just turned into a radish. "What? And have her think we're nosy? You know if I ast' somethin' like that, Rose is just gonna clam up."

"An' we ain't *nosy*," Maggie said. "We're *concerned*."

Before I could stop them, my eyes rolled into the back of my head.

"Aint no call for eye-rollin'," Maggie said snippily.

"*'Concerned'* about *what*?" I asked.

Just then Rose came back into the room. "Of all things, Wash wants ice-cream. On a day like this!"

"*Humph*," Maggie grunted, "He'd eat ice cream if he was standin' out in the snow butt nekked."

**\*\*\*\*\*\*\*\*\*\***

We left Mama's with enough food for a small army. She said once our power was back on, we'd need something to cook, and cook proper. There was no use arguing with her.

"Did you have a good time?" Brendan asked as we drove onto the road.

"Um."

"What does that mean?"

"My family," I said, "is as nosy as they come. Mama actually had the nerve to say she didn't think you'd made it out of your kilt!"

"Whoa. Did you tell her?"

"Brendan, she'd never let me live that down."

Brendan smiled. "*I* may not, either." And he gave me a wink.

# Chapter 22    *Of Mice and a Man*

It was a beautiful honeymoon. We ended up staying at the *Dearbháil* and never made it to our trip away, even though the snow had begun rapidly melting. The power came back on by Thursday, and we were so happy to be in our own home that we decided to stay there for the rest of the two weeks. We bought paint and made plans to start rejuvenating the house.

"I hope you don't think I'm boring," Brendan said as we were loading the paint into the car.

"Why would I think that?"

"Here we are just married, and instead of a honeymoon trip, I take you out to buy paint!"

"Not just *paint*," I said. "*Honeymoon* paint!"

We would start working on it the next week. That night as I lay in bed, I was excited about it. I giggled.

"What?" Brendan asked.

"I was just thinking about painting and fixing up. I feel like a kid at Christmas!"

He laughed. Getting into bed next to me, he put his arm around me and kissed me. "You're easy to please, Mrs. Fitzgerald."

Then I heard it. Something moved in the attic.

"Has to be the house settling," he said. "We've had all this snow, after all."

There it was again. Something was moving across the attic floor.

"Didn't you say this house was haunted?" Brendan asked, his eyes getting wide.

"Hogwash," I said. "It's the house settling or something."

"How do you know?"

"Bren, you just said so yourself!"

We lay in silence for a moment and heard no more noise. This went on for three nights in a row. On the fourth night, after making a racket over the ceiling, something ticked down the attic stairs.

"What was that?" he asked.

"I guess you'll have to get up and see."

Brendan looked at me. He pushed the blankets back and got up. "All right, but if I come across some old dude hanging by his belt, I'm *not* inviting him to breakfast."

Brendan stepped out into the hall and snapped the light on. I could no longer see him, but I assumed he was making his way toward the attic stairs. In a few minutes he was back, getting into bed and putting his cold feet on me.

"What was that for?"

"My feet are cold, and all over *this*." He handed me a pecan. "It was in the hall at the foot of the stairs. Mo, I do believe we have mice."

**********

There was something about setting mouse traps that made me queasy. We'd decided on the traps instead of poison. If they didn't work, we'd bring out the big guns in the form of warfarin. We'd placed traps all through the house. Up in the attic, Bren and I were freezing as we set about finishing our task.

"I hope this does it," I said, setting my last trap down. "They can be awfully tricky, mice."

"We'll get them one way or the other. Look. There's a lot of junk up here that needs to go out. We'll have to wait till the spring, though."

I looked around in the dim light. I could see some old chairs and end tables. "Hey, this may be the beginning of my antique shop," I said.

"Could be. Well, love, that's it. The last trap. Let's go downstairs and get warmed up!"

In the days that we had spent at the *Dearbháil*, we decided we'd move in permanently. We'd planned to stay at Mama's, but after seeing all that needed to be done, we came to the conclusion that it would make more sense to stay in town and live there while we worked on the house. It would present some annoyances, such as having to move furniture back and forth, but we decided to do it anyway.

"We'll be sitting with our feet under our own table," Brendan said.

The house was in good shape considering the neglect. All the woodwork was original—the moldings, the built-ins, the wainscoting. The dining room still had the original built-in buffet. The kitchen cabinets were original. They needed cleaning and polishing and maybe some new hardware. We felt so blessed that the house had not been abused in all the years it stood empty, passing from hand to hand. The plumbing and electric, as Mrs. Kennedy had informed me, had indeed been updated already.

We lay in bed on the last night of our honeymoon. We were exhausted. We'd gotten the cabinets cleaned and the kitchen walls painted. Our appliances had arrived, and we'd eaten a nice hot supper cooked on a real stove. I felt we had accomplished a lot in our little time away from the rest of the world.

"For our first anniversary, I'll take you on a trip to Ireland," Brendan said after we'd had our prayers.

"Ireland, is it? That'll do just fine." I could barely hold my eyes open.

He continued speaking in the dark. "I've enjoyed this holiday with you more than I can say, even if it did turn out to be work instead of a honeymoon."

"Oh, I loved it," I said sleepily. "We're making our home together. Whoever would have thought that a blizzard would bring a couple so close?" I smiled.

"You're amazing, love," he whispered, kissing my eyelids. "Good night."

"Night."

Sometime during the night, I woke up to a *swish-swish* sound somewhere in the room. I thought I was dreaming, but I sat up and rubbed my eyes to make sure I was awake. There it was again. *Swish-swish* **thump**. *Swish-swish* **thump**.

"Brendan, Bren, wake up." I shook him till he came around.

"Wha—what's the matter?" He sounded alarmed and sleepy at the same time.

"Listen to that," I whispered.

"What?"

"*That*."

*Swish-swish* **thump**.

"What in the world?" he said. "It sounds like it's coming from inside the room."

We listened again.

*Swish-swish* **thump**.

Brendan reached over and turned on the light. We looked around the room. Looking on my side of the bed, I let out a squeal. A mouse had been caught in a trap, by the foot, and was dragging it along as he tried to make his escape.

"Brendan!"

We both jumped out of bed and watched the hapless mouse as he tried to make for the bedroom door. "Oh, Brendan, *now* what?"

"What do you mean, '*now what*'?"

"What do we do with him? The poor thing!"

"*Poor thing*? Girl, it's a *mouse*! He and his family of dozens have taken over our *home*! Don't let his cuteness fool you." He looked around for something to put the mouse in. "Oh, boy. The only thing is, now *I* have to do the job the trap didn't."

"You mean you have to kill him?"

"Of course I have to kill him! That's the whole idea of the trap!"

"Oooooh, I can't watch!"

"Hand me that pillow case," he said.

"Not my new pillowcase! It's 400-count Egyptian cotton!"

"We'll get a new one, girl. I have to have something to take him outside."

I took the case off the pillow and handed it to him. He dropped it over the mouse and snatched it up again with the end wadded up. Then he headed out the door and downstairs. I wondered how he would finish the deed, but then I didn't want to think about it.

After a bit, I heard him come up the stairs again. He came into the bedroom empty-handed.

"Did you wash your hands?" was the first thing out of my mouth.

Brendan looked at me. A look passed his face, and he said, "Of *course* I washed my hands. Do you think I want blood and death all over me?"

"Oh, no!" I felt sorry for the mouse, in spite of his disease-carrying nature.

"Actually, Mo, I let him go. I managed to get the trap off his foot without him biting me, and he looked at me with those big brown eyes, and I just couldn't do it. I let him go with a warning to tell his friends."

"Oh, Bren, you softy."

"Huh," he snorted. "No telling what I have unleashed. Tomorrow," he said, getting back into bed, "I'm bringing out the big stuff."

"Warfarin?"

"Peanut butter. It's impossible to get that off the trap and not get properly smacked." He turned the light off and left me sitting in the dark.

"I guess you should have killed him," I said.

"Why do you say that *now*?"

"Well, I was just thinking. He has a broken leg now. What chance does *he* have at survival? He might suffer terribly, freezing to death out in the cold. Maybe killing him would have been kinder."

Brendan raised up on his elbow and turned in my direction. "Girl. I don't want to hear any more about that mouse. I hope I don't have to drive out to Mama's so I can get some sleep."

"Oh, Brendan, you know she'll talk you to death."

Before I knew it, Brendan had rolled over and had me pinned down. I burst out laughing.

**\*\*\*\*\*\*\*\*\*\***

Almost all the traps had been sprung with no mice to be seen. These were some pretty crafty mice. Brendan reset all the traps using peanut butter. By the next day, the same thing.

"Good grief. How are they doing it?" He was puzzled.

That question was answered that evening when I went into the butler's pantry. I'd heard a trap spring, so I went right away to see what we'd caught. There in the corner sat the fattest mouse I'd ever seen, licking the peanut butter on the sprung trap. He looked up at me with little interest, then went on licking his chops. I backed out of the pantry.

By the time I got back with Brendan, the fat mouse was gone. "I tell you, he was *gargantuan*!"

Brendan looked skeptical. "How big can a mouse get? Are you sure it wasn't a rat?"

"No. I know a *rat* when I see one. This was a big ol' juicy *mouse*. Huge! I swannee I've never seen one so big!"

"Must be all that good living here at our house. Well, that's it. Warfarin. I'll give him a snack he won't soon forget!"

By Friday, we heard no more stirring, no pecan-rolling, no shuffling in the attic. All was quiet at the Fitzgerald household. "Suffice it to say that we got the little devil," Brendan said with pride. "And the others, I'm sure."

**\*\*\*\*\*\*\*\*\*\***

In the evenings after work we always did some work to the house. One Monday in February, we decided to paint the butler's pantry, a tidy little room between the kitchen and dining room. We'd start right after supper.

It was nice coming home after being gone all day. I hummed as I started putting together a light meal. Brendan came in the kitchen through the butler's pantry.

"Do you smell that?" he asked.

"What?"

"There's a pong in the pantry there."

I went in and took a deep breath. It was the smell of death. "Oh! *Minging*! It has to be mice. *Dead* ones."

We looked at each other helplessly. Then with hesitation, as though something would jump out at us, we began opening the cabinet doors.

"Oh! Ugh! Found it!" Brendan groaned. There was the fat mouse, dead as everything, piled up in the lower cabinet. "Good grief! Look at the size of that thing!"

"I *told* you," I said. "I *told* you he was gargantuan!"

We were stooped over, looking at the mouse propped up in the corner as though he were sitting in a chair, and marveling at his size.

"Just look at him," I said. "Why, he looks like Joe from *The Pickwick Papers*!"

Brendan went out back and retrieved the shovel. Scooping up the dead beast, he quickly made his way back outside, dumping it in the trash can outside the door. He tied the plastic liner in a knot and slammed the lid down. "Good riddance!"

I could hear him washing his hands in the bathroom off the back porch. When he came in the kitchen, he looked rather smug.

"The mighty Nimrod," I said, handing him a jar of relish. "Open, please?"

"The mighty Nimrod has been reduced to opening jars? The shame of it all!"

So were our days living in the *Dearbháil* of Cork Street.

# Chapter 23    Springtime

I was looking forward to St. Paddy's Day and the yearly festival. It would be the first time I'd be wearing the Fitzgerald tartan in public. The evening before, I started feeling sick, however, and I wondered if I'd picked up something from work.

"Ugh, there's a nasty stomach bug going around," I told Brendan, "and I think I may have it."

Before he could respond, I had to run to the bathroom. I just barely made it before losing all my supper.

"Are you alright?" he asked through the door.

I washed my face and held on to the sink for a few seconds. "I think so. Something didn't agree with me."

I felt better. I went back to the kitchen and sat down.

"What was that all about?" Brendan asked.

"I guess my stomach doesn't like my cooking."

During the night, I slept fitfully. I kept waking up feeling sick, feeling hot, then feeling cold, and this went on all night. "I'm definitely coming down with something," I told Brendan in the morning.

"You should stay home."

"I'm not running a fever, so I think I'll go in and have Dr. Liske look at me. Maybe I'm just run-down."

I had dry toast for breakfast and managed to keep that down. By the time I got to the office, however, I had to hit the restroom right away.

"Girl, you look like death warmed up," Jean said when she saw me that morning. "You can't be sick today. It's St. Paddy's!"

"I don't think my stomach cares," I moaned. "I hope Dr. Liske can fix me."

When he came in, he looked at me and frowned. "Mrs. Fitzgerald," he said, "you look a little blue around the gills. Go to one of the examination rooms and let me take a look."

I obeyed. I was looking forward to feeling better.

Dr. Liske and Jean, acting as temporary nurse because it was too early for Ol' Soggy Bottom to be in, came in the exam room. He washed his hands and began feeling the lymph nodes in my neck. Then he looked at my throat and listened to my lungs.

"You'd better hurry," I warned. "I think I need to vomit again."

"Have you been doing this all night?"

"A few times."

He handed me an emesis basin. "I think you've gotten dehydrated. Let's get some fluids in you and see how you feel, shall we?"

I started feeling better once the fluids got into my system. I lay on the exam table and nodded off. When I woke up, Brendan was standing over me.

"Hey there, love," he said quietly. "How are you feeling?"

"Oh, hey. I feel a little better, actually." He helped me sit up. Dr. Liske took the IV out of my arm and put a *Peanuts* band aide on the spot.

"You go home, Missus," Dr. Liske said, "And get some sleep. I gave Brendan a tablet in case you get sick again, yes?"

"Don't worry about a thing, Sweetie," Jean cooed. "You just feel better."

Brendan took me home and I went right to bed. I slept several hours before waking up again. I then got up, went into the bathroom and took a shower. I would make it to the St. Paddy's festival after all, or what was left of it. I went downstairs in my bathrobe and a towel on my head.

"Swami." Brendan smiled at me. "You must be feeling better!"

At that very moment, I caught a whiff of broccoli soup and had to dash to the bathroom.

\*\*\*\*\*\*\*\*\*\*

It was another long night. I had taken the pill, and that helped, but I couldn't rest. First thing in the morning, Brendan drove me to the office. I was still in my nightgown.

"Oh, my," Dr. Liske said when he saw me. "I think you need more fluids. You look worse than *death*!"

"Gee, thanks, Doc," I said. I looked at Brendan. He looked concerned.

Dr. Liske sent me into the bathroom with a little cup. When I came out, he started the IV.

"Okay, let's see what's going on with you. I'll have Nurse come in a draw some blood also." I dreaded the thought of Ol' Soggy Bottom sticking me with a needle. Dr. Liske patted my arm and smiled at me. "Don't you worry. We'll get this worked out."

"How do you feel, love?" Brendan asked. "Fluids helping?"

I nodded and kept my eyes closed. I was afraid if I said too much, I'd be sick again.

Dr. Liske breezed in rubbing his hands together and smiling from ear to ear. "We have a diagnosis! We won't be needing that blood work after all."

"What's wrong with her?" Brendan asked.

"Oh, nothing is *wrong*," he said, beaming. "Mrs. Fitzgerald is having a *baby*!"

**********

I would be 40 by the time the baby was born. In all the years I had been married before, pregnancy eluded me; with all my difficulties, I finally gave up hope and figured I would always be childless. According to Dr. Liske, I'd most likely gotten pregnant on my honeymoon. I thought about all this in the car on the way home. I was unbelievably happy, yet terrified.

We arrived home and sat in the driveway in silence. Finally Brendan said, "Maureen. We're having a baby. I'm sorry you're not happy." The pain in his voice killed me.

"Oh, Bren, I *am* happy. I'm just scared. A baby at *my* age? Why am I so sick? Can that be a good sign? I have so many thoughts going rogue in my head right now..."

"Listen, if you don't think you can do this...I mean, if you can't..." He was struggling for the right words. Finally he said, "Whatever you decide, I'll understand."

"What do you mean?"

He looked at me, searching, and the sadness in his eyes was unbearable. I understood.

"Brendan, oh, Brendan." He reached across the seat for me, and we cried. "I don't know how I can be having this baby, but I know I'm already in love with him. He's part of you and me, and I will love him no matter what happens. I'll be strong, I promise. I don't ever want you to think I have any regrets."

"My love," he sobbed, and there was no need for any more words. We were going to be parents. I was going to be a mother. It seemed too unreal. Suddenly I was extraordinarily happy.

"Let's call Mama and everybody and invite them over," I said. "I can hardly wait to share our news!"

\*\*\*\*\*\*\*\*\*\*

The Irish Hurricanes blew in, and once everyone was settled, Brendan said, "We're glad you could make it! Maureen and I have some great news!"

Mama put her hands on my shoulders and looked at me. She smiled. Without taking her eyes off mine, she said, "What is it, Brendan?"

"Maureen and I are expecting a baby. In October."

Mama hugged me in such a grip that I lost my breath. There were whoops going up from the MacKenzie women. The house was filled with noise and voices of everyone talking at once. There were hugs and tears all around, and then the camps were divided between the men and women. Brendan, Wash, and Uncle Clive stayed in the front room; Mama, Maggie, Aunt Melba, and I migrated to the kitchen.

We called Rose and told her. She was crying into the phone.

I looked at my relatives and knew I was blessed. God was in control; He'd see us through all the difficulties. I had no doubt about that.

\*\*\*\*\*\*\*\*\*\*

That night in bed, Brendan and I cuddled underneath the extra quilt. It had turned colder.

"How do you feel, love?" he asked, kissing my hand.

"Sick!" And I laughed. "What's all this about *morning* sickness? This is more like *all day and night* sickness!"

"Can I get you anything?"

"I have everything I'll ever need," I said.

We said our prayers, expressing our deep gratitude for our baby and our life together. I fell asleep right away and slept all night long, not remembering any dreams in the morning.

**********

The sickness continued, every day, almost all day. I plowed ahead, though, and managed to get to work every morning. Dr. Liske was ready with whatever help I needed to get through the day. Jean pampered me, not letting me do anything that might be a strain. I was beginning to feel like an invalid, but I did appreciate her concern.

The work on the *Dearbháil* had come to a halt. The only rooms that had been cleaned and painted were the kitchen, butler's pantry, our bedroom, and the upstairs bathroom. We would have to get a nursery ready, but that would have to wait for warmer weather and when I felt better. I didn't think the sickness would ever stop.

One morning toward the end of April, the nausea and vomiting stopped as quickly as it had come. I woke up without it, and I lay in bed for a bit just to make sure. Slowly I sat up. No nausea. I felt wonderful after having been sick for so long. On top of that blessing, spring was in full force, and the trees and flowers were all in bloom. I looked out the window as I put on my bathrobe and felt as though I was seeing a whole new world.

Brendan had already gotten up and was just starting breakfast, something he'd begun doing while I was sick. I walked in and hugged him.

"Good morning!"

"Good morning, love!" He held me at arm's length and studied my face. "You don't look sick this morning. You look *beautiful*!"

"Get on with you."

"No, I'm serious. You're radiant!"

"I don't *feel* sick this morning. Not a bit! I feel fantastic!"

"Praise God," he said and hugged me. "I'm so happy that you're better!"

We had prayer together and thanked God for His wonderful mercies. For the first time in almost two months, I actually felt like eating, and the smell of food didn't make me feel queasy in the least.

"What are you making this morning?" I asked as I sat at the table.

190

"I'll make whatever you want! Name it."

"Pecan waffles!"

"Hey! I have a great idea! To celebrate your feeling better, let's go to the Waffle World. We can be dressed in a snap!"

And so we did. That was the most delicious pecan waffle I had ever tasted, and I ate every single crumb of it.

# Chapter 24    Mama on the Move

May came in in typical South Carolina fashion; it quickly became hot and humid. There was no air conditioning at the *Dearbháil*, and I was beginning to feel it with my pregnancy.

"Murdah," I said, fanning myself with a piece of cardboard, "I won't make it through the summer!"

It was Sunday morning and Brendan was painting the front room. "It *is* hot," he agreed, "and will only get hotter." He put his brush down and sat down on the floor next to me. "Maybe we should consider putting in central air."

"Can we afford that?"

"Sure we can. We sold my old house, so we have money put by for fixing this one. We can shop around and see what we come up with."

"I don't want to get rid of the radiators, though," I said. "I love my radiators. Now *that* is *heat*."

"You wouldn't want central heat?"

"No. I had it before and nearly froze to death."

"Well, by all means, we'll keep the radiators and just have cool air installed. Tomorrow I'll make some calls and see what we can get." He kissed my head and got back up to resume painting.

"Sorry I'm not much help," I said.

From the ladder, Brendan looked down at me and smiled. "I like having you there to look at. My wife and future baby in the room with me."

I smiled up at him. I felt my throat get tight and my eyes were stinging. I was so emotional that anything sweet set me off.

"You know, I'm here on the floor. I could be cutting in along the base boards. I'd like to make myself useful."

So Brendan and I had the room cut in in no time, and then he rolled the rest of the walls. Our front room was going to be lovely. We'd been shopping around for antiques and had found several nice pieces that we loved. Our home was starting to come together. We were still basically living out of the bedroom and the kitchen, so having another room ready would be a welcome change.

**\*\*\*\*\*\*\*\*\*\***

Mama called and said that Rose was coming home for a visit.

"*And*," she said, "she's bringin' that Italian professor with her!"

"Mama, you're kidding me!"

"Nope.  I told her I wanted to see her—an' all y'all-- about somethin', an' she asked me if it was alright for him to come along, and I told her okay.  So I can hardly *wait* to see who has *Rose* hooked!"

She would be coming in next week, right after the school's graduation ceremony.

**\*\*\*\*\*\*\*\*\*\***

We all sat around Mama's kitchen table, waiting for Rose to show up.  Brendan and I had been to church and drove to Mama's right after. She'd cooked something vegetarian just for us.

"Bren," she said, dishing out the food, "I don't know how you let this little gal talk you into givin' up meat!"

"It was my idea, actually, Mama.  I didn't want Mo to have to cook two meals, and it seemed crazy to go in after she'd cooked and then make something for myself.  So...it just seemed like a good idea."

"*Humph*," was her only reply.

Brendan looked at me and smiled.  I smiled back and patted his knee under the table.

"None of *that*," Mama said as she put a baked potato on my plate.

I was curious about Rose's beau, but I was also eager to hear why Mama wanted to get us all together.  What was so important that she couldn't do it over the phone?  I knew there was no point in asking her what it was about. She would keep her lips sealed until Rose arrived and we were all together.  Maggie and I had discussed it earlier between ourselves, and we concluded that maybe Mama was telling us she was getting married. We later discarded that idea because, as Maggie put it, Mama wasn't acting goofy enough for someone about to announce her approaching nuptials.

After lunch, Wash and George got up and headed to the front room to watch television.  Brendan stayed behind and continued to sit with me.

"Aint you goin' in with th' boys?" Maggie asked.

"Oh, I suppose so. As long as I don't have to watch those old reruns of *Miami Vice*." Brendan looked pained.

"Good grief," Maggie muttered. "I think they fixin' to watch some Wyatt Earp movie."

At this, Brendan's face brightened. He loved westerns. From the front room, Wash yelled, "Come, on, Brendan! We startin' a movie!"

"Well, ladies, I'll take my leave." He leaned over and kissed the top of my head.

"So what's the matter with *Miami Vice*?" Maggie demanded to know.

Brendan gave her a pitiful look and said, "Oh, *Margaret!*" as he left the room.

Mama said, "Nothin, except you play it on the TV all the time. We all sick of it. I was sick of it when it was new, and bless Pat, I'm *really* sick of it *now*."

"Comin' from a woman who still watches *Hee Haw* reruns," Maggie said flatly. "You shouldn't-a bought me them DVD's then."

The three of us chatted, but it wasn't long before we heard the rental car come up the driveway. Everyone headed for the windows.

"Y'all get away from there!" Mama demanded. "Sit down and act like citizens!"

So we stood back and waited. Finally we heard the front door open. "Mama?"

"Rose! Come 'ere, girl!" Mama hugged her in a death grip, and then she turned her attention to the man standing next to Rose.

"Mama, this is Benigno De Luca," Rose said proudly. "Ben, this is my mother, Elizabeth MacKenzie."

Mama's mouth was open, as were all of ours. Benigno De Luca was considerably older than Rose, shorter, and was sporting a little bald spot on the back of his head. He was nothing like I had imagined.

"Mrs. Mackenzie," he said with an Italian accent, "I am so honored to meet you." He kissed her on both cheeks.

The introductions went around. Ben was giving us all little kisses on the cheeks, even the men. It didn't bother Brendan because his parents had always done it, but the look on Wash's face was indescribable. We all sat down in the front room, and the silence was awkward.

"Mama," I said, "I'll put on some coffee and we can have some of that nice pie you made. I'm sure Rose and Ben could use some refreshment."

Mama looked embarrassed that she hadn't thought of it. I could tell that she was so flabbergasted that she had even forgotten her manners. She blushed and thanked me.

Maggie got up and followed me. "I'll help you," she said. She and I could not get in the kitchen and out of sight fast enough.

"*He's* what's got Rose so twitterpated?" she said in a fierce whisper.

"I can't get over it," I said. "I *never* would have *thought!*"

By the time we got back with the coffee and pie, the conversation had gotten lively. Ben De Luca was entertaining everyone with stories of Italy and his father. Brendan's face was red, he'd laughed so much.

We set the trays down and Rose got up to serve. She handed Ben coffee and pie, and he looked at her with adoration and said, "Thank you, Kitten."

Mama, Maggie, and I exchanged glances. Maggie, frowning, mouthed, "*Kitten?*" Mama had to pretend to cough to stifle a laugh. I knew the conversation among us later would be a scream.

**********

Rose and Ben De Luca would be staying with Mama, Rose bunking in with Mama and Ben taking the white room. Ben was insisting on staying in a hotel, but Mama would have none of it. There was never any use in arguing with Mama. Once they were settled in, Mama called us in the front room. Finally we would be getting down to the business of getting us all together.

"Elizabeth, this is a family meeting. I'll go outside," Ben said.

"Pish," she said. "You'll do no such a thang. It ain't like it's a big secret or nothin'. You sit with Rose and make yourself at home."

I looked at Ben. I could imagine him in his professor robes, presiding over a senior class of young men just like in the old movies. I smiled at the thought. I looked at Rose and she was looking at me.

We were finally all seated and quiet, except for George, who was playing with his phone.

"Boy," Wash said, "you fixin' to lose that thang." George put it away.

"Well, I know y'all want to know what's goin' on, so let me get to the point. I've decided to move into town an' put the house on the market."

There were audible gasps from all us girls.

"Now before you get your drawers in a wad, let me say that before I do that, I'm offerin' it to any of you what wants it. It's the family home, and that's the only right thing to do." She waited for someone to say something.

"Mama," Rose was the first to speak, "why do you want to move into town? You've lived here all our lives."

"Well, girl, I'm gettin' on in years, and I ain't got no business out here alone in these sticks. It was okay when I was younger, but now I got to start thinkin' about what happens when I get *really* old. I got to be close in in case I ever run into trouble."

"Mama, you know as much as I love this house, I can't pick up and leave New Mexico. I have a life there," Rose replied, looking down at her lap as though she had somehow let Mama down.

Mama looked at Maggie.

"I guess me an' Wash'll have to talk it over, Mama...I like livin' in town."

"I guess that leaves *you*, girl," Mama said, looking at me.

"Well, Mama, Brendan and I already have our house, so I guess we won't need to make an offer," I said. It hurt me to think of never being able to come to this place anymore. Brendan squeezed my hand. He seemed to know what I was thinking and understood.

Wash spoke up, something he rarely did. "Mama, I got a' idea for ya. You thank about it before you answer. What if we traded houses?"

"What?" Mama and Maggie asked together.

"Now, Maggie, I know you say you like to live in town, but you also want a bigger house, and we ain't got no more room fer buildin' on. We can take Mama's house, and I'll build on to it all you want. You always said you wanted a room big enough to do your quiltin' in. Well, now you can have it. It's got all them nice apple trees Papa planted, too."

We all looked at Maggie.

"'Course, it all depends on what Mama wants," Wash went on. "I was just thankin' that if we was to trade houses, she wouldn't have to spend her time lookin' for one and havin' to take on debt." He turned his attention to Mama. "I got a lot tied up in that property, Mama. I done built on to it, even added another bathroom. It's a bigger house, but I know this 'un's more land with it, so I'll pay you what you want fer it. I want to live in the country ag'in."

Mama regarded Wash. "You let me study on it tonight, Son."

Wash nodded and said no more. In all the years I'd known Washington Connolly, I don't think I'd ever heard him speak that much at one time.

**********

It was late when we left Mama's. I fell asleep in the car on the way home. I woke up with Brendan gently shaking my arm. "Wake up, Kitten," he said. Half asleep, I giggled.

I barely got my teeth brushed, I was so tired. Brendan was still getting ready for bed when I pulled the sheet over me. I fell right to sleep.

The sun was high when I woke up the next morning. Brendan wasn't in bed. It was nearly nine o'clock. I turned over and just lay there. The cool morning air felt delicious. Running my hand over my swollen belly, I thought of our baby and how anxious I was to see her. I had no idea of the sex of this little life, but I was hoping for a girl. I ticked off the months, and I still had five to go.

I heard Brendan coming up the stairs, and he walked in carrying a tray.

"Good morning, sleepyhead!" he said cheerfully. "How'd you sleep?"

"Like the dead! Ooo, breakfast!"

"I thought you might want a little pampering, love," he said, kissing me. Together we sat in bed and had a feast.

"What a blessing you are," I said, putting a little jelly on some toast. "You're spoiling me, you know."

"Good!" Brendan unfolded the morning paper and perused it. "So what do you think about Wash's proposition?"

"I think it's a good idea myself. Maggie's house is move-in ready. You know she keeps it clean as a whistle. Mama won't have to paint or anything unless she wants to. Wash'll be back in the country where he's wanted to be for a long time."

"And Mama will be closer to us here. That'll be nice."

I looked at Brendan and smiled.

"I think Maggie will be the nut to crack," I said. "She likes her house, and she likes it in *town*."

"Yes, but I can't see Maggie wanting the Homeplace to go to perfect strangers."

"You're right about *that*. Well, I guess we'll have to see!"

Brendan was still looking at the paper, but I knew he hadn't read a word of it. "So...what do you think of Ben?"

I smiled. "Honey, hush."

"Come on. Tell me."

"Well, at first I couldn't believe how much older he is. That was a shock! And Rose is *taller*! But when I saw the way they looked at each other, I was impressed. He seems to be a nice man, with major intelligence. I can see why Rose is attracted to him. And Papa was way older than Mama, so I guess that's alright."

"Do you think they'll get married?"

"It wouldn't surprise me. Rose hasn't been serious about anyone in years. And you know how she feels about nicknames. She lets him call her *Kitten*!"

**********

Mama had a long discussion with Maggie about Wash's proposal. She told me all about it later.

"I told her that Wash has always been the one to give, give, give. 'It's *your* turn to give,' I says, and you shoulda seen her face. I says, 'Girl, you know Wash is a country boy, an' he's been pinin' away for th' country ever' since y'all got married. He bought you that house in town 'cause *you* wanted it, and he was wantin' to do anything to make you happy. Well, it's your time to think about *Wash's* happiness. If that ol' boy wants to get back in th' woods, you let him! He's done said he'd do whatever you want to th' house.' She didn't like it none too much that I was gettin' bossy with her, but she thought about it. Then she got to lookin' 'round th' house and started gettin' ideas about all she could do to it. She decided to go for it!"

198

Mama looked happy as she sipped her coffee. "I always have liked Maggie's house. She's got a nice porch for sittin', an' the sun comes up right where my bedroom'll be. You know I like *that*."

Mama, with her short hair and beau, had certainly changed a lot since I moved back to New Ulster. Although she was older in years, she somehow seemed younger.

"So how is Reuben?" I asked. "I haven't heard you say anything about him lately."

"Had a lot on my mind, girl," she said, not looking at me. Then she was silent. I wasn't about to let that go.

"Such as?"

She took another drink of coffee then slowly put her cup down on the table.

"Well, to be honest, ol' Reub's done hauled off an' ast' me to marry him."

"Mama!" I nearly shouted. "Why haven't you said anything? And what did you tell him?"

"I told him no," she said, looking as if I should have known the answer right away.

"Why? He's terrific! And I thought you were happy with him!"

"All that's true," she said. "But I ain't cut out for no farm-livin'. You've been to his place—he lives out in th' middle of nowhere. I enjoy his company, sure thing, but I don't want to be out in the countryside like that no more."

"Is that why you wanted to move to town? To have an excuse not to marry him?"

Mama frowned at me. "Mo, you know *very well* that I don't need no excuse to do what I want to do. I'm movin' to town for the very reason I give you girls already. That an' the fact that you're havin' a baby, and I want to be close to all y'all."

In the weeks that followed, Mama and Maggie began packing up their belongings. Brendan and I had air-conditioning installed in the *Dearbháil*. It was just in time for one of the hottest summers in my memory.

# Chapter 25    A Familiar Face

We had stopped going to church on Sundays. There was so much work to be done on the house, and with us both working during the week, it became a big day for chores. I asked Brendan the same thing every Sunday morning: "Are we going to church?" His answer was always the same: "We went yesterday." I also noticed he always planned ahead for the Sabbath. One Sunday morning after our prayers, I came out and asked him again.

"Are we going to church or not?"

"We went yesterday, love," he said. And then, "As a matter of fact, I've been wanting to talk to you about that. I want to be baptized. I was before, as a child, but I want to be baptized the *real* way—under the water! And with it being my own decision. After all, Jesus wasn't baptized by a little sprinkle on His head."

"No, He wasn't."

"I feel this is what God is calling me to do. Even before I met you, I was asking God to show me the right way, to show me what He would have me do with my life. I really feel this has been an answer to prayer. And I think it would be really confusing to our baby if his parents had conflicting ideas about church. I've been doing a lot of studying and praying, Maureen. I guess you've maybe noticed that I've been trying to keep the Sabbath—and it's been such a blessing."

I jumped into his arms and cried. It had been an answer to my prayers as well.

**********

I decided I wanted a new dress for Brendan's baptism. It was time for one anyway; my dresses were getting tighter by the week, so I needed to break down and buy an actual maternity dress. Mama and I made a shopping date one Sunday afternoon.

We drove by a little place called Fran's Fashions. It was relatively new, owned and run locally like most everything else in New Ulster, and the windows were dressed so smartly that Mama insisted we stop and go in. I was hoping to find something nice right away, hating the idea of having to go over to the next county to shop at the mall.

A sales lady approached us, but I brushed her off by saying we were just looking. But after a while, my feet began hurting from all the walking and standing and coming up with nothing. Everything I tried on made me look horrible. Instead of looking pregnant, I just looked fat. I was having no luck whatsoever.

The sales lady approached us again, probably after seeing the distress on my face. She was dressed very fashionably herself, and as she came over, Mama whispered, "Let her hep you this time!"

"Could I help you find something?" she asked, eyeing me up and down. I thought her accent was "big city" and just a little put-on.

"Yes, please. I want something nice for church. Nothing complicated, nothing flashy. Just comfortable and pretty," I said.

"Well, I think I have *just* the thing. I saw you looking around, and I thought, *Now, what would I dress her in?* And I immediately thought of this."

She led me over to a rack and pulled off a dress. It was a light blue, and I loved the color. I started to make a comment about it, but before I could, she said, "Now I *know* what you're thinking: *Me? As big as I am? In* **crochet**? But I think it suits you beautifully. And it just says *summer*. No one will even *notice* those extra pounds."

I noticed Mama had turned away and had gone over to look at slips. From behind, I could see her shoulders shaking; I knew she was laughing.

**\*\*\*\*\*\*\*\*\*\***

.

The whole family had been invited to the baptism. There were going to be two other baptisms as well. It would be a high day!

"June second and hotter than you-know-what," Brendan said as he put on his tie that morning.

"You're not kidding. I'm glad you put in the air-conditioning!" I had put my hair up so I would be a little more comfortable at church. No matter how much I played with it, I couldn't get it right.

"We're going to be late, Mrs. Fitzgerald."

"Well, I don't want to go to church looking like trash."

"Trash? Girl, you're the most beautiful woman in town! No one would ever mistake you for trash." Standing behind me in front of the mirror, he put his arms around me. "Is it time yet?"

"Four more months!"

He kissed my neck and just held me. "Listen," he said, "I want to tell you something."

I stopped fussing with my hair and listened.

"I took some of the money we made from the house and opened a savings account for the baby, for college." Our eyes met in the mirror. "I know it's early, but college is getting more expensive by the day. I figured we'd better start saving now, putting some by every week. I was going to wait and surprise you after the baby was born, but I decided I should go ahead and tell you."

"You know something, Bren?" I could feel myself getting emotional again. "You're going to be the best Da in the world."

**********

With our family and the guests of the other two men being baptized, the little church was about to burst. My family alone took up an entire pew: Mama, Aunt Melba and Uncle Clive, Uncle Richard, Aunt Ida Rose, Aunt Minnie and Uncle Russ, Maggie, Wash, and George. Uncle William and Aunt Doris were so scandalized by the turn of events that they refused to come. They had sworn that Brendan was just man enough to rescue me from "that crazy church," and when the table was turned, it was more than they could take.

Maggie and Wash weren't too keen, either, but they at least said nothing and showed up. Brendan was so pleased seeing everyone. He was, after all, the newest member of the family and still didn't have all the cousins' names straight yet, so he was touched that so much of the family came to share this special day. We invited Reuben, but he bowed out, saying he had things to take care of at the farm.

After the offering was taken up, we sang the doxology, and then Pastor Yates instructed the baptismal candidates to come to the back with him and make ready. Brendan kissed my cheek as he got up to go. I was already choking back tears. The congregation sang a couple of hymns. Then the curtain in front of the baptistery opened, and Pastor Yates was standing in the water.

He said, "This is a high Sabbath! We have three men here today who have professed their love for God and faith in Jesus and have all chosen to be baptized in the same way as our Savior. It has been my pleasure getting to know all of them, and I know that you will welcome them with open arms as your new brothers in Christ." He asked Brendan to step down into the water.

"Brendan Fitzgerald comes to us today by way of Roanoke, Virginia! Some time ago, he met our dear Maureen MacKenzie, and what can I say—the boy was stuck on her! He's been faithfully coming to church here every week. He called me several weeks ago and said that there had been a revival in his heart. So here we are today. Brendan, why do you want to get baptized?"

"Because I love our Lord and Savior Jesus Christ, the Son of God, and I want to serve Him in His will all the days of my life."

Pastor Yates put his hand on Brendan's back and the other he lifted up. "Brendan Fitzgerald, because you love God and accept His Son Jesus as your one and only Savior, I baptize you in the name of the Father, and of the Son, and of the Holy Spirit." Then covering Brendan's nose with a folded handkerchief, Pastor Yates fully immersed him into the water and brought him back up to the surface. I heard myself shout, "*Amen!*"

The other two men were then baptized, but I was lost in a fog, thinking only of Brendan. While waiting on him to change and come back to join us, I leaned over to say something to Mama, but she had a distressed look on her face. I said, "What's wrong?" But all she did was shush me and stare straight ahead. I couldn't figure her out. Had someone said something to offend her?

Brendan came back and sat down. His hair was still wet, but it was combed and neat. His face glowed. He put his arm around my shoulder and pulled me to him. I started crying again. He reached in his pocket and gave me a tissue, kissed my temple and whispered, "You little cry-baby!"

"I know!" I answered, crying and laughing at the same time.

After the service, Pastor Yates was standing at the door with Brendan and the others so the congregation could meet them as they filed out. I noticed Mama hanging behind.

"Mama, what is the matter with you?" I hissed. I found her behavior bewildering.

"Nothin'. I'm just waitin' on the crowd to thin, that's all."

I decided not to wait and went on and got in line. I of course greeted Brendan with a holy kiss, and smiled at him, shook the hand of the second man, Roy Athens, and then I came to the third man, Okey Montgomery.

I shook his hand. "Welcome," I said.

He smiled and shook my hand with relish. "I believe I know your mama an' you."

"Oh?"

"You don't remember me? Well, it's been a long time, and you was just a little gal. I used to live in that little two-room house next to yourn."

I recalled a couple of people living there over the years.

"I had me a little dawg, and your mama took him one day."

*Creeper Man!* I nearly said it out loud. I could feel my heart start to pound.

"But that's alright, that's alright. I was a mean rascal back then. Your mama really got me with some bi'lin' water when I come back t' get my revenge." He gave a little laugh, still holding on to my hand. "I got sent back to th' Big House for that, for bein' drunk an' stupid. I want you to know, though," and his voice got choked, "that while I was in prison for the umpteenth time, I come to know th' Lord. I come to see that my way was all wrong, and only Jesus could save me from my life o' sin. Altogether, I spent twenty years o' my life in an' out o' prison, but the last ten I been preachin' the Word to the other inmates, 'cause I know they lost without the Lord Jesus. I couldn't wait to get out so I could get baptized good an' proper!"

This man had such a sweet smile, and his face was so radiant with God's love and forgiveness, that I had to hug him. I couldn't wait to tell Mama who he was.

Brendan leaned up and looked at me to say, "It's getting crowded here!"

Okey Montgomery laughed and said, "Sorry! I was holdin' this little gal up. I used to live next door to her. She done growed up into a nice lady!"

I went to find Mama. She was sitting on a pew, pretending to be interested in her fingernails. "Mama! You'll never believe who I just met!"

"So it was *him*, was it?  Creeper Man?  I thought I recognized him."

"He recognized you, *too*.  Mama, he's a changed man!  Come say hello!"

She got up with hesitation and then went up the aisle toward the door where Okey Montgomery stood.  She hugged Brendan, shook Roy Athens's hand, and then came face to face with ol' Creeper Man.

"I swannee," she said.  "It *is* you."

"Miz MacKenzie, I want to apologize to you.  I did wrong by comin' to your house that day.  I aimed t' do you harm, and God saw fit t' protect you.  After I got saved, I promised God that if I ever had the chance, I'd apologize t' you.  It's been a lot o' years, but I shore would like t' hear you say you fergive me."

Mama saw the radiance, too.  I saw her face flush fully red and her eyes tear up as she saw first-hand the power of God at work in this man's life.  I knew her heart was soft toward him, her brother in Christ.  "Of course I do, Mr. Montgomery.  God's changed you, and that's all that matters now.  Welcome to the family of God!"

**\*\*\*\*\*\*\*\*\*\***

We had a huge dinner at Aunt Melba's after church.  After her approval, and Mama's, Brendan and I invited Okey Montgomery to eat with us.  It seemed only right, because he had no family.  He had a big appetite for such a thin man.  Aunt Melba seemed happy to see him eat so much.

Mama told the story again of how we had rescued the little dog.  Mr. Montgomery said, "That was the best thang that coulda happened to that little critter.  I was awful mean to him.  I was mean to *ever'thang*.  I was hot as a firecracker at the time, but later on I was glad you did it."

George spoke up and asked, "So *you're* the one they called Creeper Man?"

Mama and I immediately wanted the floor to swallow us.

Mr. Montgomery said, *"Creeper Man?"*  He slammed his hand down on the table, threw his head back, and let out a holler of laughter.  He laughed and kept laughing.  Finally, he caught his breath and said, "Why, George, I been called a lot o' names in my time, but *that* beats 'em *all*!"

"I'm so sorry, Okey," Mama said, humiliated. "We just didn't know your name."

Mr. Montgomery patted Mama's hand and told her it was alright, that he was a creeper man then, but not anymore.

"The Lord turned my life around," he said. "I was in prison, and a man come in an' visited me. He got permission to visit anybody that didn't have no family, if we wanted him to, and I did. It's hard enough bein' in prison, but bein' in there with nobody on th' outside t' keer about you, well, that's just the hardest part. He ast me if I'd ever heard o' the Lord Jesus, an' I said, 'Only when I was cussin'.' An' he'd come an' visit me ever' week, and ever' visit, he'd tell me a little more about Jesus. He even give me a Bible.

"One night I was readin' the book o' Matthew, and I come acrosst Chapter 25 an' verse 36: 'I was nekked an' you clothed Me; I was sick an' you visited Me; I was in prison an' you came to Me.' I thought about my friend, Mr. Ezekiel—believe or not, that was his name—an' how he was so faithful t' come see me an' witness to me an' be my friend when I didn't have nobody. I knew then that th' Lord God had sent him to me, an' I saw that God had sent Jesus t' die in my place. That same night, I fell on m' knees an' ast Jesus to come into m' heart an' clean me up an' live there, that I wanted to serve Him for th' rest o' my life. I had got to that place all 'cause one man keered enough about me on the inside o' them prison walls t' give o' his time an' tell me about Jesus. He'd-a been here today, 'cept he done passed right before I made parole. He was a man all about *God*."

There wasn't a dry eye around the table. I even noticed that Georgie was wiping his face.

"Well, praise th' Lord," Wash said, and we all said, "Amen!"

*********

That afternoon when things were quiet and most everyone was sprawled out on sofas and chairs to nap, I stepped out on the front porch. There was a nice breeze in the late afternoon sun.

"Oh, hey," I said when I'd noticed Georgie in the porch swing. He moved over so I could sit.

"What are you up to out here all by yourself?"

He shrugged his shoulders.

I sat back in the swing and ignored the shrug. I remembered he was a little quiet over dinner, too. So we sat together, quietly, listening to the distant hum of an air conditioner.

He opened his mouth as if to speak and then closed it again. I waited, wordless. Finally he said, "How do you s'pose a man like Okey Montgomery come to believe in God?"

"Well, he told his story right there at the table. Someone followed Jesus's advice and ministered to those in prison. Okey didn't have anybody. I'm sure it made him feel good to know that this gentleman came all the way out to the penitentiary just to see him. He had no debt to Okey, but he had a debt to Jesus. I'm sure he saw that he had decent food, soap to bathe with, and God's Word to give him hope. As he said, it's a terrible place when there's no one on the outside who cares. And it was a blessing all around. This Mr. Ezekiel was a blessing to Okey, and Okey was a blessing to him. And eventually, Okey brought others to the Lord. Being introduced to our Savior has changed their lives forever. These men are forever brothers in Christ. With God, Scripture tells us, *all* things are possible."

Georgie was silent and turned his head from me. I could feel that he was struggling.

After a while, he mumbled, "I didn't tell you, but I asked Lydia to be my girlfriend."

I smiled and put my arm around him. "I'm so happy," I said. "I wondered then about you two!"

"Well, don't be *too* happy," he replied, almost snarling. "She said that while she liked me as a person, and even had considered wanting me as her beau, she said she couldn't allow herself to be unequally yoked. Unequally *yoked*? What in thunder does *that* mean?"

"Well, it's advice from the Bible. Most people see it as council on not marrying someone who is an unbeliever, but it certainly stretches further than that. Business partners, for example. How can you conduct your business with an unbeliever when his moral views are different from yours?"

"Well, enough about that."

"I'm sorry I get so preachy," I said, feeling a little embarrassed.

"This business with Okey, when he told his story today. After all them stories all y'all told, I expected him t' come in brandishin' a machete! But here was this quiet little man, holdin' his Bible like it was his life's blood. Aunt Mo, there just has to be more. I mean, what's in it for him?"

"Eternal life," I answered. "The key, Georgie boy, is not to expect that everything in this life will go your way. It won't. What you *can* expect, though, is His hand holding you though it all." Suddenly I remembered Mama's words to me when I was so depressed. "'*See? I have engraved you in the Palm of My hand.*'"

"Do you hate that ol' thang you were married to before?"

I sucked in some breath. "Ohhhhhh, I used to. I used to, Son. It was only by prayer asking that the Holy Spirit love him through me. I just didn't have the power on my own."

We were quiet for a few minutes. Finally I said, "I may be jumping the gun a bit, and I'm sorry if I have it wrong, but I hope you don't start getting serious about church again just to win over Lydia. Christianity is a life style change brought on by a heart change. Don't pretend you have a relationship with God just to make her love you. Nothing in that but disaster."

His silence made me wonder, but I said no more.

George ran his fingers through his red hair and then sat forward, his elbows resting on his knees. "I love you, Aunt Mo. I need to tell you that more."

"I love you, too, George."

With that he got up and opened the screen door to go inside.

"Going to church in the morning?" I asked softly.

He hesitated in the door for just a second. "I'm studyin' on it," he said.

# Chapter 26    *A Hot Summer*

Independence Day came again, and we nearly called off the party because it was so hot. Mama's house was ashambles because of the move, so Aunt Melba and Uncle Clive were hosting it that year. She was planning to have us all eat on the huge expanse of a front porch she had. I was dreading it because of the heat, but she assured me that the ceiling fans out there would not only keep us cool as cucumbers but would keep the flies away as well.

My chore was to make something vegetarian, "Or y'all gon' hafta eat meat like the *rest* of us!" Aunt Melba had told me.

Brendan suggested a spinach lasagna. "I know that's not very Fourth of July-ish, but I've been wanting some of it," he said, and his eyebrows were up in a "Please?" position. Of course I would. I got an early start that morning so I could beat the heat. Even with air, the kitchen got hot with the oven on.

"Murdah," I said, "if Aunt Melba thinks it's going to be cool under those fans, she needs to think again!"

Brendan began fanning me with a paper plate.

"Be ready with that out at the party!"

We also were taking a huge watermelon, something I craved on almost a daily basis. "Just put that at my place," I had said when we bought it. "I'm not sharing."

When everything was done and cooled enough to pack, Brendan started loading the car. I stood on the front porch and watched him and inwardly cursed the heat. It hadn't rained in over a month.

"I don't suppose," I remarked as he came back up on the porch, "that we're going to have fireworks this year."

"Oh, no. Uncle Russ already told me we wouldn't. Fire ordinance."

We went back in the house. "Well, I don't know about you, love, but I'm changing clothes." He was wearing a polo shirt and shorts. "It's not even noon, and I'm about to cook in this shirt. I hope you don't mind, but I'm going to wear a tank top."

"No, I don't mind. You may as well be comfortable."

I had put on the coolest thing I had, a thin cotton sleeveless maternity shift and flip-flops. My hair was piled on my head as well.

Brendan took two stairs at a time toward our bedroom. "Girl, I feel like shaving my head!"

"I hope you're kidding!" I shouted after him. I waited for the sound of the razor. After a few minutes I was satisfied that his hair was safe, and I went back into the kitchen for some water. He came in a few minutes later, wearing a white tank top, shorts, and flip-flops. I smiled. His arms were very muscular, and I couldn't help blushing at the sight of them.

"Ready to go?" he asked, not understanding my smile.

"Now or never," I said.

\*\*\*\*\*\*\*\*\*

There were a few cars parked at Aunt Melba's when we got there. Cud'din Willie was there with his family. I was surprised to see Uncle William and Aunt Doris. She came with the same sour expression on her face that I'd become accustomed to over the years. I wondered if she looked that way in her high school yearbook; Little Melba, much to Aunt Melba's delight, came down for the party; Uncle Richard, Uncle Michael and Aunt Sally were on their way; Ida Rose; Ida Rose's twin Lois and her husband Martin; and Aunt Minnie and Uncle Russ came in last. Except for Cud'din Willie's children, there were no young cousins.

George had invited Lydia. He seemed to be stuck on her, alright. She had grown even prettier since I'd last seen her. I wondered why she decided to come since she'd turned down his proposal of his being her beau. But here she was, and he seemed happy.

Uncle Clive kept the grill busy, and he was sweating profusely. Brendan gave him a hand with it so he could go under the porch fans and cool off a little. I was watching Brendan flipping hamburgers, and he certainly seemed to be enjoying himself. He caught me watching him and said, "Oops! I didn't want you to see me having fun with meat!" Then he began laughing at the ridiculousness of what he'd said, and from the look on my face.

I laughed. "You're a grown man, Brendan Fitzgerald! Do what you want." He then made a great show of flipping the hamburgers higher. He was quite good at catching them.

I helped Mama and Aunt Melba with the plastic dinnerware and paper plates. Unfortunately for us, the fans were blowing them around, so Aunt Melba decided to anchor them down with a chicken leg. When she turned her back, Uncle Clive took the chicken leg and began eating it. Plates drifted everywhere.

"Clive! What in tarnation are you *doin'*?" she snapped.

"I'm hungry. I thought you put that there for *me*."

"I swanee," she muttered. After we gathered the plates back together, Aunt Melba held them down with a full pitcher of sweet tea.

Dinnertime came, and what a feast. The fans were on full-blast and did indeed keep the flies away, as well as the paper napkins. Even over all the den of everyone talking at once, I heard Aunt Doris complain about her food getting cold. I watched as Aunt Melba and Mama exchanged looks. Mama rolled her eyes and went back to chewing. The food on the plates *was* getting cold, but the day was so hot that I didn't care.

Brendan leaned over and said, "This lasagna is delicious, love."

"Thank you. I'm glad you're happy with it. I noticed everyone *else* passed it over."

"Well, Mo, you know these guys are *hard-core*."

I giggled. He was right. I looked at everyone else's plates, and they were covered in ribs, burgers, and various chicken pieces. I noticed that Cud'din Willie had barbeque sauce on his nose.

"I'm saving room for that watermelon," I said. I had been craving it all day.

Reuben had brought horseshoes and after lunch was setting everything up to play. I wouldn't be playing because it was too hot, but after the game got started, it looked like so much fun that I wanted to try my hand at it. I hadn't played horseshoes for years. I watched Brendan for a few minutes, and for someone who had never played, he was quite good. I couldn't let him out-do me.

I walked out to the yard and stood beside Reuben. "Oo-wee, it's hot, gal," he said. "You need to sit down?"

"No, I'm okay. All this shade is nice." We were standing under three sugar maples that loomed in the back and offered shade for the entire yard.

"Ol' Brendan's pretty good for a city boy," he remarked.

I felt proud. "Yes, he is. He sets his mind to something, and there's no stopping him."

Brendan had finished his turn and came over. "Mo, what are you doing out here? You need to be under those fans, or else in the house."

"I'm alright. I thought I'd take a turn at horseshoes. You played so well that I wanted to see if I could beat you."

Brendan snorted. "That's mighty big talk for a little mama." He regarded me for a moment then said, "One game. But if you get too hot..."

"Yes, sir, I'll go sit on the porch like a good girl."

He wasn't one to boss me around, but in my condition, he took a little extra care. He still remembered how sick I'd been. I hadn't forgotten, either.

"We're all just warming up right now," he continued. "I got a ringer and a leaner. See if you can beat *that*."

I went out and studied the situation. I threw the first horseshoe and got a leaner. I turned around and looked at my opponents with a smirk. Brendan bowed to me, and Reuben clapped. I threw the second shoe with overconfidence, and it landed a foot beyond the stake.

"Your game, gentlemen," I said, as I breezed past them and headed back to the front porch.

"Aren't you going to play?" Brendan called after me.

I kept walking and didn't turn around. "I have a date with a watermelon."

Reuben laughed.

"I do declare, look at all them napkins on the ground," Aunt Melba said. She and the other women were cleaning the tables for dessert. I heard the watermelon calling my name, but I said, "I'll pick them up, Aunt Melba."

There were dozens of paper napkins scattered in the front yard. Those fans had done a great job of liberating them. The front yard, unlike the back, had no shade trees, just bushes and a few short evergreens, so I decided to make quick work of it and get back under the shelter of the front porch.

Stoop, grab, shove in plastic bag. I hummed in rhythm as I worked. About the tenth stoop, grab, and shove, sweat was pouring down my face, and I felt light-headed. Before I knew it, I had hit the ground like a stone.

I came to with Brendan leaning over me. Mama was wiping my face with a wet cloth. Maggie was standing over us with a black umbrella to keep the sun off. Everyone else was standing around watching and offering help. In the distance, I could hear an ambulance siren.

"Mo? Mozie, can you hear me?" Brendan asked, panic written all over his face. I tried to speak but felt a little confused.

The paramedics arrived and jumped into action. They put me on the gurney after checking my vital signs and decided I need to go to the emergency room. I heard one of them tell Brendan that he wasn't allowed in the ambulance; he would have to follow in his own vehicle, but they assured him that I was going to be well-taken care of, and that taking me in was just precautionary measures because of the baby.

On the trip to the hospital, the paramedic in back with me kept asking me questions. "How do you feel, Mrs. Fitzgerald? Do you know where you are? How far along are you?"

I answered the questions, and she seemed pleased. She gave me a spoon of chipped ice. "Just let that melt in your mouth, honey," she said. "I can tell you're dry. We have some fluids going, and that will help you, too."

I thanked her and asked for more ice. Nothing tasted so good.

In the exam room in the ER, I was given a sonogram to check on the baby. The nurses were very professional and kind, and when all the activity was over, I was overcome with exhaustion and fell asleep. When I woke up, Brendan and Mama were there, each holding my hands.

"Hey, Mo," he said, kissing my forehead. "You gave us quite a scare." He smiled down at me, the worry on his face fading as he saw me smile back at him.

"I'm sorry," I mumbled.

"Not to worry. The doc says you and the baby are just fine." His voice was so tender that it made tears come to my eyes.

"Girl, if I'd a knowed you was out there pickin' up them stupid napkins..." Mama's voice trailed off. "Well, I reckon you too old for a whoopin'." She smiled at me and wiped her nose with a tissue.

"I'm okay. Mama. I'm okay."

"They're going to let us take you home now in a minute," Brendan said, "as soon as this last fluid bag is finished. Are you warm enough? Can I get you anything?"

"Watermelon," I said.

**\*\*\*\*\*\*\*\*\*\***

I stayed the rest of the day at home in the bed. The cool sheets felt wonderful. Brendan came up with a bowl of chunked watermelon, just like I liked it, seeds removed.

"For you, love," he said and sat on the bed facing me. He was grinning.

"What are you up to?" I asked.

"I was just thinking. Oh, what we men will do to keep you MacKenzie women happy!"

I didn't understand what he was getting at.

"Reuben came over a while ago to go over an idea with me. He would have come up to see you, but he said you needed your rest."

"That was nice of him to come by."

"Well, we started talking and I asked him about Mama. I just came right out and asked him if he had any plans that involved her. I felt like it was my duty, after all."

"Duty? Oh, Brendan, you're just being *nosy*! You've been around the MacKenzies too much!"

He smiled. "Let me tell you what he said, Mo! He told me he was going to turn his farm over to his son and move to town—*if* Mama would agree to marry him!"

"Brendy!"

"You women seem to cast a spell on us. Must be the red hair."

"I wonder what she'll say?"

"I hope she says yes. I think Reuben is a great guy, and he sure seems to care a lot about Mama. And you, too. Let me tell you why he came here in the first place."

He leaned over and ate a piece of watermelon.

"Bren, stop stalling."

"He had the idea to come over and clean the woodwork and get all the painting done. He says you're not up to it, and we need to get this done before the baby comes. We *do* have a nursery to fix up! So we're going to start tomorrow. The women—Mama, Maggie, and Aunt Melba— are coming in the morning to wash and polish the woodwork. Then tomorrow afternoon, Reuben, Uncle Clive, George, and I will start painting. Wash will be over as soon as he gets off work."

"Brendan, it'll be finished in no time!"

"Yep, and then you and I can go furniture shopping for the baby's room." He was giving that broad smile of his that I loved so much.

**********

The work began the next morning. Mama, Maggie, and Aunt Melba all came together in one car. I thought this was odd because they all complained about each others' driving. But here they were, and in they came with buckets and rags and a couple of bottles of wood soap. No one would let me do anything, so I just made sure I had plenty of sweet tea and ice ready. I sat down a lot like I promised, and all of us chatted while the washing and polishing was going on.

"After we get all this done," Maggie said, "we should go ahead and roll out the paper to keep the floors clean. Then when the men come in, they can get to paintin' right away."

"Good idea, Maggs," Mama said.

Mama was washing the window frames, Aunt Melba the doors, and Maggie was on the floor washing the base boards. They were pretty quick and very thorough. I was sorry I couldn't join them. I was itching to do something to help.

"Anybody want tea?" I asked.

Maggie sat on her bum and puffed. "Tea would hit the spot right now!"

The others agreed. I was happy to finally be doing something. I loaded up a tray with ice-filled glasses and the tea pitcher and headed for the dining room. I poured everyone a tall glass, and we sat for a few minutes and they rested. Before I was ready, they all got up and started to work again, all of them cleaning the wainscoting, and when they finished they changed their cleaning water and made their way into the hallway. It was long and had wainscoting, too. I brought a kitchen chair into the hall and sat.

"Can't I do anything to help?" I asked.

"You can be quiet and make sure you keep that baby healthy," Aunt Melba said.

There was a duet of "uh-huh" from the other two. I got up and went back in the kitchen to think about lunch. While I was considering what I would be making, I had some watermelon.

I got up from time to time to make sure they had plenty of tea, and I noticed that they worked like a swarm of bees, never getting out of the others' sight.

By the time lunch was ready, those women had every bit of woodwork on the first floor washed and polished and shining like new. The window panes gleamed. I was very pleased that everything looked so beautiful. I couldn't thank them enough.

"Well, let's have lunch!" I said, feeling very happy.

"I hope you made meat," Aunt Melba said.

"Sissy!" Mama chided, "Leave that girl alone about *meat*! We'll eat whatever she's fixed and *like* it."

"Mama, I *do* have some *chicken*! It's store-bought, and I had to have someone deliver it. I knew you'd want something more than what *I* eat."

Maggie put her arms around me and squeezed.

"Bless you, child," Aunt Melba said.

**\*\*\*\*\*\*\*\*\*\***

The men came in after lunch and began painting right away. They were thrilled with Maggie's idea of having the floors already covered. The women all went home to rest, so I only had my sweet tea routine to keep me busy. The men weren't chatterboxes like the women, and they also didn't work in a pile—they were scattered around and each starting a different room-so I decided to go to my room and read. Before I knew it, I was asleep.

Brendan was getting into bed when I woke up. My reading lamp was still on, and my book had fallen to the floor.

"Bren? What time is it?"

"A little after 10."

"Oh, my! I've slept for hours!"

"You must have needed it, love."

"I guess. So everyone's gone? I was going to make y'all supper!"

"Not to worry. I found plenty of leftovers, and everyone had their fill. I cleaned up the rest of that lasagna, by the way." He lay down close to me. "Do you feel alright?"

"Yes, just a little confused. I feel like it should be morning!"

"Hmmm, I sure don't. I'm bushed! But it looks beautiful, Mo. We'll finish up this week for sure. All we have left are the second coats and touch-ups. We did all the walls and ceilings. Tomorrow the women will come in to wash the upstairs, and we'll finish painting downstairs then start up here."

"No wonder you're so tired! My hard-working love."

"You know," he said, "this is another one of those times when God has taken something awful and turned it into something beautiful. You and the baby are okay. On top of that blessing, our family and Reuben were willing to come here and help me get this painting done. Maureen, there was no way I was going to have this done in time for the baby. Once again, we've been blessed."

"Yes, we have. We are surrounded by people who love us."

Brendan smiled and said, "Those women."

"What do you mean?" I asked.

"Maggie passed the word on to us to all stay in the same room."

"*They* did that."

"You know why?"

I shook my head, frowning.

Brendan gave a little laugh. "They wanted to stick together in case something happened."

"Something happened? I don't understand."

He waved his hands in the air and said, "Woooooooo!"

I couldn't believe it. "They really think this house is haunted? Oh my *word*!"

"They'll get over it eventually," he said, smiling, and closing his eyes.

I needed to get up and get ready for bed, which seemed an odd thing to do since I just woke up. I said, "Brendy, let's have prayer and then I'll go brush my teeth."

He didn't answer. I sat up and looked at him. He was fast asleep. Quietly I got out of bed and slipped out of the room. I couldn't wait to see what the house looked like.

# Chapter 27    The Arrival

Summer was coming to a close. We survived August and Dog Days when the rains finally came again. By mid-September, I was training a new girl to take my place at Dr. Liske's office.

Brendan and I decided that I would quit work the week before my due date and stay home once the baby was born. I loved the idea. He said we'd get by on one income because we'd put by, and also we had no mortgage. "We have whiskey in the jar, as the saying goes," Brendan said. If we were careful, we'd be fine. Any sacrifice would be worth it to be able to keep our baby at home and see him grow every day.

Jean took the news hard, but she certainly understood. She had her own announcement to make; she was having a baby in the spring. "Ol' Doc may be havin' a whole new office staff by next year!"

The *Dearbháil* was finished on the inside as far as fixing up, thanks to the beautiful gift of time and work from our family and Reuben. Every Sunday, Brendan and I went furniture shopping. We completed the nursery first. I thought it was beautiful. Then we found some really great antiques to furnish the sitting room. Piece by piece, Brendan told me, we'd be a fully-functioning house.

The last Friday in September was my final day at the office. Dr. Liske and Jean threw me a little going-away party at the lunch hour. Brendan left his office and came over. It was a bittersweet afternoon. I kept crying and laughing in cycles.

As I was getting ready to leave, Dr. Liske asked me to step into his office.

"Yes, sir?" I asked when I'd closed the door behind me.

"Sit down, Maureen," he said, waving with his hand. I did. He sat on the edge of his desk. "I just wanted you to know how much I will miss you. You have been an excellent employee. To be honest with you, I think you probably saved my practice here, taking things in hand and getting it straightened out."

I started to speak but he held up his hand to stop me. He wasn't good at speaking from his heart, and he wanted to get everything said at once.

"I will never find another Maureen MacKenzie! You have been a blessing to me, Maureen. Not just here, but in my home life. You are such a godly woman—oh, yes, I have been watching you!—and I have learned a lot about faith from you. It has brought me closer to my wife. And even more, it has brought me closer to *God*."

By this time I was choking back tears. He silently handed me a box of tissues from his desk.

"So," he said softly, grinning, "what are you going to name that baby?"

As I wiped my eyes I said, "Elizabeth Doyle if it's a girl, after my mother. Timothy Brance, Brendan's middle name and my father's first, if it's a boy."

"Those are nice choices."

"Thank you," I said and smiled. "I hope the baby thinks so!"

He took my hand as I stood up. "I hope we will see one another again. Let me know when that Fitzgerald baby is born. If he is like his mama, he will come into the world red-haired and screaming."

At this, I laughed through my tears.

Dr. Liske then reached in his jacket pocket and pulled out an envelope. "I wanted to give you this in private. It isn't much, but use it for however you see fit. Thank you, Maureen. Thank you most kindly." Dr. Liske hugged me. I could see that he had tears in his eyes.

"Thank you, Dr. Liske. Thank you for giving me this job when I really needed one. It has been a blessing to *me*, too."

Brendan and I said our goodbyes to the staff. I had to hug Jean twice, and we cried like babies. Brendan made a trip to the car with all the gifts we'd gotten.

Jean hugged me again. "Don't you *dare* forget me," she said.

"Never!" I cried.

Brendan returned, and saying our goodbyes again, we closed the office door behind us for the last time. We got settled in the car and I was still blowing my nose and wiping my face. On the drive home, I remembered the envelope. I took the card out and read it. It had a pram on the cover, and inside, Dr. Liske wrote a short but sweet note. *To the Fitzgerald Baby. You are blessed!* I choked up again.

A small paper was folded up in it, and I opened it. Dr. Wolfgang Liske had given us a check for one thousand dollars.

**\*\*\*\*\*\*\*\*\*\***

I was getting impatient for the baby to come. My due date came and went, and it didn't seem that it would ever happen. Mama came over one afternoon to keep me company, and as she and I had a cup of decaf—which she saw no logic in, but drank it anyway—she asked me had she ever told me the story of my birthday.

"Yes, Mama, you've told me."

"Well, sit still, 'cause I'm fixin' to tell you *ag'in*.

"I was like you, expectin' all through the summer, and I was just *miserable*! It hadn't rained in a good while, but the day you was born, the sky opened up and the flood waters come down! I declare, all of heaven opened up! Well, I commenced t' havin' contractions, so Brance, he got me out in the car in all that pourin' rain, along with Rose an' Maggie, 'cause they wadn't nobody to stay with 'em. We got out to the car, and your Da could barely see t' drive, the rain was comin' down so hard. We finally made it to th' end of th' road an' got to the bridge, an' bless Pat, it was *gone*! Mangy Creek had flooded and washed that bridge right out! There wadn't a thing to do but turn around and go back home.

"When we got back an' got in, he picked up the phone to call the hospital, and hanged if *that* wadn't out, too! We didn't have no neighbors back then. There was the Creeper Man house, but it was empty. This was all countryside, and the nearest neighbors were on the other side o' *that bridge*!

"I was in bad shape by now. You was comin', and in a hurry! Brance got Rose an' Maggie and took 'em to their bedroom and says, 'Rose, you a big girl now, an' I need you to look after our Maggie. I don't care what you hear on th' other side o' that wall, *don't you come out that door*, you hear? You stay here with Maggie, *no matter what*, until you hear me call your name.' I heard Rose say, 'Yes, Papa,' as brave as she could, but I could tell she was skeered. Heck, *I* was skeered!"

I was cuddled in a throw on the other end of the sofa where Mama was sitting. "So what happened *next*, Mama?"

"Well. Your Da put me to bed and then went to th' kitchen, put some water on t' boil, got the sharpest knife he could find, all the clean towels, some twine, an' come back to the bedroom, rollin' up his sleeves. He says, 'Bess, I guess we it. We got to do this thang.'

"I was so skeered, 'cause yo' sisters had been borned in the hospital, and the daddies wadn't allowed back in the room with the mamas, so I didn't know what Brance thought *he* was gon' do, not ever havin' seen a birth before. He put some clean towels under my bottom, talkin' to me the whole time to try to keep me calm, says, 'Bess, you need to be prayin', Sweetheart, 'cause it won't be long *now*.'

"I had his hand in a death-grip, prayin' out loud to beat the band, just askin' our sweet Jesus to help Brance out, and help me not to be skeered. Your Da says, 'Bess, I be needin' my hand back now!' The last contraction come, and I thought I was dyin', and he was tellin' me to push as hard as I could, and I swear, I thought it'd kill me. They give me somethin' when your sisters were borned, so I had no idea how hard havin' a baby could really be.

"Then all of a sudden, it was all over, and out you come, and Brance went to work on you like he knowed what he was doin'. He got that cord tied off and cut, and got you wrapped up and handed you up to me. 'We got us another little gal, Bess,' he says, an' he looked so happy. He then set to gettin' me cleaned up, and moppin' up all the blood. He got me a clean night gown an' helped me get that on. I says, 'Brance MacKenzie, how in tarnation did you know what to do?' An' he says, 'Bess, love, I had to deliver my baby sister when I was only 13. I ain't never forgot that. My mama talked me through th' whole thang.'

"Well, I'd never heard tell of such a thang! All I knew is that I had been blessed by God with Brance MacKenzie, and He saw fit to bring us another baby girl, all safe an' sound! Then your Da, he took the placenta and went an' buried it out under one o' them apple trees."

"Third one down by the fence," I said.

Mama nodded. "Third one down by th' fence."

"And *then* what happened, Mama?" I asked.

She smiled. "Why, she growed up to be the purtiest lady you ever saw, and had her a sweet husband, an' her own baby, and lived the rest of her life happy as a clam at high tide."

**********

A cold front came in in mid-October. Brendan decided to turn the boiler on for the radiators to knock off the chill in the house. We got ready to go to bed that night, and I said, as I had for over a week, "Maybe tonight." We said our prayers and went to sleep, cuddled together under the blankets.

During the night Brendan woke me up. "Mo, Maureen, wake up. I think you wet the bed!"

I sat up and pulled the blankets back.

"No, my waters broke! Brendan, my *waters* broke! We need to get to the hospital!"

He dressed quickly, and I put on sweat pants and a pullover sweater. Brendan grabbed the bag, and we were out of the house within minutes. On the way to the hospital, I gave the maternity ward a call to expect us. Then I called Mama. She was already in bed asleep.

In her new house, she had a phone right by the bed.

"Hello?" she asked sleepily. "This better be good at *this* hour."

"Mama! We're on the way to the hospital. I'm in labor!"

Mama didn't say anything. She slammed the receiver in the cradle. There was a fire lit under her. I knew she'd call Maggie and everyone else, and because I was having a contraction, I left the phone alone.

"Oh, love, are we almost there?"

"Almost. Not far at all." He was doing such a good job keeping his face calm, but if I'd closed my eyes, I would have sworn I was in the car with Aunt Melba behind the wheel.

The hospital was only another block away. Brendan careened into the parking lot and parked under the emergency entrance. He helped me out of the car, but I was having another contraction, so we had to stand there for a moment. A nurse saw us through the glass and ran out with a wheel chair. She got me wheeled inside and Brendan went back out to move the car.

"Name?" the lady behind admitting asked.

"Maureen Fitzgerald." I handed her my information. She seemed to be in no particular hurry.

Brendan came in. "Honey, why aren't you upstairs? Ma'am, she's about to have this *baby*!"

"I can't help that, sir. I got to get her information."

That's when my calm, sweet husband lost it. "Well, then you can follow *me*! I'm taking her upstairs, so if you need to know anything, you need to grab a pencil and *come on*!"

He had that wheelchair spun around and headed for the elevator before she could get up from the desk. She yelled something to him, but he kept going. We got into the elevator, and the doors closed on the yelling voice.

"They're probably going to have security waiting for us," I said.

"Well, as long as I get you where you need to be, I don't care."

Sure enough, when the elevator door opened, a security guard was standing there waiting. Brendan was tall, but this man towered over him. Brendan didn't flinch.

"You Fitzgerald?" he asked.

"I am," Brendan said.

"Well, you need to get on to the maternity ward. They're expectin' you with your missus. That gal downstairs? Let me handle *her*. You get your wife settled and then you worry about that paper work." He shook Brendan's hand and then patted mine. "God bless you, Sister." Looking back at Brendan he said, "Straight down the hall, to the left." Then he got in the elevator and the doors closed.

I was about to say, "What a nice man," when Brendan jerked that wheelchair around and pushed me down the hall. I was hanging on for dear life. We made it to maternity, and they took me right in. "You'd better go take care of business," I told him. "I'll be alright. I'm in good hands. I promise I won't have this baby till you get back."

I had a few more contractions while he was gone. I was beginning to be afraid that I *would* have the baby without him. Shortly, Mama and Maggie blew in, huffing and puffing.

"Girl! We saw Brendan downstairs! Is everything alright?" Maggie gasped.

"Yes, I'm fine. He's just getting me admitted. He shouldn't be long now."

They sat down in the chairs and caught their breath.

"Lawsey me, when Mama called, I thought I'd have a heart attack!"

"I don't even think I said goodbye, did I, Mo?" Mama asked.

I giggled. "No. You just slammed the phone in my ear, and I figured you were either on your way, or you thought I was an obscene caller."

They laughed.

"Well, I got Maggie on the phone. She drove to my house and picked me up so we could come together. Wash is comin' later. He said *somebody* needed to get some sleep."

"I'll call George tomorrow," Maggie said. "No use wakin' him up in the middle of the night when there ain't a thing *he* can do. I *did* get Rose. She said she would work something out to come. She sends her love and says you and Brendan are in her prayers."

"Thanks for takin' care of all that, Maggs," I said.

"Hey," she said, "I brought you this. Just finished it today. Sorry it's not wrapped."

Maggie handed me a folded quilt, baby-sized. Both sides were made from the Fitzgerald tartan, and the quilting on it formed the Fitzgerald crest. I had never seen anything so intricate.

"Maggie, this is *beautiful*!" I said. "It must have taken you forever!"

"It did! I wanted to have it ready for you to bring the baby home in it. I'm almost glad she's not in any big hurry, or I wouldn't have got it to you on time!"

Maggie hugged me and kissed my cheek, something she rarely did with anyone.

I felt another contraction. I groaned.

"Girl, have they give you anything yet?" Mama asked.

I shook my head no.

"*Um.* Well, I guess they don't give that twilight sleep anymore, do they?" she asked of Maggie.

"Mercy, no. That was some awful stuff. They give a' anesthetic of some kind, but it ain't like that old stuff they used to use."

"How do *you* know so much?" Mama wanted to know.

"I *read*," she said, sounding insulted.

Brendan came in, also huffing and puffing. The hospital had seen a lot of running on this night. "Mo, are you okay?"

"I'm fine, love. No baby yet, though. I told you I'd wait!" I smiled at him.

He pulled up a chair at the head of the bed. "How are y'all?" he asked Mama and Maggie.

"We made it!" Mama said. "Now that Brendan's here, Mo, get on with it. We want to see this baby!"

"Brendan, look at the quilt Maggie made!" I spread it across me so he could see it.

He traced his finger along the stitching. "This is the *family crest*!" he said. "Maggie! This is incredible!"

Maggie blushed. "Well, I went back an' forth about what quilt pattern to use, an' then th' idea came to me to just use the tartan and stitch the crest on it. I found a picture of it an' traced it out on graph paper." She looked pleased, but she was embarrassed to talk about herself or her craft.

"You're a true artist," he said and got up and hugged her. Maggie blushed again.

"I can't believe you didn't want to know if it's a girl or boy," she said to me, looking down.

"Well, it won't be long now till we find out," I answered.

The night wore on. The contractions kept coming, but nothing was happening.

A nurse came in and gave me an injection through my IV line. "This will help you relax," she said. "It'll help relieve some of the pain."

"Thank you," I said, and I could feel the effect immediately.

Maggie said, "Oh! I forgot to tell y'all what happened two nights ago! You know Wash spent th' night out huntin', and that was the first night I'd be by myself at Mama's house."

Mama said, "It's *your* house now, girl."

Maggie smiled and went on. "Well, I put th' cat out earlier in th' evenin'. I was fixin' to go to bed, an' I looked out the winda to see if she was ready to come in. Well, bless Pat, what did I see but a *man* layin' out in th' *yard*!"

"A *what*?" we all asked together.

"Yep, he was layin' out in th' yard, near the porch. I went t' one winda an' then another, an' sure enough, there he was, an' I thought, 'They's a man out in my yard, an' he's just waitin' on me to go to *bed*! Then he's gon' come up here and *tear th' door down*! Well, I'll just tear *him* up *first*.' So I went and got the pistol..." at this, Brendan's jaw dropped and Mama gasped, "...and I commenced to goin' from this winda to that one, and finally it come to me that I'd better turn the light on an' give him a chance to run. So I flipped on the light, an' it wadn't a blame thang but a *nandina* bush, leanin' over makin' a shada! But I tell ya, it looked just *like* a man! You could see th' *eyes*! I was glad I didn't call 911, or I woulda been in th' *mess*!"

I laughed, but it was a small one, because I felt so close to sleep. I started to tell Maggie how crazy I thought she was, but Mama was talking, and I began drifting in and out of sleep. Somewhere in the distance I heard Aunt Melba rush in, saying she wasn't allowed to stay and had to go back out. Because I needed sleep, Mama and Maggie decided to go to the waiting room with Aunt Melba and let me rest. Brendan stayed with me.

"I love you," he whispered as he stroked my hair.

"I love *you*," I said groggily.

"I'm sorry you have to go through this," he said. "I wish it didn't have to be so painful."

"I'll be alright," I whispered. "It's for our baby."

Brendan said, "I want to tell you something before the baby comes because I have a feeling it's going to get busy in here soon!"

I was feeling groggy, and his voice sounded far away. "What is it?"

"I was thinking this morning about how blessed I am. These days with you have been extraordinary. God has blessed me in more ways than I could have ever hoped. If I had to go through everything I have in the past, all the loss and grief, just to get here with *you* today, I would do it. I am the most blessed man in the world, Maureen." The expression on his face was one of pure love.

"I know God led me to you, Brendan. He was holding my hand through that dark path. It was worth going down, finding you at the end."

I slept. Sometime in my sleep, a contraction woke me. I turned on my side and groaned. Brendan wiped my face with a cool cloth. Was I dreaming? I tried staying awake but couldn't manage. Brendan was speaking to me, and I wanted to answer, but I was so tired.

This went on all night. I turned on my other side, and I saw daylight just coming through the window. "Is she here yet?" I think I may have asked.

"What did you say, Mo?"

"Brendan?"

"I'm here."

I gripped his hand as I had another contraction. "Help me," I said. "Help me. Will this ever be *over*? Oh, *Brendan*!"

"I'm sorry, Mo," and I could hear the hurt in his voice. "I'm so sorry, love."

When the nurse came in again to check on me, he asked her how much longer she thought it would be.

"She's not dilating very much," she said. "I can give her a little more for the pain."

"Please," I said. "*Please* help me." As the medicine went into my arm, I could feel myself going to sleep.

Her voice was fading away as she said, "The doctor will be in soon."

I dreamed about Papa. He was with Mama and delivering their baby. I said, "Papa, do you need any help?"

"I need you to pray, Daughter, an' pray hard, or you'll likely not be borned!"

"I'm prayin', Papa! I want so much to be borned!"

"Mo, who are you talking to?" Brendan asked, close to my ear.

"I have to help Papa," I answered.

"You must be dreaming." He kissed my forehead.

"I need to get *borned*."

"You're right here, love." His voice was so soft and sweet.

"Brendan, I love you. I've missed you so much!"

"I've been right here. I'm right here."

Dr. Williams came in. Through the fog I could hear him ask me how I was feeling. He was checking me out, and I felt embarrassed because Brendan was sitting right there, and I felt exposed to the whole world.

"You haven't dilated as much as you should have, Maureen. We may have to consider a caesarian."

"No, I can't. I promised Brendan he could be there. I have to have this baby." I forced myself to say through the medication.

Dr. Williams grinned and pulled the sheet back over me. "Well, *Baby* may have more to say about *that*. We'll wait a little longer and see what happens."

"Mo, if you need to have a caesarian, then that's what we'll do. I can't see you going through this all day like you did all night." Brendan spoke firmly, yet kindly.

I fell back to sleep. I woke up to another contraction. "Oh, God, help me," and I began to cry. I was determined not to scream out, but it was hard not to. "Oh, God, oh, God."

Brendan hit the buzzer for the nurse. She came in right away. "She can't take this anymore," he said. "Get Dr. Williams and tell him I want this caesarian done as soon as possible."

"Nooo, Brendan," I cried. "I want to have this baby myself. *Please.* Dr. Williams will help you!"

"Mo, you don't know what you're saying. Please calm down. I'm trying to do what's best for you and the baby."

"I'll call him," the nurse said.

I was crying. Another contraction came, this one so much harder than the others, that I rolled over again to try to get away from it. Dr. Williams came in.

"I'm glad you changed you mind," he said, patting my foot.

"No, it was my idea, Dr. Williams. "If she can't have this baby naturally, I'm all for the caesarian. She's been at this long enough."

"Well, I'll get the nurse to prep her and get her upstairs. I think that's wise, Brendan. We want this baby to be as healthy as possible." With that, he turned and left the room.

"No!" I cried. "You can't let them *do* this, Brendan!" I began having another contraction. I felt like I was being squeezed to death. "Oh, God—please, *please!*"

The nurse came in. She lifted the sheet off and gasped. "Why, honey, you don't need *surgery! You're having your baby!*" She pressed the intercom to the nurses' desk and said help was needed STAT. "We're having a baby down here!"

Suddenly pandemonium seemed to break loose. I felt a pain that I had never had in my life, but I stifled back a scream.

"She's crowning," a nurse said. "No time to get her to delivery! Maureen, honey, I need you to push as hard as you can!"

I was crushing Brendan's hand, but he never complained. "Oh, please!" I begged one last time. Then suddenly there was a huge relief, and I felt everything let go.

The three nurses gasped all at once. "Oh, he's beautiful!" one of them said.

Then I heard a hardy cry from a baby, our baby. Brendan was kissing my face. I felt his tears fall into my eyelids. "My love, oh, my love," he sobbed.

The nurse placed our baby in my arms. Red-haired and screaming, Timothy Brance Fitzgerald had come into the world.

# Epilogue

aureen, that doesn't sound very *manly*."

"Well, he *isn't* a *man* yet. He's still a newborn!"

Brendan and I were sitting in the porch swing of the *Dearbháil*. It was the first week of November, and a chilly morning, but we had decided to have our tea outside. There wouldn't be many days left that we could enjoy the swing.

"I still think you ought to just call him by his name," he said.

"We haven't *decided* what we're going to call him yet," I countered. "Timmy, Tim, Timothy, which I think sounds too grown-up, or Brance. So for now, he's my Butter Bean."

Brendan took a drink of his tea and regarded our son. "I just hope he doesn't go into kindergarten telling everyone his name is *Butter Bean*. 'Well, hello, Mr. Bean,'" he said in a mocking high-pitched voice, "'I'm Miss Toma*h*to! If we find one of the Okra children, we can have succotash!'"

"Oh, stop it," I laughed. I covered the baby with my shawl and began nursing him. "Ooo, look! He's a *hungry* Bean!"

Brendan put his arm around me and kissed my cheek. "He's a big eater," he said. "Takes after his Da!"

I grinned. "Yes, and he'll be eating pecan waffles before we know it!"

"You look beautiful this morning," he remarked, looking at me with his clear green eyes. I felt myself blush.

"Thank you," I said, and I felt happy. I put my head on his shoulder and dozed off while the baby nursed.

The house phone rang.

"Murdah," I said, coming around. "Ignore it. I'm having a nice time in the quiet."

"Sounds good to me. So when are you going to let me have the baby? You've been hogging him all morning."

I laughed. "Well, I think he's finished, so I guess I can turn him over to his Da for a little while."

Brendan's cell phone rang.

"Oh, good grief," I said. "Well, you might as well answer it. Something must be going on."

"Hello? Hey, Mama. Yeah, she's right here. What?" He laughed. "Hold on."

I traded the Butter Bean for the phone. "Mama?"

"Girl, are you sittin' down?" Mama asked.

"I sure am. What's going on?"

"Well, ol' Reub done give up his farm to his son. He said he didn't want that to stand in th' way o' happiness, and asked me ag'in if I'd marry him. Said he'd move in here with me, if that's what I wanted. So I told him I would."

"Mama!"

"We gotta haul off an' make some plans, 'cause we gon' tie th' knot in December. I reckon we'll all be over now in a minute to get started!" With that, Mama hung up the phone.

"Well, I declare," I said, "Mama's going to marry Reuben Delaney after all!"

"Great! I like Reuben, and I think he and Mama are a good match."

We sat in the quiet, enjoying all of it, because we knew it wouldn't last. The Irish Hurricanes would be blowing in any time now, probably unleashing all kinds of pandemonium in the form of wedding plans.

After a while, with Brendan happily snuggling a sleeping Butter Bean, I went inside and started coffee and got out the tin of cookies. Shortly I could hear Mama, Maggie, and Aunt Melba jumbling in, all fussing over Brendan and the baby. Then the Hurricanes barreled into the kitchen and sat at the table, all talking at once.

Looking at these women who had been with me all my life—all God's gift to me-- I felt an overwhelming sense of love and gratitude. The day that I had come back to live with Mama seemed so far away now. I then had no idea what was going to become of me, but now my life felt richer than it ever had. I was with my family, my husband, and our new baby. These were the days of blessing.

I noticed that Brendan, holding the Bean, was standing at the kitchen door, taking in all the ruckus. We looked at each other, shook our heads, and smiled. I thought of a verse from the book of Jeremiah. "For I know the plans I have for you," declares the Lord, "plans to prosper you and not to harm you, plans to give you hope and a future." I didn't know *what* the future held, but I knew *Who* held it. And knowing that would be enough.

www.ingramcontent.com/pod-product-compliance
Lightning Source LLC
Chambersburg PA
CBHW070616130626
46556CB00001B/384